# 2 STREET

CHRIS BAUER

SEVERN RIVER
PUBLISHING

Severn River Publishing
severnriverbooks.com

ISBN: 978-1-64875-499-9 (Paperback)

# ALSO BY CHRIS BAUER

*To South Philadelphia and the people who live there.*
*A strange and wonderful place.*

# 1

## THE STORM AND THE ARMORED CAR

Friday night, December 4
South Philadelphia
Number of days to the New Year's Day Parade: 28

Frank Tisha had one more stop to make. His hands in his pockets this god-forsaken night, he leaned into the snow caking his knee-length cashmere coat. He pushed west along Snyder Avenue toward Front Street and entered the corridor beneath the concrete spans for I-95, escaping the blizzard for a few moments.

I-95 reached north and south on trestles a few stories above street level, the traffic's din on the span overwhelming the soundscape underneath it, even in the storm. South Philly exits, jammed during rush hour and on Philly sports teams' game days, were as quiet as the prairies in Montana in a heavy snow like this. Visibility on the street in the storm was shitty, which made walking under the trestle almost pleasant. Hatless, even in this weather, was how Frank rolled, the snowflakes defrosting in his ears and pooling there. He brushed off his eyebrows, shook his upturned collar almost clean, and stomped his feet. He walked half a city block through the corridor surrounded by concrete, a respite from the severe weather.

Frank blew into his hands, emerging at the traffic light. At one-fifteen a.m., with the city in the grip of this freak Alberta Clipper weather system, car traffic was a trickle at street level, the blizzard subduing it more than the late hour. Foot traffic was nonexistent and would stay that way until bartenders served their last-call drinks then shoved their drunk patrons out the door into this white, wintry night.

Patting his coat's breast pockets was a habit, feeling for the edge of his bookie notepad inside. In bad weather he kept it in zip-locked plastic. Its blue-lined pages and his scribbles on them were in soft number-two pencil lead, and they would smear if they got wet. The plastic bag was a job hack, something he'd picked up from his predecessor, a longshoreman who'd had an unfortunate accident on the docks, crushed between two large pallets of offloading motorcycles. Not a called hit on the guy, but Frank often wondered.

Now three years retired from the local Teamsters front office, Frank had been giving too much of his pension and social security to the Atlantic City casinos, so he quit gambling and went to work for Dizzy Punzitore and the Massimo family the day after the family lost the longshoreman. Transportation for high-end escorts, collections work, and old-school illegal "street" numbers that paid 800-to-1, which bettered the Commonwealth's legal numbers odds of 500-to-1. The bettors were blue-collar city folks mostly, with a few local high rollers layered in, all recorded with a nubby pencil in Frank's rice paper notepads, their collection the product of a few miles of shoe leather, day and night. This record-keeping method worked fine for the numbers game spanning multiple decades before him, and it worked fine for Frank Tisha during the current one.

He owned a cell phone but didn't trust using it for this business. He set fire to each two-buck notepad after it filled up. If anyone ever dimed him out and sent the cops to his house, he could toss the one he was using in one of the buckets of water he kept around the house, and the water would dissolve the rice paper. But taking pictures of the bets, then texting them to his handler—not a good idea. In his mind, the internet let all that shit float out there in the clouds forever, where the Feds and local constabularies could find it. Old school was best.

A block past Front Street, Danny Boy's Corner Saloon loomed, its green and white shamrock lights blazing its marquee at the intersection, lighting up the miserable night.

A woman leaned against a second-floor railing of a covered balcony on the other side of the street, a pair of French doors open a crack behind her. Her cigarette tip glowed, burning through the curtain of falling snow. Frank could hear low music through the open doors—saxophones, trumpets, banjos, a jukebox in the background, all of it smooth and non-obtrusive even in these wee hours. In less than a month—on New Year's Day—dancing, prancing, and marching Mummer bands with histories of forty or fifty years or more would overwhelm Philadelphia's Center City streets in a parade with live music, skits, and fanciful outfits, their inebriated performers spilling into the South Philly neighborhoods afterward.

He watched her watching him from the terrace. The carriage lamps below her lit up the large black letters painted beneath where she stood, across the width of two stucco rowhomes. *"Downbounders,"* the letters boasted, which was the social club hangout for an entry with the same name in the parade's Mummers string band division.

"Nancy," Frank called, no more than a *hi, how are you* acknowledgment, a verbal tip of the hat suffixed with a hand wave.

"Otherway," Nancy said, using his street nickname. "Stay warm, honey."

She exhaled a plume of smoke, their greetings deadened by the white curtain that made them each little more than silhouettes to the other. A ritual for them, three, maybe four nights a week, unless he stopped to trade additional pleasantries. Too cold and monstrous to do that tonight. Little time for him to stay long at this last bar, either, because he wanted to get home. He got after his coat collar again to shake it clean, then pulled it closed around his neck.

With a hard pull at a carved wooden door, Frank entered Danny Boy's. This time of night the drunks were either passed out and draped over the bar, or on the floor, or on their elbows in the booths. Tonight, Danny Boy's was dead.

"Line one up for me, please," Frank called to the bartender, a woman.

Ruddy white face, strawberry-blond hair, and chunky, she reminded Frank of his wife Teresa's primary care doctor, a mick.

"You bet, Mister Otherway."

At home he was Francis or Frankie to Teresa. Elsewhere, it was Tisha, Frank, or Otherway. It all worked. Frank squinted at the rear of the bar.

"He's waiting for you," the bartender said, her chin pointing.

A given. At the paneled taproom's farthest end, one beefy occupant sat in a two-person booth, his back to the bar.

Frank nodded then barely turned his head, the booth already within his peripheral vision. People thought Frank "Otherway" Tisha's lazy eye was his superpower, but his peripheral vision was no better or worse than anyone else's, he just let people think it was, especially his grandkids.

He downed the shot of Dewar's, headed back to the booth, and sat across from Michael, sixties, the bar's teetotaling owner with cherry cheeks and no neck. Majorly overweight, Michael fed his face with leftover jalapeño poppers, overwhelming his mouth like a hoarding chipmunk.

"Want some?" he asked Frank, chewing through the question.

Frank waved him off. "No sleep if I eat shit like that this late. I need to finish up and head home in good enough shape to do Christmas shopping tomorrow. What do you have for me tonight, Michael?"

"The snow put a dent in it, Frank. Here."

One sheet of paper, fourteen one-word names on it, fourteen three-digit numbers alongside the names, fourteen bets, all the info handwritten. Frank took out his notepad and rewrote the entire list, left Michael to dispose of his piece of paper. No money changed hands.

"Settlement day tomorrow, Michael. You ready?"

"I will be. We had a good week, no accounting for tonight."

"You did at that. Good to hear you're flush. After you get the call and the drive-by tomorrow, maybe I stop back and do a few of those poppers with you? Around dinner? Maybe I bring Teresa?"

"You and that silver fox? Sure, Frank."

"Hey. That's my wife you're talking about."

"Nothing but respect, Frank. See you then."

Frank left Danny Boy's, trudged up Second Street, "2 Street" to the locals, no one else ahead of him on foot. The snow fell serenely in big flakes now, not swirling, the high wind and blizzard conditions easing off. Christmas decorations adorned rowhome after rowhome, the houses all narrow, all two stories, all with front stoops. At street level, a conga line of parked cars were all quietly getting snowed in. Some TVs flashed their lights on upstairs bedroom walls, but most people were tucked into their beds, weathering the crazy early December blizzard.

A black armored truck idled near the corner, commanding his attention, sitting higher than the parked vehicles on the street. A "cash in transit" vehicle, or CIT.

A cigarette break? Midnight lunchtime for the truck's graveyard-shift guards?

The only truck on the residential street, it blocked a snow-covered fire hydrant. Its headlights and parking lights were off, the truck's cab dark. Out of place at this hour, in the middle of the night, and out of place as a solid, boxy, commercial vehicle on so narrow a street for any time of day or night. Frank kept his distance from it. He reached the corner, made a left, and stayed his course west on Mifflin Street.

He heard the armored truck's engine rev and the transmission shift. Its headlights still off, it made the left turn, dieseling slowly up the street on Frank's tail with no reason to be following him, so it probably wasn't.

But it was officially out of place now. The street was one way, the truck moving in the wrong direction. Frank mumbled a what-the-fuck and quickstepped to the street's other side, putting a curb and a tight row of parked cars between him and the truck.

No approaching traffic. The truck bucked once like the clutch had been popped, lurched forward, and drove past him a few lengths in second gear. The single back door suddenly swept open, banging against the truck's rear wall. The interior remained unlit as the truck rumbled farther up the street, nothing visible inside. Two seconds, three seconds ahead of him, two bodies fell out in succession, sticking their landings on the white-covered blacktop. He flinched with each thump.

Frank being there, seeing this, was not a good thing. He moved behind the protection of a parked car, his head lowered. He craned his neck for a peek, the light from a streetlamp reduced but not canceled by the falling snow.

The first body was face up, a Black male, his head leaking from a massive wound. The second body was also Black, had landed on his stomach, the exposed side of his face shredded like beet-stained lettuce. Frank's assessment was these were victims of gunshots at close range. The snow under their heads turned red quickly like cherry water ice.

A third body fell out. A truck occupant hopped out of the door that had given up all three bodies. Camo jumpsuit, black beard, black watch cap and gloves. He turned the third body over, the victim now toes up. He reached back inside the truck's rear door and swept his arm side to side along the floor. His gloved hand reemerged, holding a banjo.

Frank shielded his eyes from the darting, icy snowflakes. Something about the body was off.

Through a squint Frank watched him lay the banjo on the victim's chest. The camo guy climbed back into the rear of the truck where his gloved hands reached for an interior door handle and yanked the rear door shut, but it didn't latch. The truck's engine revved once, twice, and when the CIT moved forward in first gear, the door flipped open again. A canvas satchel dropped out, yellow-white with brown handles, the size of a gym bag. Easy to miss in the snow, so much of it swirling in the air.

To Frank, the bodies had been pushed out and left there on purpose, but the canvas bag...

The snow got heavy again, blinding, returning to blizzard conditions. Headlights approached from the opposite direction two blocks away, the visibility sketchy, the vehicle creeping up the one-way street the right way.

Frank, on the sidewalk, stayed a crouched, cashmere-coated snowman halfway between the bodies and the bag, the CIT a few lengths away.

He wasn't armed, and he could barely feel his hands, or his face, or his feet, some because of the cold, some because of the tension. He had no business being here, witnessing this, probably the only witness to it, but the bag... what the hell was in the bag?

The truck lurched, its spinning tires dredging up a spray of snow like a dog burying its business in the backyard, further covering the canvas bag. Alighting snowflakes pelted the bag's off-white, stenciled canvas that bore one word only, *Dominion,* in blocked, blue letters, the same stenciling as on the rear panel of the armored truck. The truck's transmission reengaged, pushing it up the street until it reached the corner. Frank kicked his way through a snowdrift and waited before entering the street. The armored truck turned the next corner and was gone.

The approaching car crept forward, its headlights illuminating the parked cars and the twinkling Christmas wreaths and lights hanging on in the blizzard for dear life on rowhome doors, railings, and light posts. To Frank, he was in a scene from a Hallmark card, in this case the South Philadelphia Collection, the bodies the clincher. The car stopped, bathing the body with the banjo in its headlights, the street now as bright as a shopping mall parking lot at midnight.

Oh my. The body was headless.

The car suddenly spooked and slammed into reverse, backing up all the way to the prior intersection. It skidded to a stop, banged into drive, and disappeared onto another side street.

Frank stepped around the first two bodies for a look at the third, ignoring the satchel. It was a husky male in long gym pants and Air Jordans, wearing a heavy winter coat. The banjo was upside down and turned over, its banjo neck running from his thighs north to the round, sheep-skinned cover that reached above the man's shoulders, sitting above the space where his head should have been. The stretched drumhead cover bore a crude frowny face drawn in black marker. What the hell was that all about? And what was in the dead guy's two coat pockets, so bulky, protruding from them?

It was currency. Stacks of hundreds peeked out of each pocket, the stacks half in, half out. Except—

On closer look, it wasn't currency. It didn't hang like it, was too thick, too stiff.

Fake money. Cash-tracking devices, each the size and shape of currency, made to blend in and look like the real thing. Frank knew exactly what it was because of the business he was in and the people he worked for. The devices had been fished out of whatever the proceeds were for this little heist and left behind. Smart crooks. The money on this truck was now free and clear.

He hustled back between the cars and returned to the sidewalk. He tapped a contact on his phone and listened to the ring while quickly retracing his steps.

"This better be good, asshole," came the greeting.

"Sorry, Diz, something happened—"

"Otherway? That you? It's two a.m. I was about to bust a nut with the old lady."

Frank stopped his stride, looked back up the street, peered through the snow and the fog his breath was making. "You're never gonna believe what just went down—"

Three bodies, two of them for sure armored car guards, but the third probably not, a banjo where his head used to be. Dizzy Punzitore heard Frank describe all of it, the armored car, the guy in a camo jumpsuit, and where it all went down, 2 Street and Mifflin. Frank checked his watch. "The whole thing took less than five minutes..."

But he made no mention of the canvas bag he'd kicked out of sight between parked cars before the spooked car had arrived, a heavy curtain of falling snow shrouding him while he did it. He had a good idea what was in that bag, and he'd know for sure in a few minutes when he returned for it in his car.

## 2

# DEAD MAN WITH BANJO

**Saturday, December 5**
**Northeast Philadelphia**
**Number of days to the New Year's Day Parade: 27**

"It's three-oh-seven," Rhea said in answer to Philo's question. She grabbed her ringing phone. "In the morning," she added, preempting any confusion.

"You're killing me, Ibáñez."

A declaration with no real malice, only a slight edge. Emerging from so deep a sleep, it was all Philo could manage because, after all, it was three-oh-seven in the morning. Rhea put up her hand as she spoke into her phone, a request that he shut the hell up.

Fine. Eyes open. *Owww*. Eyes closed again. A headache now, whiplash from the jolt he'd gotten from the phone call, plus not getting enough sleep, plus him straining, trying to eavesdrop. He dropped his head back on the pillow and ran his hand through his rooster mane.

"I'm not in the city tonight, sir," she said to the caller. "I'm in the Northeast with no car... Because I'm off duty, sir. SEPTA would take me two hours in this storm... C'mon, sir, that's personal. I need a pass on this one... Thanks. Bye."

Philo pushed his tongue between his lips, stuck together by what was supposed to be five to six hours of pasty-mouthed slumber after their two bottles of wine and an hour of lovemaking, which had exhausted them both. Or maybe it was only twenty minutes of lovemaking, or ten, or five, or maybe he fell asleep beforehand, he couldn't remember. It didn't matter, he was the bona fide victim here, rousted by the three a.m. phone call.

Rhea left the bed, more awake than him but not by much. Philo dragged a hand to his chest, then to his eyes. He rubbed at them, improving them to slits. Rhea tossed her phone onto a pile of clothes on the armchair, went to the bedroom window, and twisted open the blinds. Stripes of amber street-light bathed her naked body and the bed behind her, Philo's lanky body under its ruffled sheets. Next to the bed on an end table, a Sig Sauer hand-gun, his.

"You signed onto this routine," she said, not turning around, a delayed response to his complaint, "the first time you kissed this Philly detective, lover." A declaration, no snark or malice intended. She peered out the window at the snow.

"Yeah, well, for the short term maybe," Philo said, still horizontal. He lolled his head in her direction, hoped his smile would soften the sarcasm. His cottony gaze settled on her Latina silhouette, an apparition awash in soft yellow light akin to heavenly visages of saints and angels and saviors. This "short term" of theirs had turned into ten months. Philo was good with it so far, good with all of it, even these late-night police-business calls, and even if it meant coitus interruptus. Hell, he was even okay with the sleep deprivation. He and Rhea together were a good thing.

"Longer than most for me," she said.

"Stop, Rhea, you're making me blush," Philo said.

"The *relationship*, lover. Longer than... forget it, you're hopeless. Damn, it's monstrous out there."

Her phone rang again. She retrieved it from the pile of clothes. "Ibáñez. What now, Sergeant, sir?"

Philo sat up, un-gunked his sleepy mouth with a sip from a bedside water bottle. Rhea listened to her caller, her supervisor, a sergeant in Philadelphia's Third District, South Philly, her move to the precinct recent, a transfer out of Philly's Sixth. Philo slid his feet onto the floor, sat on the edge of the bed listening to her grunt a few nays then a few okays while he pulled on his gym pants. Yesterday had been rough for him and his Blessid Trauma Crime Scene Cleaning team, cleaning out a meth lab house, the aftermath of an explosion and kitchen fire that killed two people. A lot of furniture and appliance moving, multiple floors needing remediation. The job still wasn't done. He needed a trip to the bathroom for a shower just thinking about it, plus there was all this wine wanting its release from his bladder.

On his feet now, he tested his bed legs, stabilized himself. He opened the bedroom door. No one else in the house except for Six the Cat, his Calico, his bestest buddy, the reason the door was closed.

*Meow... MEOW...*

"Hey, sweetums. Yeah, I know it's early... no, use your litter box. Get."

Philo entered the hall, Six the Cat squeezing between his long legs as he lumbered to the bathroom, she following him. Rhea, still in the bedroom, was having her final say on the phone.

"Fine... *Fine,* Sarge, I'll find a ride. Carl shouldn't have to handle it alone. I can be there in under an hour, depending on the storm."

Rhea appeared in the bathroom doorway and leaned against the jamb, a long-sleeved sweatshirt now covering her as far south as her hips, but not quite south enough to make her fully decent. Philo was at the sink washing up. Six sat on the bathroom scale, preening.

"So. Philo. You and that nasty military commando vehicle of yours need to drive me to a crime scene in South Philly. Two Street and Mifflin, near Snyder. Multiple bodies."

"It's a Hummer, Rhea," he said, splashing his face with water, "and far from military. Just has some big tires."

"It's a beast, and there's more than a foot and a half of snow out there. Is that a yes?"

He toweled his face off, smiled, and pulled her to him. They shared a full-body embrace against the sink and a deep, suggestive kiss.

"Sure," he said. "Y'know, with all that snow out there, it might just take a little longer than you said to get downtown. At least that could be your story..."

Her hands reached up and cradled his face. Her thumbs massaged the hard angles of his cheekbones, absently rubbing at the raised scar tissue there like it was a smudge of dirt, three stitches' worth, knuckles to bone. Hadn't bled much, from what he remembered. Bareknuckle boxing, totally illegal, anywhere he could make a buck from it: an earlier life for him, premilitary. There were other scars, physical and mental. After she folded her arms around his neck, he lifted her onto the counter, eliminating their substantial height difference. Another passionate kiss.

"I notice how you, um, now want to finish what you didn't finish earlier," she said, her smile questioning but warm.

"See, yeah, sorry about that, I was really tired, and..."

"Shhh," she said, whispering in his ear. "Consider this an advance against the gruesome work ahead of us. Or at least ahead of me. C'mere, Mister Philo Trout..."

Philo's H2 Hummer crushed its way through the accumulated snow to the I-95 ramp before settling into a slow march behind a trio of staggered snowplows, the SUV champing at the bit in the leftmost lane. Four-ten a.m. now, the precip reduced to snow flurries. They consumed donut shop coffee and bagels at thirty-five miles per hour. Tall, piercing, stadium-quality lighting illuminated the highway. Great visibility, all lanes, from the soaring bright lights and their glimmer onto what the winter storm had dropped, the plows pushing the snow aside but the road still completely white, no asphalt visible.

"You're positively glowing," Rhea said, sipping at her cup, the SUV wipers on intermittent. "A slam, bam, thank you, ma'am moment back there for you."

"And you're projecting," Philo said. "Look how awake we are now. And it was more than a moment."

"Not much more, Philo dear. And I'm awake now more because this coffee has two espresso shots."

"Not fair. We had a time constraint. Something about a triple homicide."

"Yes, there is that."

Philo's choice had been to overshoot their destination via I-95, passing Center City, the high rises, the historic district, then the floating restaurants and the longshore docks wrapping around South Philly. They exited the interstate farther down and approached their destination from the south. Four-thirty a.m. now, still dark, the city still asleep. A steady push up 2 Street and they found the police activity ahead of them, the east-west block of Mifflin Street. It was like an after-hours block party, a T-intersection of spotlights, idling police and EMS vehicles, and residents outside their homes on the sidewalks, moving from foot to foot in the cold, their phones in the air, each of them kept at bay with crime scene tape and uniformed cops.

"Park here," Rhea said near the corner. "This is close enough."

"But there's a fire hydrant."

"I know people, remember?" she said, giving him a look.

Rhea closed the door and waited for him, her takeout cup in a leather-gloved hand. The snow crunched underfoot, Rhea badging her way past a cop while vouching for Philo as an under-contract crime scene cleaner. After a walk up 2 Street to the intersecting street then around the corner, they ran into an impromptu cop convention.

"Carl," Rhea called at her partner. A veteran detective like Rhea, Carl had his hands inside the pockets of his bomber jacket. The two were trans-fers from elsewhere in the city, teamed together after their moves to the Sixth District. Philo liked Carl.

"Rhea," Carl said, then a nod. "Philo."

"'Sup, Carl."

"Fill you in, Rhea?" Carl asked.

"In a minute." Rhea walked ahead, leaving Carl with Philo.

"Then I'll tell the crime scene cleaner instead," Carl said to Philo, who was matching his steps. "Two vics near each other in the street. Black males, both shot in the face. Bloody snow. A third victim maybe thirty feet farther up the street. A banjo on his chest, upside down, the banjo covering where his head should have been. Weird. That's about it so far. Probably won't need your cleaning people, from what I can tell. A hose will wash this all away after the snow melts. But what do I know."

"Not here on business, Carl."

"Oh. Pleasure, then?" Carl said, eyeing Rhea. "Nope, sorry, forget I said that. Don't tell Ibáñez."

"No problem. Long as you recommend Blessid Trauma the next time you need a deep clean at a scene. To clarify, Rhea needed a four-wheeled ride down here. My Hummer and I were in the vicinity."

"Copy that, amigo," Carl said, adding a wink.

Rhea sipped her coffee as Carl and Philo closed ranks behind her. She eyed the brick and stone façades of the rowhomes on both sides of the snow-covered street, people gathered outside on their frozen stoops or peeking through the curtains in their windows. "Okay, Carl, get me up to speed," she said. Canvas throws covered the two bodies head to toe, the body placement haphazard.

"These two were executed at close range," Carl said.

She nodded. "Identified yet?'

"Yes. Armored car security guys, their IDs intact. Still armed, their guns holstered. Both were shot-gunned to the head, their bodies tossed out of the truck. Dominion Security Services employees, just like the uniforms say. A check with the company says the vehicle was done with its run and on its way to an overnight bank repository to drop off its receipts. It never showed up. No intel on its location yet."

"Why not? No GPS tracking on the truck?"

"It stopped working."

"How about on the money?"

"Yeah, about that. The perps found the cash-tracking devices in the bags. They left them with the dead bodies."

"What the fuck. So where's the bank repository?" Rhea asked. Behind Rhea, a woman in uniform approached on foot, a determined gait in the middle of the street, a uniformed man keeping stride with her.

Philo squinted. He knew the Philly police commissioner even at a distance, from higher profile jobs he'd done for the city. She'd become a city darling with some of the news coverage she'd received.

An unaware Rhea pressed Carl with a *C'mon*, still checking info on his phone.

"I've got it somewhere... here it is. Repository's at Thirtieth and Market. Near the IRS," Carl said.

"Across town. Was this the normal route for the truck?"

"Yes and no. This block, maybe no. Otherwise, yes."

"Murder weapon recovered?"

"No." Carl checked his notes. "Each truck crew has a shotgun, so if it's still with the truck when we find it, we'll check it out."

She got in a crouch next to one of the bodies, pulled on a pair of nitrile gloves, and reached for the cover. Philo and Carl peered over her shoulder as she pulled it off. Black male, shotgun pellet holes prickling his double chin, a large, bloody cavity swallowing his mouth and nose. Eyes open.

"Someone got right into his face to do this," Rhea said.

Carl answered yes, then his eyes darted past Rhea, alerting her they had company.

Rhea turned. "Cold night, Commissioner," she said, then, acknowledging the commissioner's male assistant, "Lieutenant Yonder." The lieutenant nodded.

"That it is, Detective," Police Commissioner Darnell said. "You and Detective Norman, follow me please. The third vic is up the street."

Valerie Darnell. Commissioner Val to the Philly media, who were in love with her. It belied her Black ethnicity, Philly known for not being overly kind to its minorities. But things had changed in the last few decades, and they would continue to do so if Commissioner Val had anything to do with it. And swagger was something the people of the city always embraced, if the person could back it up. Next to her stood Lawrence Yonder, fifties, slender, college-educated, and white. A long-term Philly cop who Philo had pegged as a bone spurs kind of guy. Rhea never liked him, calling him a brassy-assed bureaucrat who got in the way of getting things done.

Rhea's slight hand signal at Philo told him to stay behind, this new adventure needing to be with police personnel only, for the moment at least. He abided, blew into his hands, and watched them hoof it up the street, the commissioner's male cop assistant also in tow. The narrow street had residents on their stoops, chattering with each other, with others poking their hands and faces through their curtains, drapes, and blinds, watching the action.

Philo had seen Commissioner Val in operation, had dealt with her because of his crime scene cleaning contract with the city. She took no bull-shit from the politicians, the Philly police rank and file, or the brass, or from back-to-back city government administrations either. Her cops, males and females of all ethnicities, would die for her. It was respect she'd earned as a beat cop in her twenties and thirties. She'd been shot twice, had been shot at three times as many, and had killed perps that ran the ethnicity gamut.

"There you are," Rhea said to Philo, no Carl, no Commissioner Val with her. "I'm allowed to take you back, so you can see what you missed. The coroner's here, so make it snappy. He wants the bodies. You're welcome."

The coroner sucked on a cigarette as he pulled back the cover again. The third victim was on his back in snow that was once fluffy but now tamped down by cops and detectives and Philly police brass, maybe even a witness or two before anyone from law enforcement had arrived.

And no lie, there was a banjo. It rested transversely and upside down on the body. An eerie-looking, demented sight, the banjo's head resting above the shoulders, its stretched, off-white sheepskin cover graffitied with black marker. Two bold dots for eyes but no nose, and below them a frown, the lips unparted, both lips full. An emoji, or a racist caricature? Why not just a simple line for the mouth?

"Yeah. It took more effort to draw those lips," Rhea said. "Just spit-balling here—"

Philo eyed the vic's clothing. Long gym pants in black around a trim waist. Red sports jersey visible under an aviator bomber in navy, unzipped to the waist, its alpaca collar covered in blood, some of it frozen. Air Jordans on his feet, in black. If this guy was in the armored truck, he hadn't belonged there.

"... but the brass might be looking at this as a hate crime in addition to a robbery," Rhea said.

"Hate crime?" Philo said. "Against who? Banjo players? The

Mummers?" He wasn't serious, but after all, there was the banjo, and in Philly, banjos often meant Mummers.

Rhea shook her head. "No, against minorities. Philly's white supremacy people have been loading up lately, getting bolder. They're taking their cues from that freak Jack Maguire and his movement. That exaggerated drawing..."

"Okay, okay, I get it," Philo said. He'd seen them in action in the neighborhoods. A major arm of a national group called The Real Proper Punks had taken root in the city, imported from the white supremacy incubator cities in the Midwest and the Pacific Northwest. "Irish" Jack Maguire was getting a lot of press, the Charlottesville protests and violence major photo ops for him. Philo segued away from the theoretical, back to the practical. "Any info on the missing head?"

"AWOL at this point."

"Ibáñez," Carl called, "I just got a clarification from Dominion Security." Carl tucked his phone away and arrived alongside them. "About the money the truck was carrying—"

"A wild guess. It's casino money," Rhea said.

"Yep," Carl said, landing hard on the "*p*."

"Not a surprise. How much cash on the truck?"

"Dominion's people said just over seven figures," Carl said, "combined."

"*Combined?* Meaning what?"

"Two bags. Still no GPS signal from the truck itself, but they were ecstatic to tell us that the signals from the devices in the bags are all working just fine."

"All the tracking devices, meaning they're all accounted for?"

"Yes indeed. All broadcasting their signals from right here, our busy little crime scene."

# 3

## BLAME GAME

Saturday, December 5
South Philadelphia
Number of days to the New Year's Day Parade: 27

Frank "Otherway" Tisha could say he'd never had this much cash in his possession ever, but only if he had the inclination to tell someone about it, which he didn't. A restless sleep got him out of bed before six a.m. like a kid on Christmas morning, aware that the fat man in the red suit had dropped his load under the tree. Hell, even the season was right. Alone in his basement, he'd had enough time to count it.

Five hundred twenty-seven thousand, three-hundred dollars. Twenties, tens, ones. Not in a lock box needing a key or a combination, or a combination of keys and combinations—just cold cash racked and stacked in bundles going full commando inside the canvas bag, its tracking devices back on Mifflin Street in the coat pockets of a dead body, no other tracking devices found.

Bank ATM replenishment cash or other bank money? It didn't matter, because it couldn't be traced. Retail store money? Same answer. Casino money? More of a concern. With the truck on the South Philly streets at that time of night, there was an outside chance that this was what it was, casino money. And taking money from a casino could be the biggest mistake anyone might ever make—if it could be traced. Someone in the truck made sure that it couldn't.

Weighing heavily was the South Philly Purolator armored car story from the eighties. A similar circumstance, in the same neighborhood: the money fell out of the back of the armored car company truck, its finder Joey Coyle got paranoid, couldn't keep quiet about it, and was eventually caught. Coyle's antics were made into a movie. But in addition to Frank being a wise guy in mob parlance, Frank *was* wise. No one would learn about this money, now his money, because he knew to stay quiet and not call attention to himself. For the time being, it would go into the trunk of his Chrysler.

Seven a.m.-ish. Teresa called him upstairs from the basement for some eggs and bacon, her silver curls above a workout headband, her slim hard-body belying her age. Frank got a call on his cell and stopped chewing his breakfast to answer it.

"Yeah, Diz, what's up?"

"Noon at Carmine's. I'll buy you a sandwich. See you then."

A man of few words. Not a free lunch, Frank knew. Dizzy would be looking for an update on what had happened—additional play-by-play about what Frank had seen go down in the blizzard last night.

"Let the dance begin," he mumbled after Diz ended the call.

"You say something, Frankie?" Teresa said.

"I need to see Dizzy about what happened last night after the last pickup. No biggie, sweetheart."

"It's on the news. Commissioner Val's talking up the investigation. Three murders. You and the crew better be clean here, honey."

"We are. Oh, you and I will be eating at Danny Boy's tonight. Can you be ready by six?"

The Dominion cash bag, empty of its bounty, snapped, crackled, and popped in the fireplace. Teresa was still out shopping, all bundled up for a trip to the butcher's. A stop at the butcher's also meant stops at the bread guys, the dry cleaners, and the Hoagie Ladies Deli for lottery tickets and gossip, all on foot, the snow be damned. Frank watched his fireplace flame up and burn its contents. He had maybe another twenty-minute window to poke at the burning bag and turn it over and over along with a few seasoned logs, but he saw now he wouldn't need all that time. The canvas was gone, the leather handles charred black but not burning, their brass brads liberated, mixed in with the cloth ashes. The leather would have stunk up the place if it weren't for Teresa's glowing Yankee Candles masking its pungency on both floors of their rowhome. He used tongs to lift out the half-moon handles, shrunken from the heat, and dropped them into an ash bucket. A few scoops with the fireplace shovel deposited the bag's hot ashes in with the leather. A layer of tap water covered the bucket's contents and put out the last of the fire. The mucky ashes and curled leather fit snugly inside two empty cans of *Chock full o'Nuts* coffee.

Outside his back door, his army-green trash receptacles sat side by side against a waist-high chain link fence that separated his tiny yard from his neighbor's. Frank brushed the snow off the lids to his plastic barrels and dropped in trash that filled them to their brims. In two days, their trash would be collected. Enough time for someone to locate missing evidence before trash pick-up, if they knew where and what to look for. A prohibitively unlikely circumstance. Maybe a coupla days of light anxiety for him, but no real danger.

Last night, best as he could tell, there'd been no witnesses to him leaving the scene with the canvas bag in the blizzard. Mifflin Street was one lane for cars to drive and one lane for them to hug the curb for parking, the width of the driving lane tight enough that people turned their side mirrors in to keep them from getting sheared off by passing traffic. Easy retrieval of the bag ten minutes after he first left the scene: he crept up the street in his Chrysler 300, left the car to clear off his windshield by hand, bent down for the bag hidden in the snow, and slipped it into his open door. He'd then backed his way out.

Carmine's Taproom, South 7th Street, was close enough to Frank's house he could walk to it. He entered, saw Dizzy at the rear corner table where he normally conducted business. Frank waved off a hostess. He removed his coat and sat across from his mob boss.

"Ordered you a grilled pepperoni and mozzarella panini," Dizzy said, "just to keep things moving. I'm telling you, Frank, your arteries gotta look like the Schuylkill Expressway at rush hour eating that greasy shit."

Dizzy Punzitore, broad-shouldered, had a bull of an upper torso. Thinning white hair, long white sideburns. Sixties. One of the capos in Salvatore "Big Sal" Massimo's crime family.

"Nope and nope, Diz. The amount of walking I do day and night, I'm clean as a whistle."

"Fine, there's that. There's also that I don't actually give a shit, either. Tell me what happened last night."

Sandwich, curly fries, a bottle of beer. Frank talked while he ate. Diz sipped his Scotch and listened, enough direct eye contact between them that Dizzy for sure had to know Frank was telling the truth, nothing but the truth, just not the whole truth. It turned out that Dizzy's line of questioning was going in a different direction.

"The police commissioner held two news conferences this morning on this already, eight o'clock from her house, nine o'clock from the Roundhouse. The lady sounds like she means business, and that makes us happy as shit. Know why?"

The Roundhouse, on Race Street in downtown Philly. Shaped like a pair of handcuffs, the iconic building and its curved architecture were not long for this world as the city's police headquarters. The cops were moving out, taking their complicated existence to a new location that was previously the home of the *Philadelphia Inquirer* newspaper.

"Because the family had nothing to do with it," Frank said.

"Bingo. Tell me this. The guy you saw. The one you said was in a camo jumpsuit and was doing all the heavy lifting..."

"He pushed the bodies out the back of the truck. What about him?"

"Hawaiian? Or maybe one of the Muslin Gang?"

Frank finished his beer. The taproom's waitstaff already had a bottle in waiting for him at their table. Standard M.O. for Dizzy and his guests.

"You mean Muslim."

"Don't correct me, Frank."

"Sure. But I dunno, Diz. No idea. He had a beard, and he wore a black or navy-blue watch cap that covered his head."

"How'd his face look, and his eyes? Dark? Hawaiian or what?"

"C'mon, Diz, I really don't know. It was snowing too hard."

Dizzy pounded the table, a fist that made Frank's beer bottle and lunch dish jump. "I'm telling you, you Otherway motherfucker, he was Hawaiian, damn it. He had to be. Think hard. Those Ka Hui pricks, they did this."

The Massimo crime family was feuding with other mob factions who'd been making inroads around the city: the relocated Hawaiian mob family known as Ka Hui; the Muslim Mafia; the Kosher Mob; the Northeast Philly K&A Gang in the Badlands, mostly Irish; the Greeks; and the Vors, the made men of the local Russian mob.

Frank made searching his memory look realistic enough, Dizzy's eyes drilling him. "The guy's eyes were dark, not light," Frank said. "I guess I can't say he *wasn't* Hawaiian, but—"

"I knew it. Ka Hui. Those fuckers, hitting us in Mummerland. The casinos in *our* neighborhoods..."

*Casinos?* Uh-oh.

"It was casino money in the truck? Not bank ATM or retail money?" Frank said.

"You betcha."

Sonovabitch. Frank's heart skipped a beat, but Dizzy didn't seem to notice, still all fired up about Ka Hui.

"... Big Sal gonna need to flip the switch on these guys after this one."

"So, ah, Diz, what did the Philly commissioner have to say?"

Dizzy downed his drink, looked pissed when he didn't find another one lined up next to the last. A death stare at the bartender got the guy moving. "You say something, Frank?"

"I said, the Philly Police commissioner, where is she on this, 'cause, you know—"

Frank made an implicating gesture at himself with his hands. If, quote, "organized crime" was involved, the commissioner might have said something to that effect.

Dizzy sipped from his new Scotch. "Don't worry, they don't know nothing about you, or at least they ain't letting on they do. If there were any witnesses, no one's talking. We've got eyes on that block. People who know people who know us. No chatter, nothing."

Frank's assessment, too, was there'd been no witnesses. All except whoever was in the car that backed away from the scene in a hurry, but the car was too far up the street to get a look at someone walking in the snow. That person probably made the 911 call to get the cops involved.

"You ever going to get that friggin' ambyio-whatever eye fixed?" Dizzy said out of left field. "You need to get that taken care of, Frank."

"Amblyopia. Too late for that at my age, Diz. Tell me—that second police press conference, what came out of that?"

"Identities of the victims. Two of them anyway. Confirmed as Dominion Security guards. The third one, the one with the banjo in street clothes, no info yet. No head yet either."

"Was the third one Black?"

"Yeah. Or brown."

"Huh," Frank said, a placeholder while this all registered. But the largest part of what registered was there was no mention of a canvas bag, or—

"What about the truck, Diz? The commissioner mention the truck?"

"The truck's GPS tracking stopped working after it got on northbound 95. The cameras on the interstate picked it up. They lost it somewhere in Newtown, way up in Bucks County, where it left the highway."

"Huh."

"What's this 'huh' shit? You don't believe me?"

"No, no, Dizzy, that's not it. It's just that, who's big in Newtown?"

"No one's 'big,'" Diz said, air-quoting him, "but every town's got a connection to *someone*. Look, I don't give a shit about that truck or what or who was in it, and Big Sal don't give a shit about that truck, neither."

"But it was casino money—"

Dizzy drilled a stare. Frank's poker face hinted at ignorance.

"Our skim comes before the money gets on the truck. What, you didn't know that?"

"No." Frank went for his beer, took a pull, hopefully hiding his relief.

"Well, now you do. Whatever was on it, no loss to us. But it's the perception. No respect. Someone did a big job in *our* territory, took a big shit on one of our streets, and didn't clean up after themselves. Fucking Hawaiians."

"But how do you know for sure it was—"

"Intuition. I hate those guys. You want another beer?"

No lost money for the family, just lost respect. Internally, Frank was feeling giddy; externally, his face stayed blank.

But hey... five hundred fifty-seven grand, with no strings to, or interest by, the Mob.

"Nah, I'm good."

# 4

## FIVE DRUMMERS DRUMMING

Saturday, December 5,
Jackson & S. Water Streets, South Philadelphia, under the Interstate 95
bridge span
Number of days to the New Year's Day Parade: 27

Rehearsal in progress, full instruments, with a few parade props, for Teddy Cangelosi and his string band. It was abysmally cold in the city, the streets still in the grip of an Alberta Clipper and the havoc of nineteen inches of horizontal and vertical snow the system dropped two days earlier. Rehearsing in the aftermath of the storm in these conditions might have been overkill, but the Old Time Philly String Band wanted to be combat ready, so here were John Edward "Teddy" Cangelosi and his bandmates gathered after dinner, under the floodlights beneath the I-95 span.

Teddy's résumé: local cover-band work, the band's crooner; some voice-overs for radio ads; and the retired stadium announcer at Citizens Bank Park, home of the Philadelphia Phillies, the voice the crowd heard over the PA system at games. But his Mummer work was now a passion, part of the city's romance with a unique hundred-year-old musical tradition. Song, dance, and costumed splendor performed live, Mummer roots had hitched a ride to a few inner U.S. cities by way of European immigrants, but they could be traced as far back as ancient Egypt. In Philly, the pinnacle of their existence was a one-day payoff a year in the making: a festive, nearly chaotic march through the city's downtown streets each New Year's Day. Fun and frivolity, and an excuse to consume large quantities of alcoholic beverages, getting sloppy on 2 Street after the parade.

The I-95 vehicle traffic rumbled three stories above them. The cold surrounded Teddy and the other marchers, the overhead concrete structure and the blacktop underfoot gripping them like the inside of an old icebox, one that needed chiseling to free up the hotdogs.

Wearing ski masks, fingerless gloves, mufflers, wool socks, and fortified with flasks, the musicians went through the paces of a raucous five-minute routine complete with dancers and tumblers. Not a rehearsal in full dress, it included tiny floats and props only, all equipment small enough to transport in pickups and SUVs. And the drumline—their new drummers, five musicians from a local community college, all of them Black—was amazing, just an absolute wow, Teddy internalized. Even in the cold, they and the entire group of more than seventy-five performers were simply outstanding. They were gameday ready, New Year's Day less than a month away.

George, band captain, addressed them through a bullhorn. "One more time and we'll call it a night. And stop complaining, lest—and I did say 'lest,' you cretins—I remind you why we need to win this thing this year. As for today, a coupla tequila shots back at the club later will thaw out your extremities."

A voice from within the crowd, a retort: "*Unless maybe we want to stop home first and put one of those unthawed extremities to good use.*" The speaker blew a kazoo-like note through his saxophone, eliciting chuckles.

"Hey. It's a PG-13 crowd out here watching us," George said. "Let's keep it clean, numb-nuts."

Scrawny, white, and in his early sixties, Teddy hazarded a look at Harriet, she with her fiery orange-red hair rinse and wide hips leaning back against her car, a thermos upright on the car's hood. In the thermos, hot rum toddy. Harriet took a sip from the cup, then waved her mittened hand to her boyfriend Teddy and his four-string banjo, a Mummer musical instrument mainstay. The car she leaned against was more than a car: a Dodge Challenger SRT Demon in candy apple red with 840 horsepower. In the possession of one Harriet Broglio, in her mid-fifties and arguably experiencing a mid-life crisis, it was a road terror and street bully.

"Ah, Teddy? Come back to us, Ted," George said, his bull-horned visage squawking, Teddy's eyes still full of his woman friend. "Yo, whenever you're ready, Teddy darling... Good. Thank you. I'll count us down. Five, four, three, two, one..."

The full complement of performers kicked into high gear, the string band music reverberating throughout the neighborhood, its audience of families and friends Mummer-strutting in their places in the parking areas and the paved spaces on the periphery. The theme for the band's performance this year leaned heavily on Mummer instrument mainstays of saxophones, banjos, accordions, and glockenspiels. Banjos—strummer banjos, not pickers—dominated the music, their riffs staccato and brassy, loud and punchy. A unique blend of John Philip Souza, Scott Joplin, and John Williams of *Star Wars* fame.

Taking up space in Teddy's head along with the music were the two reasons that this year was so important. First, a freakish head-on auto accident after last year's parade left two Mummers dead and a third passenger in serious condition. The driver of the other car, in the process of fleeing from the police, was charged with multiple homicides.

The second reason was their new drumline. The band had gone cold turkey into diversification, effective this year. Their statement was they would no longer tolerate any bigotry. No more blackface routines and no more "punching down," a practice endemic to Mummer clubs of the past. None of their future performances would be at the expense of minorities or other marginalized groups. The Old Time Philly String Band jumpstarted their commitment by recruiting a Black drumline for this year's performance. Other bands planned similar overtures, but Teddy's was doing it. Screw the baby steps approach. The seventy-sixth edition of the Old Time Philly String Band would make a huge Mummers' strut toward full-tilt inclusion.

Harriet downed more of her toddy, light on the rum, Teddy knew, because he'd made the batch for her, and she was driving. She squeezed inside her car, parked in the pole position at the edge of the adjacent ceme-tery, and got the Demon's massive engine running, ready for a quick and easy exit when the time came, and that time was near. The band moved into the last bars of its final run-through. Teddy longed to have his strum-ming banjo fingers in the warmth of that car around a cup of hot toddy and massaged by Harriet.

A cobalt blue van entered the parking lot, crossing Teddy's field of vision as it passed behind Harriet's idling Dodge. It drifted to a stop at the end of the chain link fence separating the cars from the open performing area, cut its headlights, and left its engine running. There it would have a head-on view of the last moments of the band's routine through its dark-tinted glass. The drumline's snares provided a drumroll for the crescendo as Teddy counted through the beats of the music, strumming hard with his fingerless gloves on as he marched toward the band captain, mimicking the exit they'd all take past the parade judges.

He eyed that van. The windshield's tint was so dark it was probably ille-gal, the glass looking like it was painted black. Whatever. Just a blue van, its occupants watching their performance, waiting on band members to finish so it could gather a few of them and leave. Teddy was in lockstep with the other members, all performers wanting to nail the routine's closing number so there'd be no need for more new takes, it was too damn cold, and—

*Step, step, turn, step, step, turn, pluck these strings, massage the frets, up, down... my fingers, all numb and aggravated... we're close to finishing, and...*

*... it's so frickin' cold... Missing the high school gym rehearsals big time...*

*... step, step, turn, step, step, turn, drumline drumroll, right behind me, right up my ass...*

*... You guys got it, we are so damn killing it, I am so loving this, so proud of my band...*

Two doors of the cobalt blue van opened, driver's and passenger side, and stayed open after two men exited them. Ski masks, gloves, ski suits in black and gray, dark sunglasses, both men ready for the cold, their arms at their sides. They strode toward the back end of the band, toward the drum-mers, the five percussionists all hitting their marks, these rookies, so outstanding, the performance's grand finale...

*Step, step, turn...*

On the final turn Teddy and the drummers faced the two men from the van, and their gloved hands now held semi-automatic pistols raised to shoulder level, two guns each, the men in full stride, marching at the marchers...

The trigger pulls came from all four guns, the shells ejecting as they walked—

*Pop-pop-pop-pop...*

*Poppoppoppop...*

The shots went on forever, the bodies dropping in front of him, drumsticks skittering onto the blacktop, the snares punctured, the tangles of drums and arms and legs and heads and torsos all collapsing into themselves.

Teddy watched the carnage, a slaughter, saw it in slow motion, more *pop-pop-pop*, became part of it, a jolt hitting him through his coat, below his waist. He felt the heat searing into his ass cheek, then came the second jolt, a rip into and through his thigh, and a third...

He slipped down-down-down, into a pile of screaming, bleeding, dying humanity.

The shooters backed up, their guns still raised, waiting for someone to give them a reason for having to shoot their way out. They reached their van and slipped back inside. The driver wheeled in reverse, the van exploding out of the lot onto the street. It careened around a corner, disappearing into the night.

A stunned and angry Harriet was on Teddy like a blanket, joined by his Mummer captain who howled in shock after seeing Teddy's wounds, his eyes darting between Teddy and the crumpled body of the drummer next to him, someone tending to that victim as well. Around them it was a cacophony of screams and pleading into phones, all begging the 911 operators for multiple ambulances.

"Ted!" George, the band captain, yelled. "Hang on, Teddy, EMTs are on the way."

Harriet's eyes darted everywhere George's did, assessing the situation. Teddy keyed on her face and held her hand, smiling to ease her worry.

"I'll be okay," he said, but the pain was escalating...

Harriet grabbed Teddy's banjo strap and wrapped it around the top of his thigh as a tourniquet. "Screw this," she blurted. "Grab his legs, George, I'll get under his arms, we're not waiting, he's going with me." She looked left and right. "Him too," she decided, pointing at the college student bleeding out next to him, blood running down his snare drum. "We'll put him in the back seat. Here we go, Ted. Ready, one, two..."

Harriet's throaty two-door Dodge Demon fishtailed onto Jackson, a one-way street, and accelerated, blurring past the streetlights and the houses and the bars and the corner grocery stores, horn beeping, headlights flashing. The car decelerated, cruised through the stoplights, green, red, yellow —seven minutes per the GPS to the hospital but damn, Harriet would do it in three she was yelling, Teddy trying not to drift away in the passenger seat, whimpers coming from her other passenger in back, a cop car now chasing them. The blood from Teddy's leg was slowing now, her tourniquet working, but his ass was still a nexus of pain, still stinging, and still bleeding, much like his shoulder was.

Left on Broad Street, left on Wolf, Methodist Hospital Emergency on right. Harriet screeched up to the door and exited the car. She called to people in doctor-nurse scrubs hovering at the entrance. "Gunshot victims! Two gunshot victims in my car, need help here."

ER techs pulled Teddy from the front seat and dropped him onto a gurney, him calling to his bandmate as the techs removed the young man from the back seat. Harriet walked fast alongside them, hovering as they hauled them into the hospital, pleading with the technicians and anyone they passed in mint green scrubs to get more doctors into their ER, more gunshot victims were coming, a major shooting...

*... a fucking execution, multiple people dead, my God, oh my God—*

And then the veil dropped, Teddy's eyelids closing, and he was unconscious.

A drugged Teddy Cangelosi opened his eyes and smacked his lips. He surveyed his sterile surroundings. Outside his space it was noisy, frantic. Harriet was on a call, pacing next to his bed.

"In intensive care, stabilized," she said into the phone. "Shot three times, his leg, ass, and shoulder, one bullet passed through his thigh. Another victim is in a coma, but it doesn't look good. The others are all dead, George. Pass this along to my ex-in-laws, tonight, soon as you can. I got a good look at the van. A real good look. They want any notes on it, and I know they will, I'll be glad to oblige... The cops? Yeah, sure, guess I'll talk to them, too."

She checked Teddy, his eyes half-lidded and glassy, his smile heartfelt, its intensity drug-influenced. "I need to go, George, Teddy just woke up."

"Harriet," Teddy whispered, his mind fuzzy, his lips mostly cooperating, "darling, you look so delicious..."

"Quiet, stud. You remember any of what just went down? Why you're here, in intensive care?" She closed her hands around his, the one without the IV. "I'm sorry, Ted honey, so sorry. The kid in the back seat..."

Tears breached the levee, trickling down her plump cheeks. Teddy so loved this beautiful woman, her smile so sweet, so genuine, complementing her dimpled, full face...

"... at least four of the drummers are dead..."

The words pierced his fog. A shooting. *My, my, my...*

"I don't remember an ambulance. How did I...?"

"My car."

It came rushing back. Him bleeding all over her black leather seats. Horns blaring, mostly from Harriet's car, tires screeching, the car slip-sliding in and around the nighttime city traffic.

... the college kid in the back of her car, coughing, whimpering... dying...

"I don't remember much of the ride either, honey," she said. "We picked up a cop escort who wanted to talk to me about reckless driving and what happened back there and what I did to get you here but it's all good, you're here now, and they're taking good care of you."

"Philo. Harriet, you need to talk to Philo. His girlfriend will fix it with the cops..."

"He called already, before I could call him. It's all handled, honey. Please just relax. Know that I love you very much, Teddy honey..."

# 5

## THE HEAD

Sunday, December 6
Wynnewood, Pennsylvania
Number of days to the New Year's Day Parade: 26

The attack on the Mummers ambushed the morning national news cycle while overwhelming local Philly coverage. The carnage had turned it into a middle-of-the-night, all-hands-on-deck event for Rhea's district, leaving Philo with Six the Cat his only bedfellow for the rest of his prior evening.

Philo returned to Blessid Trauma's current work-in-progress, a seventy-year-old Cape Cod on a quiet residential street in Wynnewood, just outside Philadelphia, on a tiny lot with nosy neighbors on all sides, but apparently not nosy enough. The new owners, a young family, had less than two years in the neighborhood. Their two-story frame addition gave the house a full family room, a powder room, a massive master bedroom, a spa-like second bathroom, and a second-floor laundry. And the renovation masked the conversion of the basement into a major-league methamphetamine lab. The explosion took the lab out of business and, sadly but stupidly, the young parents' lives. Two adults dead, the parents of two toddlers who were in daycare when it happened. The toddlers' relatives were fighting with the insurance companies for whatever they could salvage financially of the newly parentless lives facing the kids going forward.

Philo checked his phone messages and texts again. Nothing new from Harriet about Teddy. Awake and talking as of last night, but still in intensive care.

The first day on this job was yesterday for Philo, Hank, and Miñoso, three of the four employees of Philo's Blessid Trauma Crime Scene Cleaners currently on the payroll. Grace, Hank's wife, with fragile breathing from double-lung replacement surgery, was sitting this remediation out. The client home had lost half its usable above-ground square footage, the fire and explosion hollowing out the entire basement. The blast found a release up the chimney from volatile chemicals kept too close to the furnace. *Ka-boom.*

His phone whistled a few bars from *The Good, the Bad, and the Ugly.*

"Your phone, *Señor* Trout," Miñoso said when no one reacted.

"Yeah, thanks, but we talked about this, Miñoso. We're going with 'Philo,' right?" he said, correcting him. "Not this '*señor*' crap?"

"*Si, campeón, si,* I will remember."

"Not 'champion,' either. Not *señor,* not mister, not *campeón,* just Philo. We're informal around here, remember? Tell him, Hank."

"Let it go, Philo. Maybe Miñoso will even things out versus what, you know, Grace calls you."

Grace Blessid. Hard-ass, former heavy smoker who damn near put herself into an early grave with her cigarette habit and the chemicals she inhaled during her decades as co-owner, along with her husband, of Blessid Trauma. New lungs, new life, new zest for zinging profanity at whoever tested her ire, especially Philo, the company's new proprietor and her frequent target. Per her own admission, she'd been the personification of sex, drugs, and rock 'n' roll throughout her twenties. Her health problems and the sale of the business had slowed her down but hadn't sidelined her attitude. It had instead emboldened her.

Miñoso was the newest addition to the team, filling in for Patrick 'Ōpūnui, the absent and slightly brain-damaged fifth employee who was still in Hawaii. Patrick was rediscovering his roots after years of dissociative amnesia from a blunt force trauma incident during a street robbery that took both his parents. When Philo bought Blessid Trauma, Patrick was part of the deal.

Philo tilted his hazmat mask hood above his head and checked his phone to see who had called. Rhea. He called her back. "What's up, Detective?"

"We found the head."

"Uh-huh," he said, humoring her. "Remind me, whose head again?"

"The third victim of the armored car heist. The banjo guy."

"Glad for you, Detective, good, but I need to get back to this meth house cleanup. We're almost done, so if you don't mind..."

"It was stuffed into the takeout window for a Chinese food restaurant. Happy House. That name sound familiar?"

"There's a Chinese restaurant called Happy House a block from my house. They've got a weird Plexiglas walk-up window for their takeout, you don't need to go inside..."

"That's the one."

"Huh. But like I said, Detective, honey, do I need to know this now? We're kind of busy here."

"There's ink behind his ear that you might be familiar with. For my money, I think it's a Navy SEAL tattoo. The one with the eagle, the anchor, the pistol..."

And the trident. Same tattoo as Philo had on his leg. A reward that some SEALs gave themselves after finishing basic training. She now had his attention.

He took the stairs from the basement up to the first floor and found his way outside, Rhea, still talking: "The tattoo is small, camouflaged by other artwork, but one of the M.E.s figured it out."

Philo removed his hazmat hood and set it down inside the rear of their step van. "Let me guess. The tattoo is only an inch tall."

"Good for you. Yes. Wait. Size is important?"

Philo let that one go, rubbing his forehead as he spoke. "Yes. Navy regs say face and scalp are off limits for tattoos. Behind the ear or on the neck is fine, but it can't be any larger than an inch. What you have there says he could be a SEAL."

"And we're pretty sure he was a Mummer, too. We're contacting all the local bands and clubs. No leads yet, although I don't understand why. It's not like there are a lot of Black Mummers out there, and now, you know…" Her voice trailed off.

*And now there were a lot less after what had happened last night*, Philo finished in his head. "You maybe want me to pull some strings with the Navy?"

Philo's phone made a funny noise from another call he let ring through to voicemail.

"The coroner's office is already on that. I want you to see what we have here, the head, the tattoo, like, now, please. Then we can talk more about it."

"Where are you?"

"At the Chinese food restaurant."

～

In his Hummer cruising Roosevelt Boulevard into Northeast Philly, Philo returned the call that he'd let ring through, expecting, needing, to hear a certain familiar voice.

"Philo?" was the greeting on the other end, weak and weary, the voice not sounding like Harriet's in-person voice. Harriet Broglio sounded bereft. Philo's heart sank.

Beyond a "yeah" in response, Philo was breathless and on edge, now expecting her to speak the worst news. Something that would make his day a whole lot more unsettling.

"He's in stable condition but improving. They moved him out of intensive care," came the words he wasn't expecting. "The wounds were life-threatening but repairable. The other guy I took with us—he's gone, Philo. Checked out while he was in my back seat. What a waste, damn it."

Philo exhaled, but after Harriet delivered the news, she broke down, sobbing into the phone, the crying turning into her cursing like a longshoreman, her voice full of the kind of threats that could only come from the hot-headed Italian woman she was. Threats that, Philo knew, her acquaintances could deliver on.

"Swear to God, Philo, if they find out who did this, I—"

The "they" weren't the police. The "they" were her in-laws, most of whom she'd disavowed so she could move on with her life, distancing herself from their questionable activities after her ex-husband had died. She'd married into it, had become "connected," then begrudgingly enjoyed what that meant, for a while at least. But she'd eventually soured on it and divorced her husband, which divorced her from the family. Then came the full break when her husband died from the big C. No kids between them. But none of this meant anything to Philo at the moment. He knew the history only because her manfriend Teddy Cangelosi, one of Philo's closest buds, had told him of Harriet's former connections. Their personal history, Teddy and Harriet's, had originated from Teddy's amazing job as a stadium announcer and her position as a food company executive for the company that catered Philadelphia's sports venues.

"Look, I get it. Take a breath, let me speak with Teddy. He good to talk?"

"Sure. He's still loopy, but here he is. Teddy, it's Philo…"

"My man Philo! Good to hear from you. How's Six doing, shithead?"

Philo's cat. Six the Cat was gaga over Teddy and vice versa. "She's good, she's doing fine. Tell me how you're making out."

"The drugs, man. I should feel like a cesspool but the drugs, they're keeping my spirits up, except… those guys, Philo, my new Mummer brothers, they're all gone, the new drumline, all five of them, just, gone…"

Philo listened to what Teddy could remember of the shooting, heard him turn maudlin inside his drug cloud, heard how he expected to be released in a few days, and how Harriet had saved him.

"I'm still marching. They're patching me up. I'm still going to make the parade."

Harriet objected loudly in the background, but Teddy's reassuring voice pushed right through her stop sign. A moment later, a nurse said the discussion was over and Harriet signed off the phone for him.

Philo parallel parked on Frankford Avenue. The Chinese restaurant would have normally been open if not for the police activity, which had drawn a crowd. The fog from his breath surrounded him when he exited the Hummer. He stepped onto a concrete sidewalk that fronted the takeout eatery only two blocks south of his own rowhome.

First floor was the restaurant, second floor an apartment, presumably where the owners lived. He approached the storefront, its vinyl-clad facade and glass front door combined to parallel the length of two cars in tandem, the lettering for the restaurant name in red and the phone number in white, tall letters painted by a professional across the entire front. He leaned in closer, over the yellow crime scene tape wrapped around sawhorses on the sidewalk to keep the neighborhood gawkers away, Philo now one of them. The restaurant's short, metal exterior counter, elbow high, supported a walk-up window box, a cube the size of a microwave and made of thick Plexiglas. The front of the clear cube hung down by a hinge left in the open position. A closer look gave up why: the spring-loaded mechanism for the hinge had been snapped.

The crime scene activity was on the inside of the cube, but no one would have guessed this, the plastic box clean, no indication a severed head had been in there. Philo squinted for a closer look into the restaurant's front door, shielding his eyes. Rhea's partner Carl was interviewing the owners inside. Philo checked out the other storefronts, but it was Sunday, so most of the shops were closed.

"Philo—over here."

Rhea called from beside a car double-parked on the side street leading from the restaurant, its flashers on. Not just any car: it was an unmarked coroner's vehicle. Philo arrived alongside Rhea. The woman next to her, a city medical examiner, still in her plastic gloves, was packing up. Rhea introduced Philo as a crime scene cleaning expert.

"Mister Trout consults for us. He needs to see the victim's head, Doctor. Specifically, the tattoo."

The liftgate of the coroner's vehicle was raised. The gloved doctor reached inside, into a picnic cooler. Philo stopped her with a hand gesture. "Wait, hold on, Doctor, please."

Philo's brows knitted. He leaned over, to check out the plastic bag with the head in it from a few angles. "Double bagged. Turn it, please, so I can get a full frontal of his face."

She repositioned the dry ice, moved the bagged head so Philo could get a better look at the victim through the plastic.

Black male, forties maybe. Diamond studs, both ears. Hairless, his crown to his chin, the crown looking as shaved as his jaw. Ragged neckline below the Adam's apple. Not a surgical separation, anything but a clean cut. The man's head had been hacked at multiple times to separate it from the body.

Philo's heart dropped. The face. He knew this man.

The doctor moved to turn the bag over. "Here, I can show you the tattoo…"

Philo ran a hand across his mouth, an absentminded swipe, trying to make sense of this. "No, Doc, don't. Leave him be." He followed a head shake with a hard swallow. "I… I know who he is, Rhea."

Rhea moved closer. "Philo—you sure? How…?"

"Ed Bounce. He served with me. Yeah, I'm sure."

*Shit.* His one hard swallow became two, choking him up. He willed himself past it and cleared his senses for a closer look at the victim. He had questions. Inside the nose and mouth, was that "… ice in there? Those little crystals on his nose hairs, and his tongue and teeth?"

The medical examiner said yes, it was ice, inside the head and around it, some of it mixed with congealed blood.

Philo turned to Rhea, after the M.E. closed the liftgate: "You guys thinking the ice was put in there to preserve the head?"

"At this point, no. That would make no sense, right? No reason to preserve it. And it's not like someone wasn't going to find it preserved, sitting in frigid temperatures in a clear takeout window."

"It was found in these zip-locked roaster bags? That would make the bags the perp's, right?"

"Looks that way," Rhea said.

"The ice…" Philo said, thinking aloud. "If you're thinking ice wasn't added to preserve it, it could have been water in the head that turned to ice in the frigid weather after the head was left outside."

"Seriously?" Rhea said. "Water that froze, melted, refroze, and is now melting again? We pretty much got that far on our own. We're not looking for you to solve this thing, Philo, I just wondered about the SEAL tattoo. The fact that you knew the man, that's huge. It validates my reason for having you look at it."

"I don't like the ice in there, inside the head, in their bag," he said, persisting. "It came from where?"

"Look around. Two feet of snow in the city, and it's still crazy cold. They could have dropped the head in it, maybe in South Philly, maybe elsewhere, then brought it here."

She grabbed his elbow and led him away from the M.E., appreciative of his input but losing her patience. Philo's visit to the scene was over.

But back at his vehicle, with his hand on the door handle, he did an about face. He had more to offer about the victim.

With Rhea again. "He's from Arkansas, Detective. I had no idea he was up here. I did know he played banjo. It took the edge off things, you know, him and that banjo, during training for our SEAL missions together. He could sing, too. Have you checked with the Philly string bands?"

"We will, now that he's been ID'd." She paused, shook his hand, and held it for a few extra beats. "We'll find the connection, Philo. Go, get back to your meth lab cleanup. I'm good for now."

Still curbside, he dialed up Hank Blessid from the truck to see about the meth house clean-up before making the trip back. "We've got it under control," Hank said. "We'll finish the job today."

Good. That left him free to head downtown instead, to check on his good friend Teddy in the hospital.

Sad. *Friend* and *hospital*. Two words that made him uncomfortable when used in the same sentence. Adding *slaughter* to the mix rendered the situation obscene.

# 6

## ID'D

Sunday, December 6
Methodist Hospital, South Broad Street, Philadelphia
Number of days to the New Year's Day Parade: 26

Philo resisted asking for a "Teddy" Cangelosi at the information desk, but when the sixtyish woman with the hospital's patient room info behind the counter heard him ask about John Edward Cangelosi, she went right at it.

"Teddy's on the fourth floor, dearie," she said, her smile warm and empathetic. "The city of Philadelphia is pulling for him."

Philo didn't belabor her familiarity. Teddy's celebrity was low key, but it was real. His baseball connections with the Phillies as a stadium announcer spilled into his local celebrity as a Philly string band Mummer and banjo player with a cover band. Philo never understood any of this shit, the costumes, the music, the adulation, and the excessive alcoholic lubrication that took days for Mummers and their beloved 2 Street in South Philly to recover from each New Year's Day celebration, but it was old-fashioned, working-class Philadelphia, and it was real, and his good buddy Teddy was a part of it.

Adding to Teddy's celebrity was his friendship with an aging Phillies ballplayer: Allen Dixon, one of the most feared hitters of the sixties and the seventies, and possibly all time. Baseball Rookie of the Year, a Most Valuable Player, and seven times an All Star. His MVP year single-handedly saved the Chicago White Sox, another of his teams, from moving its franchise to another city. Only the second Black ballplayer to play for the Phillies, and the first to stay with the parent club for longer than a cup of coffee. Dixon had suffered from horrendous bigotry at the hands of the fans and the media in Philadelphia. Philo knew this from a cause Teddy championed, a busy campaign by way of social media involving the press, the city of Philadelphia, and the nation, to get Allen Dixon into baseball's Hall of Fame.

And now with Teddy, the lone surviving gunshot victim from the massacre of five Mummers, here was the seventy-eight-year-old Allen Dixon, in his hospital room, a surprise visitor. Dixon was on his way out, steadied by two personal nurses and another man. He tipped a stylish hat as Philo entered the room, Philo nodding in return. Dixon ambled slowly down the hallway, a nurse at each arm. The man swiped at his moist eyes before turning a corner.

"Wow. Allen Dixon," Philo said when he entered the hospital room. "I'm impressed, Ted."

Philo leaned into a hug with Harriet, with her doing a poor job of stifling her tears. She murmured a soft thank-you into Philo's ear. Philo moved in closer to Teddy's bed for a handshake and a kiss on Teddy's cheek.

Teddy nodded, tears forming. "Yes. And Allen's son. I love that family to the moon, Philo. They came all the way across the state to see me, sick as he is with cancer. Against his doctor's orders, his son told me. I... I'm overwhelmed. Next year, Philo. Next year he gets in."

The Golden Era of Baseball's Hall of Fame vote, on Teddy's mind the past fifteen years, was an annual thing each December. Teddy was the No. 1 cheerleader for Allen Dixon's candidacy.

"Copy that, Ted. And it looked like he loves you right back."

"Some of that emotion's for me, but a lot is for those murdered young men. I'll get to walk out of here, they won't. Harriet, please get me the nurse, the drugs are wearing off. I don't want as much this time..."

Her fiery hair a little mussed, Harriet squeezed Teddy's hand, then left the room. Teddy wasted no time getting to the point.

"Your Rhea needs to figure this out before Harriet does, Philo. Harriet wants to get her ex's family working it even though she hates them. And trust me, if they work it, it won't be pretty."

"What's that mean, 'if they work it?'"

"Ouch." Teddy rubbed the back of his thigh. "This is the closest I can get to where the bullet ripped a chunk out of my ass, me rubbing the muscle near it. Harriet's been an angel, massaging me back there." A mischievous smile warmed his face. "You wanna be a dear and rub it a little—?"

"Ah, no, Ted. Back to my question. How would Harriet's connections"—Philo went with air quotes—"'work it?'"

"The usual. Roust people, threaten them. Get other families, in Philly, New York, Chicago, Detroit, to look for that van. Make in-person visits, hassle car chop shops. You can't argue with their effectiveness, but I worry Harriet will get too close to it. She promised me she'd let the police handle it, but I don't know if she'll abide by that promise. This struck a nerve with the crime families, Philo. I want her to stay out of it, have her stay safe..."

Teddy eyed her outside his room, standing at the nurses' station. She was getting more animated. "Something tells me more drugs are forthcoming."

Harriet reentered the room looking triumphant, a nurse in tow behind her, carrying a tray with a syringe. In thirty seconds, Teddy was in lalaland again. Harriet pointed at two side chairs next to the bed, wanting Philo to sit.

"This thing, Philo, this... slaughter," she said, "the entire Mummer community is crying over it."

Philo eyed her demeanor. Her knotted face said she, personally, was past the crying stage and had moved into the anger-and-kickass retribution stage.

"Tell me what's going on, Harriet."

"I'm worried the cops might drag their feet on this, or not take it seriously enough."

"Because?"

"Because maybe it's a white against Black problem, or maybe it's Black against Black, or maybe it's neither. But when you net it out, it's just another five Black men dead from inner city violence."

She eyed her boyfriend resting comfortably from the drugs. "Teddy's string band... they're committed to including marginalized groups, going all in this year and all years going forward. Someone needs to figure out who did this, and fast, so the Mummer community doesn't lose that traction."

Philo was worried about who she thought that someone should be. "Let the police work it, Harriet. My detective friend—her associates, plus the Feds—this thing is superhot. They can make things happen. You need to concentrate on getting Teddy out of the hospital so he can be back with his Mummer buddies in time for the parade."

"I promise to make that happen," she said, "because it means so much to him. But I'm not promising anything else."

"Harriet, Teddy's worried and—"

"Someone's going to pay for this. Five people were gunned down. Five executions. They were kids. College students. I saw it happen. These Mummers' roots... they run deep, Philo, just like many of the ethnic families here in Philly. I swear to God, whoever did this, they hit a nerve. They screwed with the wrong people."

Philo stepped out of a late afternoon shower, refreshed physically and emotionally from a day that had him all over the city. A meth house, a beheaded friend from his military past, plus another friend shot multiple times, still alive but hospitalized. He finished toweling himself off and slipped on gym pants.

Noise, downstairs, in the living room, at the front door. The door's hardware was rattling. With a Sig in his hand at the top of the steps, he leaned down to get a look.

Six the Cat had her paw through the mail slot, thwap-thwap-thwapping it in quick succession, attacking a package inside the storm door.

Philo arrived and lifted a protesting Six out of the way to get at the delivery. He dragged the large flat box inside. It was about a quarter the height of the door itself. He shimmied the box into the middle of the room and laid it flat on the floor. Six rubbed against a box corner, then rubbed against his leg and purred.

"Fine. Here, get out." He opened the storm door. The chill braced him, the frigid air nearly cauterizing his lungs. Six slinked past him and shuddered after a few steps onto the cold landing. She wouldn't be out long.

Philo looked left and right down the city block at parked cars still snowed in. A hearty, determined senior woman wheeled a personal grocery cart in the street, taking advantage of the snowplowing for a late-day trip to a corner food store.

No address on the package, to or from, which made it an in-person delivery by the sender. He peeled off layers of mailer tape, opened one end of the box, and peeked inside. He grabbed at what his hand could reach and slid some of the contents out.

Shrink-wrapped money. Several stacks of cash bundled together. Hundreds, fifties, twenties, tens, fives, ones. Each stack had a value written on the plastic in black Sharpie. The hundreds read "$5K," the fifties "$2.5K," etcetera. Doing some quick math, what he'd pulled out totaled $47,000 give or take. A peek inside: more of the same, a lot more. He unwrapped a stack of hundreds. Not new cash, yet the stack of bills was tight, looked clean, had been in circulation but had probably spent time in a washing machine. The epitome of laundered.

Philo went to the picture window that stretched across the front of his house and closed the drapes. He spread out the opened stacks on the floor and pondered them.

"Wally Lanakai," he thought aloud. "My $400K. Sweet."

That would be the final tally if he ever got around to counting it. The Hawaiian boxing promoter-slash-mobster wouldn't short him. Earnings from a single bareknuckle fight, his most recent and most lucrative. The last and final bout, he'd vowed, that he would ever take. Sixty-six organized fights around the world, all illegal, all of them wins, most of them during that crazy time when he was in his twenties. Extenuating circumstances had quintupled this purse, something mob boss Wally had labeled "combat pay" before the bout. It had been one of only two fights Philo had accepted in the last ten years, and both involved Wally Lanakai and his Ka Hui mob family. This one was on Wally's behalf, not against it. The delivery of the purse had been months in the making.

Here, in one package, from one fight, was what amounted to more money than all his other sixty-plus bareknuckle fights combined. A vacation to Hawaii had earned it, one planned solely as a benefit to Patrick, an amnesiac, a friend, and a Blessid Trauma employee. A vacation that had turned into anything but.

The other boxer, a former Japanese Olympian, was dead, the first time there'd been a mortal outcome for one of his opponents. Not Philo's doing, nor was it Wally's. His opponent was old-school Samurai. The disgrace of his loss made him a victim of tradition, or at least a victim of the pressures of tradition. The boxer solutioned the outcome with seppuku, a.k.a. hara-kiri, the ritual taking of one's own life.

Also in the delivered box, an unsigned note, typewritten.

*We're square now, Trout. See you around.*

His phone startled him. The display read *Rhea.* Deep breath. He'd need to play it cool.

"Hi, baby. What's up?"

She could never know about the money. Best also that he'd kept her from knowing anything about either of his last two bareknuckle fights. He'd retired from the illegal fight game years ago, he'd told her, and she was good with that. He needed to stay retired to keep her, a Philly detective, on the right side of the law. For her safety, and for something more important to her than anything else: her law enforcement career. Certainly more important than being in a romantic relationship with him because, he knew, that was how she rolled.

Rhea started. "Got an update on your banjo-playing SEAL friend."

"Okay. Why was Ed here?" Philo gathered up a few of the stacks of cash, the phone on speaker, him surveying his living room. He found space on a bookshelf for the money for now.

"One of the string bands claimed him. They'd recruited him after the mayor demanded the Mummers get more diverse. One of two Black performers for them. An ex-pat Philly Mummer living in Arkansas had given your friend Mister Bounce a hard sell on the parade and paid him to come north to try out. The other Black recruit quit the band after hearing about the attack."

"Okay, but what the hell was Ed's body doing in a stolen armored truck?"

Philo stacked more of the cash from Wally Lanakai on another bookshelf. He tilted one end of the box. One last shake and now the box was empty, the five-by-eight oriental rug in front of his fake fireplace littered with a small Matterhorn of cash money. A twinge of paranoia hit him, again checking to make sure his drapes were drawn.

"You mean other than maybe being murdered?" Rhea said. "Don't know yet. We'll learn more when we find the armored truck. One more thing: no water in his lungs. That much we know from the coroner. That rules out drowning."

"I didn't know drowning was a consideration."

"You mentioned the head was dripping water. The coroner knows her shit, and she'll be thorough, but that's one of her early findings."

"Which pretty much means the cause of death was...?"

"The beheading. That dripping water—we're going with the bad guys dropping the head in a snowbank somewhere. Or they grabbed snow or ice to keep it frozen, so maybe it wouldn't stink."

Philo heard scratching at an interior door, the one in the kitchen that led to the basement. "Hold on a second," he said. "Six is back."

Independent, indoor-outdoor Six. Philo had no choice when he brought her home eleven years ago: let her go outside to hunt, otherwise she'd claw at and destroy doors and windows trying to let herself out. He usually left the interior door to the basement ajar so she could come and go as she pleased through a pet door that led to the alley behind the rowhomes. He opened the closed door. Six was on the top step, her back to him. She about-faced then brushed past him, dragging something.

"Hold it, Six. Wait—not so fast, damn it."

A blood smear now led from the dining room to the living room, from hardwood floor to rug to the open stack of hundred-dollar bills on it, where Six pulled up short and hovered, a wildlife offering in her mouth.

*Meow...*

"Six brought a rabbit in with her," he said. "Where she found a rabbit, I have no idea."

He shooed her off the money. More cash went to the bookcase just to get it off the floor, bills without rabbit blood on them, a second shelf now full. Solutioning this on the fly, he'd need a safe deposit box or three, or maybe some offsite lockers... they all might be in the mix.

Six slinked back onto the money pile, gacked and gorked and horked up a gloppy rabbit part. Philo cursed, Six ran.

"Let me guess," Rhea said. "She consumed part of the gift herself."

"Indeed. And now it's been reunited with the rest of the rabbit carcass she was playing with. Speaking of rabbit guts—"

"No. Don't you dare..."

"We still on for dinner tonight?" he said, a smile in his voice.

"You disgust me. Yes. Pick me up at eight."

"Wait. Stay on a minute. I just remembered something."

He went to a coat closet, pulled down a shoebox, and sifted through some photos while muttering unintelligibly.

"Here. Found them. I have pictures of Ed Bounce with his banjo. When we trained together for a few missions. You might find them helpful, because, well, you know—"

As a cop, she could have finished the sentence for him, but she didn't, letting him be the one to say it as respectfully as he could, that in the pictures he had of his friend, his head was still attached.

# 7

# COMPETITION

Sunday evening, December 6
S. 9<sup>th</sup> Street, South Philadelphia
Number of days to the New Year's Day Parade: 26

Broadway Louie's had the tufted, red velvety charm of an Old-World Italian eatery despite the Jewish upbringing of its original owner Louie Silberbauer. Lou the Jew was gone. His grandson Irv was now the proprietor. It was a reservations-only place, for three reasons: one, it was small, two, the food was great, and three, it had a controversial, exotic history. Ten tables, half of them with seating for four, the other half seating for six. The dress code was shirts and shoes but was better described as mob casual, a holdover from the eighties. The place hadn't seen anyone with a dress shirt buttoned at the collar since its owner Louie worked the dining room in a suit and tie back in the day. Lou the Jew was connected and had stayed that way until he died from a single dose of lead poisoning, mob-style, from a bullet to the back of the head in the early nineties. Common knowledge was that it was a hit ordered by a boss. As was the case back then, when questioned by the police, no one knew nuthin'.

Philo and Rhea entered and removed their winter coats, the waitstaff taking them away. The host sat them at a table for four that was set for two.

Rhea straightened her silverware and ran her eyes around the place, Philo watching her. Photographs overwhelmed the walls, black and white, a few in color, each autographed with personal notes to Louie, glossies of many of the male entertainers the city called its own in the latter half of the last century. Frankie Avalon, Fabian, Bobby Rydell, Chubby Checker, Jerry Blavat, James Darren, plus pictures of Philly sports heroes, the city's consummate tough-guy politician Frank Rizzo, and even the captains of a few Mummers bands. The nostalgia might have begged the question, how could these people not have known? Weren't they aware of the sympathetic relationship between the owner and local trigger-happy gangsters of the last few decades of the last century? The answer would always be yes, of course they knew, how could they not? Some reveled in it, some rationalized it away, because the danger of hanging with crime figures gave an edge to their celebrity. A Frank-Sinatra, punk-among-mobsters affectation.

"Dinner in what used to be enemy territory," Rhea said. "This should be interesting. You should have told me you were taking me here, not surprise me with it."

An organized-crime hangout in its earlier years, back then the restaurant had frequently been bugged, the surveillance often resulting in good outcomes for the local police and the Feds. Some bad actors went to jail, and when that happened, most of the mob rackets suffered. The law enforcement wins tracing back to Broadway Louie's restaurant were the reason a South Philly "house painter," a.k.a. mob hitman, delivered the deadly .32 caliber slug to Louie's head. Regardless, the surveillance wins back then had managed only to cripple a few mob families, not destroy them.

"This reservation—it was Teddy's idea that I take it off his hands," Philo said. "I wasn't going to refuse a guy in a hospital bed. From what I remember, the food is excellent."

Rhea was unimpressed. "Chances are, that many years ago, that chef is gone." She eyed the faces in the photos nearest their table. "And I wouldn't wear your history with this place, these people, as a badge."

"My past, my cross to bear, Rhea. The good thing is, the chef is still here, still making his spicy gravy. Let's do a different topic. Anything new on Ed Bounce?"

She shared. "Today we interviewed a few Mummers in the band he was scheduled to march with, the Glockenspiel Perfectos. They're all cooperating, but we still need leads."

*The Glockenspiel Perfectos*, Philo internalized. *WTF kind of name was that?* He caught himself, realized it was no cuter, no worse than other Mummer nomenclature like the "wench brigades," and the New Year's Day parade awards for "King Jockey," "King Clown," and "Handsome Trim," and one string band named after a saltwater taffy, plus bands full of pirates, Spartans, and Vikings.

A busy night, with all the restaurant tables occupied. The owner started making the rounds. He reached their table.

"Mister Trout. Good evening. So nice to see you again. How long has it been—decades? Your friend Teddy says hi."

Philo introduced Rhea, then threw her some lighthearted shade. "A pleasure to be back, Irv. Rhea's looking forward to the meal."

The owner's smile broadened, unrelated to, but in proportion to, Rhea's glare. "Excellent. I'm also here to let you know that your meals are paid for. Enjoy."

"Wow. How'd that happen? Teddy's treat?"

Philo scanned the restaurant, waiting for an answer, now wanting a better look at the other patrons. Rhea's eyes, apprehensive, followed his. Irv stayed with the program and might have even winked. "Ahhh, Mister Trout, we can't betray confidences, can we? I'll send over some wine. Excuse me."

Rhea sipped water, glared at Philo over the rim of her glass. Irv moved to another set of guests. Rhea cleared her throat. "Ask me if I'm happy about this, Philo."

"Stop. I get it. Just... hold that thought." He picked up his phone, started keying. "And no"—he glanced at her—"I'm not being rude."

Her phone pinged. She eyed him, he nodded, she silenced her phone. She pulled up his text.

*Fraternizing at mob hangouts eating free meals. Against the department's emoluments clauses and gifts rules, am I right?*

*Teddy was only trying to be nice and just didn't think this one through. I didn't either. We'll eat, I'll leave a generous tip, in cash, then we'll leave*

Meals ordered, menus collected, wine poured, and salads delivered, they settled in. Rhea dished to Philo about her workday, her voice weary. The challenges of her caseload, having to work with the courts, the state, the Feds—she was exhausted. She grabbed her phone.

Philo's phone pinged. Her text, with more on the way, Rhea still keying. He muted his phone as well. He began reading. Her text digressed into free association.

*… they operate in the shadows, claiming they're not real. It makes prosecuting them with the racketeering statutes difficult*

*Far from the way things used to be. Some turned state's evidence joined witness protection delivered court testimonies*

*But the families are still out there. Drugs sex trafficking numbers high stakes illegal gambling*

Philo was mindful of the mob lore. More so, he was mindful of how it related to him. His turn, although his fat fingers were a lot slower.

*You realize what went on with me right? The bareknuckle fights they bankrolled when I was in my twenties?*

He ran his eyes around the restaurant. Christmas decorations. Mistletoe. A beautifully decorated evergreen in the window. Red and green everywhere, the seated female guests flush with it. His gaze narrowed on the doors to the kitchen.

*Here even, through those swinging doors. Downstairs in the basement*

*A boxing ring chalked out. Boxers throwing hands drunk refs smelly aging cheese*

*Knockouts broken ribs noses dislocated fingers. Cuts so many cuts. Blood splatter everywhere. The produce the walls the kitchen supplies*

*All in the name of surviving five minutes of bareknuckle fury for bragging rights and small purses*

Rhea put her phone down, reached across the linen tablecloth, and embraced his hands.

Philo rambled aloud, needing to vent.

"In my twenties, it was a part of my DNA," he said. "When 9-11 hit—"

He quit the fight game, entered the Navy, and did his tours. He retold it, history she already knew. Because he needed to.

"After I got back, I made peace with everyone." He paused. He choked back a lump in his throat. "Almost everyone."

"Not your dad."

"Yes, not my dad. Too late there."

She turned one of his hands up, opened it. "These scars…"

She lifted his hand to her face. Her lips and her light, warm breath comforted his fingers, their knuckles broken and disfigured from multiple bloody battles in makeshift fight venues around the city, the state, the country. The world.

When she set his hand back on the table, it returned to what was, for Philo, its natural state: a fist.

"Your hands make it easy for me to believe you, but it's not so easy accepting it when you're alone with me. Your tenderness… You've got a pass from me on that part of your life, you know that. Just don't abuse it. And don't let this place give you any ideas. You're too good a person to get back into it." She bit into a breadstick and managed a cute smirk. "And you're too old."

Philo had a rebuttal, one that could go after the snark, not the fallacy of her thinking, but he choked it back when two waitstaff arrived with their entrees. The dining room's cacophony picked up, knives and forks and spoons and wineglasses in motion at tables around the room, the patrons enjoying their dinners. A few bites into her lasagna, the grin from having the last word drained from Rhea's face. She stilled her fork, leaned right a little to see past Philo. Something in progress behind him had her attention.

He could have turned around but he didn't, already with a full view of the room in the long, tilted mirror behind her, above the bar.

A male patron at the front of the restaurant had excused himself to become the third guy to do so within a minute of two others from different tables. As soon as he left his seat, this third guy became a fourth, and the fourth became a fifth. They each entered the narrow aisle, walked single file, no nods, no pleasantries, all business, heading toward the men's room. Wrong. They passed the men's room and pushed through the swinging doors into the kitchen, which was quick to swallow them up.

Rhea reinterested herself in her meal, Philo doing likewise with his. Reflection mode for them both.

"It's suddenly a popular place back there, in the kitchen," she said between bites.

"Yeah. A real mecca." The meat ravioli and the chef's thick red diablo gravy flecked with pepper flakes was like Philo remembered. It delighted his palate but numbed his mouth.

"I'd say more like Rome than Mecca," she said.

"Fine. More like Rome."

His tongue was on fire. He went for the wine. It didn't help. He then went for his phone.

Rhea checked his text.

*I got nothing here Rhea no explanation. These guys are younger 30s 40s maybe. More like wise guys than capos. Maybe they're downstairs in the basement unloading vegetables. You feeling compromised and want to go?*

She returned the text. *Relax honey. Not before I see them when they come back plus have some cannoli and cappuccino*

Which was soon after their desserts and coffees were delivered. The swinging doors gave them up one at a time, the full complement of five returning to the dining room while Philo and Rhea consumed the massive, excellent, chocolate chip cannoli they shared while sipping their drinks. The last guy through had slipped some cash to their waiter. The wise guy families were now finishing up their meals at their tables, passing compliments to Irv while dressing themselves for a return to the briskness of a cold night. The busboys moved in.

Rhea sipped, Philo sipped, their cappuccinos so *bellissimo*—

Their waiter startled Rhea, arriving alongside her, a surprise to them both. He leaned in close.

"So sorry about this, miss, but I have something for you from one of the other guests."

The waiter's hand struggled behind his back, where he had trouble grabbing at something.

Philo's reaction was immediate, his cappuccino cup spilling, rebalancing his weight onto the balls of his feet while he catapulted forward. The waiter's jaw dropped at the confrontation, Philo moving between him and Rhea, the young man's hand shaking, unable to hand Rhea what he had for her, a business card, because his wrist was in Philo's grip.

"Oh," a sheepish Philo said, releasing him, "sorry, bud, I... Hell, my bad. So sorry." He pirouetted through an apology to the other diners. Rhea accepted the card and Philo retreated to his seat.

"Well, that was fun," she said.

"Sorry. I got a little wrapped up in the surroundings. I'll go with coffee instead of espresso next time. At least I didn't pull my, you know..."

"Your hand went under your jacket, you just didn't come out with it. Okay, let's see what we have here—"

She turned the card over, found something handwritten. She read it to herself.

"And?" Philo said, waiting.

Rhea handed it to him.

The restaurant's business card. On the back, in legible printing: *Nicky Bricks' widow put us on your armored car case. Regards to Philo.*

"So much for Teddy's Harriet staying out of it," Philo said, and handed the card back.

"This is not good, damn it." Rhea pulled her phone from her clutch and started texting, but it wasn't to Philo.

Thumbs a-blazing, she was in the zone, her eyes widening and narrowing then widening again, the focus on her handheld. Philo beckoned Irv the owner to their table.

"Do I owe you guys anything? We're heading out."

"You are good to go, Mister Trout. I hope everything was to your satisfaction."

"The food was excellent, Irv. Just like I remember it."

"Wonderful." Irv gestured to their waiter, who left the room for their coats.

"And the entertainment... it was just like I remember it, too," Philo added. He sailed past Irv's puzzled look with a "Never mind, inside joke," as the waiter arrived.

Philo bundled up, Rhea still in her seat. Philo coaxed her into standing and had the waiter help her on with her jacket. She held up her texting frenzy only long enough to get her arms through the sleeves. Philo opened the vestibule door and assisted his preoccupied detective girlfriend through it. Once past the threshold, he guided her down a step to the sidewalk.

"Wait," she said, disoriented. It was like she'd awakened from a sleep-walking episode, the cold jolting her eyes open. "Oh. We left. Sorry."

Philo draped his arm around her shoulders as they walked. "Don't be. Just tell me what's going on."

"I needed to get the word out, Philo. To the commissioner, her assistant, the city's organized crime task force, and my partner Carl."

"And that word was?"

"That some mob types fessed up to their interest in this case. I had to explain how I knew, and that became a thing, too, but so far, they say they're okay with how it went down tonight, considering the outcome."

"Explain 'became a thing.'"

"Me back there, eating at Broadway Louie's, given its history. It will be deemed poor judgment."

"Blame me."

"I did. What I didn't fess up to was their little wave to you at the end."

"Wave?"

"The 'regards to Philo' written on the card. The cop brass doesn't need to know you've got history with them."

Philo squeezed her shoulder again. "Ah. I see. Because—"

She stopped to face him. "Yes. Because more poor judgment. I like what we have here, Philo. I don't want anyone telling me I have to choose." She kissed him lightly, tenderly, on the lips. He reciprocated until her phone beeped. They stopped so she could read a text.

"The commissioner. She wants me to head into the precinct tonight. You mind dropping me off?"

# 8

## STEAMER TRUNK

**Sunday evening, December 6**
**Northeast Philadelphia**
**Number of days to the New Year's Day Parade: 26**

Philo climbed the concrete steps and reached the indented landing, the front doors of his and his neighbor facing each other across fifteen feet. The motion detector bathed the landing in stark, white floodlighting. He pulled at the aluminum storm door, its hinges squeaking, and rested his foot on the threshold in front of the shiny brass mail slot as bait. He waited and listened.

Movement on the other side of the door.

*Meow.* A paw darted through the mail slot, its claws connecting with his pantleg, roughing up the denim. The swipe left a white scratch of newly exposed cloth threads.

"Step away from the door, Six."

*Meow.*

A yellow sticky note attached just below the door knocker fluttered. He pulled it down and held it under the floodlight to read it.

*My kid's missing a rabbit from his hutch, Trout. Your cat know anything about this?* The signed sticky was from a fireman who lived in the last house at the end of the block.

"Damn it, Six, you little predator."

Six sliced at his pantleg through the slot again. He inserted his key, pushed past the delivered mail scattered on the floor, and entered his living room.

*Meow.*

Up his leg in an instant, Six was now in his arms, purring, craning her neck to nuzzle against his chin. He punched in a code to his security system, then scratched her head. "You're a troublemaker. Out. Now. While I get settled. And no more rabbits."

*Meow.*

He swept the storm door open. Six leapt from his arms and padded down the steps, waited at the curb a moment, then slingshot herself into the street from between parked cars.

Reckless. Outdoor cats lived on borrowed time, and Six was no different. But after ten years with him it was more like she'd absconded the borrowed time of a dozen other cats, probably also that of her previous owner. Six scaled the piled snow on the other side of the street and made herself scarce in the shadows.

Philo refilled Six's food and water bowls in the kitchen. He grabbed a carton of OJ from the fridge, sat at the table and sipped, musing about the long, intense day that had ended with his dinner with Rhea. At ten-thirty p.m., could he stomach the day dragging on any longer? Yes and no.

*Do some laundry,* his inner voice said, *one load.*

He pulled himself up, went to the basement steps, and flipped on the light switch on the way down.

Cleaning and lubricating one gun tonight—doing "some laundry, one load"—would be a start, would give him some leverage against the what-ifs. All those military, criminal, civil, and familial what-ifs from his past, diminished some by time, or some by short or distracted memories, or some by the shortened lifespans of vengeful, violent people who could do him harm. People who had other enemies in addition to him. He was hiding in plain sight, in the house where he grew up, doing little to avoid confrontation. He'd instead chosen to bulk up his defense rather than bow to the fear. Like Six, he was living on borrowed time. It was why he understood her so well, and why he would never rein her in.

But the only way to keep the what-ifs at bay was to treat them less like ifs and more like whens.

He owned twelve guns. He carried one Sig Sauer and one derringer, not always, and not always both, but often. The other ten he kept in working order in different locations around the house. Seven more semi-auto Sigs, a second ankle-holstered Bond Arms Snake Slayer derringer, one Honey Badger short-barreled rifle, and one Winchester pump-action shotgun. Tonight's load of laundry would be to clean and oil the shotgun.

The squat white cabinet between the washer and the dryer held his gun cleaning toolkit, behind the liquid Tide. He brought the red pimpled-plastic kit to his dad's heavy-duty homemade workbench and removed from it the carbon cleaner, bore polish, solvent degreaser, brushes, and gun oil. He unzipped the long gym bag under the workbench and lifted its content topside onto the bench. His Winchester shotgun. A fifteen-minute clean was all he had in him tonight. After he finished, he'd tidy up the workbench and grab a beer from his basement micro fridge and chill.

The shotgun oiled and a beer in hand, he dropped into a tufted cloth armchair, feathers poking through its seams, facing the basement's built-in cedar closet. The closet loomed. He sipped from the longneck bottle, staring the closet doors down, ambivalent, he told himself, but wary of the ghosts they contained.

A muffled voice came from inside the closet. Like it or not, his subconscious coaxed it out, drawing it into the open.

*We bent but we didn't break, Tris.*

His father. Not real, but he heard him plain as day in his head.

"I guess we're going to do this tonight. Okay." He gulped at his beer. His eyes moistened, and he blinked out a few tears, knowing the pain the closet held.

*Tris* was short for Tristan, his birth name. *Philo* hadn't entered the mix as a name until he was in his twenties when he started boxing. After Clint Eastwood's lanky movie character Philo Beddoe, a celluloid bareknuckle phenom with a rooster comb hairline like his own, had become a thing.

The boxing nickname stuck, but it wasn't something his father ever embraced.

*We had the final word against them Japs, Tris.*

He opened the closet's double doors and breathed in the cedar. A small overhead light came on, illuminating an upright military steamer trunk that was seventy-five-plus years old and more than half the height of the closet space. Wood corner struts fortified the trunk's varnished walnut shell, offset by tarnished brass appointments. The decals and stickers slapped onto the exterior were South-Pacific-tropical in color, the varnish sealing them in, some of them torn, some in perfect condition: *Hawaii, The Philippines, Okinawa, Japan,* and a small one near the front latch that said *The Bonin Islands.* His eyes went to the top left corner of the trunk, where the flat surface facing him bore the stenciled letters "*C.A.T., Ens., USN.*"

Clair Aloysius Trout, Ensign, U.S. Navy. His father. The same stencil appeared on all six sides of the trunk.

What had possessed his father's parents to christen their son with so feminine a first name, Clair, one that put a "Kick Me" sign on his back? Why do that to a boy?

*The streets, Tristan.*

Those tough, Depression-era, inner city streets of Philadelphia, Philo's granddad had told his father.

*The same consideration we had, son, when we named you Tristan.*

"Indeed, Pop."

More beer.

Philo swiveled one side of the upright footlocker as far to the left as the hinges would let it, exposing the steamer trunk's interior. On one side, drawers that were filled with medals, buttons, an aviator logbook, and other memorabilia ran top to bottom. The other side held a short pole where vintage clothing on thin wooden hangers hung in short garment bags pressed flat against the trunk's back wall. Inside the bags were a set of Navy officer's summer khakis with shorts, and a full set of officer's dress whites. Hooks, thumbtacks, clips, and a shaving mirror on a retractable scissored arm poked out from angles inside the trunk. Camphor permeated its interior, pungent and eye-watering.

The steamer trunk bore testimony to his father's military life as a Naval airman in the Pacific theater, 1944 forward. Prior to his enlistment, "Pop" Trout was a police detective assigned to the Northeast section of Philadelphia. Six years with the police force before WWII. The trunk told the wartime story of him as an enlisted man. A time capsule that ran the gamut, including official Navy photos of Philo's dad receiving his pilot's commission, one of him waving from the second seat of a three-person Navy Avenger torpedo bomber at Pearl Harbor's Hickam Airfield, and one from the liberation of the remaining POWs from a camp in the Bonin Islands at the end of the war. The last photos showed his father as an emaciated, grim-faced man in a crouch next to a fire pit outside his POW shack. Inside this trunk was the version the public saw about the Navy POWs the Marines had liberated, including Clair A. Trout, war hero. The untold, unpublicized narrative of his prison camp experience had come to Philo in pieces only, and in Philo's internalized spiritual communion with the contents of this trunk after his father's death.

*On Chichijima Island, we did things. Things that were necessary.*

His father's voice, in his head again, from post-war entries in his aviator's logbook, akin to a diary.

*But we were never cannibals.*

"I know, Pop." Philo twisted open another beer.

The POW camp on Chichijima Island was 700 miles south of Tokyo, 150 miles north of Iwo Jima. One of the Bonin Islands, Chichijima was where he and seven other U.S. airmen were taken after their planes went down near the island. The capture and the gruesome demise of seven of the eight men at the hands of the enemy had come to light only recently, when the media reported how a ninth airman had evaded capture altogether by flying his wounded Avenger dive bomber out to sea rather than attempt to land it. This became the storied history of a certain WWII Navy pilot, George H.W. Bush, the 41st president of the United States. Had he crash landed on or near the island, he most likely would not have survived his capture. Only one captured airman had.

*They forced us to do unspeakable things. Sickening, vile things.*

Tortured and beaten during their interrogations, his fellow airmen were executed, one by one, all of them decapitated. Then came the most despicable outcome possible for the handling of their remains: forcing the remaining U.S. captives to become butchers of their brethren, then cooks, then servers. The camp's Japanese officers were ordered by their psychopathic superior to eat their prisoners' livers and other body parts served by the POWs, and they did.

The day that Clair A. Trout, last of the eight, was to be executed had arrived. That morning, the Allies attacked and liberated the camp. He was discovered by the U.S. Marines behind his shack, poking at a raging campfire with human remains in it. In the fire, along with the remains of his last POW mate, were those of a camp guard that Pop Trout had strangled with his own hands. The Marines extinguished the fire too late to save any of the American POW's remains, but the liberators pulled out the Japanese guard's dead body by the arms, his legs on fire, his torso intact except for...

*His liver, Tris. I cooked and served it to them. I made those bastards eat one of their own.*

"Proud of you, Pop," Philo said, lifting his beer bottle in salute, "for having the last word."

Still fit for duty, his pop finished his enlistment in occupied Japan with the Office of Naval Intelligence, ONI. It added to his prejudices against the Japanese, but seeing the aftermath of the atomic bombs also turned him into a pacifist. Growing up in the City of Brotherly Love, however, had made his son Philo anything but. The love, the hate, Philo's ambivalence toward parental authority, his father was heartbroken when he embraced the local thug life. 9-11 had eliminated a reconciliation. His father was a passenger on American Airlines Flight 77, the plane that crashed into the Pentagon.

"Thanks, Pop, for these chats," he said, choking up. "Better late than never," but the "better" aspect never seemed to materialize.

The way Philo saw things, when a country's ideologies tempered by its self-preservation got the better of common sense, they turned into fanaticism, and the fanaticism became a cancer. The cancer had to be challenged and its cells eradicated. It happened throughout WWII, and it had happened many times since. Philo accepted his SEAL deployments as testaments to the ongoing malaise.

Wars. Declared, undeclared, overt, covert. Missions on the radar, or missions flying undetected beneath it. And regardless of how many notches each soldier's rifle held, sometimes the cancer came back. Stronger, and often smarter. In search of its foes and to settle scores. On the enemy's soil, but also on its own.

He was getting too maudlin. Beer. He needed more beer.

Back to his guns. He owned as many as he did because he had to.

His father never would have approved. The thuggery, the guns, the bareknuckle fights, Philo's stint as a SEAL. None of it. 9-11 had pushed Philo into the arms of the military. The patriotism was there, but avenging the loss of his father—that irony wasn't lost on him.

"I miss you, Pop, you bastard, every—damn—day." He missed his mother, too, but she didn't need to hear it. His father did.

He opened an old hatbox in the bottom of the trunk and removed his father's white USN officer's cap. His face in front of the shaving mirror, he slipped the cap onto his head and squared it up, finishing off a beer while he stared at himself.

Six the Cat pushed through the pet door at the rear of the basement. She strutted past the washer and dryer and raised her tail at the man in the white naval officer's cap, hissing at him. Philo returned the hat to the box and placed it back in the trunk. His chat with Pop was over.

Six rubbed against his pantleg.

"Hi, sweetums."

*Purr... purr...*

"What happened here?" he said, gripping and raising her chin. A tiny gash on the tip of her nose trickled blood. "Not liking this, lady. You losing your edge?"

He held her away from him and checked out the rest of her.

*Meow.*

No other damage. A few swipes with a wet paper towel from the laundry sink and a glob of antiseptic stemmed the blood from the gash. Administering the first aid gave him a closer look at her neck and her collar.

"Jeez, Six, what the hell...?"

A slash across the collar's forever-dirty red leather had stripped off a section of its beadwork, some of the turquoise beads lost to another back-alley cat skirmish. It compromised the leather, but not terminally. A shame if he'd have to replace it, because he knew he couldn't duplicate it. Handmade, no doubt one of a kind, it came with Six when he'd adopted her, and it was also—again, no doubt—at one time a fine piece of artwork by an old country artisan.

"From warrior to warrior," he said, petting his bestest feline buddy, "you think maybe it's time to hang up the gloves, Six?"

*Meow.*

Philo found another sixpack, dropped back into the chair, and recommenced staring at the closet. Six hopped back onto his lap and took a nap.

# 9

## AN AUDIBLE

Wally Lanakai peeked at his two tiles. He faced the dealer at the Pai Gow dominoes table, who like him was a dominoes player, not a casino employee, one of six players at the table. Wally called for another tile. It was another late night for him at Resorts Casino Hotel in Atlantic City. Magpie Papahani, Wally's bodyguard, hovered over his shoulder, his six-eight frame in a dark business suit like Wally's.

They had a good view of the wide aisle of bustling casino guests that ran behind the dominoes tables, separating them from the poker and blackjack tables on the other side. A few poker tables in, a casino dealer clocked out and a new dealer clocked in. Before she started dealing a hand, she gestured "get out" at one of the players seated, a male gambler with stacks of chips in front of him. Her hands, her head, and apparently her moving lips were all in agreement with her message.

Only a few things could get someone removed from a gaming table short of committing a felony. Among them were aggressive behavior, drunkenness, lewd gesturing, lewd language, being underage, or being identified as an "advantage player," someone who used legal methods like card counting to gain an unfair advantage. The new dealer was adamant that she wanted the guy removed, and Wally now wanted to know why.

"Magpie." Wally leaned back, spoke to his bodyguard over his shoulder. "See that poker table, where that female dealer is giving that chunky guy with all those chips a hard time? The guy in the basketball high-tops. Any idea what the hell is going on?"

That was Magpie's cue to check it out. He left Wally's side and crossed the aisle. Wally turned up the new domino tile his dealer gave him for a peek. Not a good hand yet.

Magpie didn't get far. The scruffy guy had committed a trifecta of no-no's, any one of which could get him tossed: foul language, finger-pointing, and a threat with a drink, all directed at the female dealer, senior to him by decades. It ended with him bolting from the table with his winnings in a chip bucket before any of the floor bosses could arrive. He threaded himself into the stream of meandering gamblers in the aisle and headed in the direction of the elevators.

Wally turned his tiles over, his hand not a winner, and waited for the next Pai Gow deal.

Magpie returned and spoke discreetly. "The dude was not having a good day. The new dealer recognized him from past tables. Get this, boss. He's underage. Plus, he's an 'advantage gambler.' She wouldn't deal him into the next hand. He pretty much sealed his own fate with that tantrum. Look, boss, here they come..."

Security was coming for him, four guards in blazers, hot on his trail.

Straight from a new dominoes hand, Wally knew from his peek that he'd win it, but he kept a poker face with his dealer. He watched security close in on the kid, who was now aware of his fate and stuffing markers into his pockets, thousands of dollars of chips, preparing to run.

Wally gave the kid an A plus for balls but an F for speed and agility, except now, with closer scrutiny, there was something familiar about him—

Wally smiled broadly when it clicked. "Ha! This is going to be hilarious."

"Excuse me? Sir?" the dealer said to Wally. "Another tile?"

He waved off a new domino and turned the two in front of him over, displaying his hand.

"Gee Joon," the dealer announced. Wally had the highest set of tiles and the best single hand possible. All the players showed their tiles in response. The dealer bowed to Wally and his winning hand.

"Great," Wally said, and tossed the dealer a chip. "I'm cashing out." He leaned back to get Magpie's attention and spoke to him. "I know who that kid is."

Magpie followed Wally's eyes and nodded. "Is that—?"

"Little Sal Massimo, Big Sal Massimo's grandkid. Casino security's about to haul his ass out of here. Massimo's got a place here in the hotel, a room he and his friends use. The kid's probably staying in it."

"The kid's like what, eighteen?"

"I don't know, but he's definitely underage," Wally said. "They'll take all his chips. Follow him and I'll catch up with you. This should be interesting."

Wally cashed out and hurried to leave the gaming floor. He reached the elevator bank. Magpie was just ahead of him, an observer as the security guards escorted Little Sal Massimo by the elbows from the elevators, back into the casino. One guard had the kid's chip bucket, another was threatening to take the teen's pants off in public if he didn't empty the chips from his pockets into a separate bucket the guard was carrying, like, immediately. Massimo's grandkid bucked and dipped, then went limp in their arms, screaming at the guards, telling them they "messed with the wrong Philly homeboy. I won those markers, they're mine, asshole. Get the fuck off me, I fucking know people..."

The guards dragged him into an alcove of business offices near the cashier windows. Wally and Magpie trailed them, then stationed themselves outside the hallway. The louvered shutters for the office window closed.

"We'll wait here a minute to see what happens," Wally said. "Get us some drinks."

With Magpie gone, Wally took a seat in the lounge next to a bar area with a good view of the gaming tables on the floor—poker, blackjack, and the Asian gaming area he'd just left—plus the slots. Next to him, the elevator bank stayed busy, doors opening and closing, its four cars discharging a steady stream of passengers but in low numbers, no over-crowding. After one elevator opened and closed its doors, Wally perked up at the single passenger who exited.

An older guy he recognized. Tall, and gaunt as a vulture, he knew him from the South Philly streets. A numbers runner for the Massimo family— the bars, the docks, the factories, the grocery stores.

"Frank Tisha." Wally mouthed the name without realizing he'd said it aloud.

Tonight was looking like South Philly mob night at Resorts Casino Hotel in Atlantic City. Wally didn't look away, didn't care if Frank Tisha noticed him. Tisha's focus was on the gaming tables and the bucket of markers he carried toward them, not whoever might be watching him. He kept walking, zipping past Wally, so close he could have tripped him, still with no awareness of his audience. He found a seat at a blackjack table.

Magpie returned with their drinks and handed Wally a tumbler. "Dewar's. You say something, boss?'

"There. Right there," Wally said with a chin point. "See that guy? The one with the oddball eye. He runs numbers for Massimo."

Magpie nodded, watching the man arrange himself in his seat, then set up his chips. "That's Otherway Tisha. Word has it he's a sweetheart, boss. The street loves him."

Frank Tisha continued arranging his chips, stacking and restacking them.

"He's got healthy stacks of markers there, boss. Looks like he plans on spending a while at the tables tonight."

Wally's nod was interrupted by a sudden awkward move by their subject. Tisha raised his head like a prairie dog who'd sensed he was being watched. He turned all the way around on his stool and faced them.

"It looks like him and that weird eye of his made us, Magpie. He can see behind his back..."

"I don't think it works that way, boss."

Frank Tisha and Wally were having themselves a moment. It evaporated when the business office alcove behind Wally got loud. Stocky Little

Sal Massimo exploded out of an open door, a bucket in one hand and a colorful T-shirt in the other. He hustled to the edge of the slot machines and slowed his stride as he entered the gaming area. His voice got louder as he raised his hand, the one that held the T-shirt. A uniformed security guard was closing on him.

"Listen up, losers! See this T-shirt? Is it worth five thousand bucks? The casino says it is. I earned these chips fair and square"—he held up his bucket—"and the casino wants to steal 'em and give me this fucking T-shirt instead. So here's some early Christmas presents to everybody—five grand in chips! Get 'em before the casino takes them back!"

Little Sal tossed the T-shirt in the air, then handful after handful of chips around the room. "Take 'em! Take 'em all!"

Slots players pounced and grabbed and pushed, snatching up chips from the floor, picking up loose, stray chips that dropped from buckets, and helping themselves to other players' markers from unattended stashes. Chaos in this small area turned into a mini-riot with punching and elbowing and grabbing and hair-pulling until security arrived, first wrestling Little Sal Massimo to the floor, chicken-winging his arms, and cuffing his hands behind his back. Other guards moved in to separate grabby casino guests from each other.

Wally and Magpie kept their distance across the aisle, sipping their drinks and chuckling, entertained by the brawl and Resorts' security coming down hard, physically and verbally, on the teen:

*Don't fucking care if you have a room... Don't care who your pop-pop is. You're the police's fucking problem now.*

"Magpie, look—see Tisha?"

"What about him?"

Frank Tisha played with his chips and engaged in a conversation with his blackjack dealer, smiling and schmoozing, with no interest in the brawl or the kid who started it.

"He saw the fighting. He knows that's Massimo's grandkid. He turned his back on him and went back to his cards. Something's not right about this."

Wally stayed focused on Otherway Tisha, and Tisha stayed focused on his blackjack hand. The Massimo grandkid shot off his mouth with a string of obscenities while they hurried him toward the exit that would take them to the parking garage.

"Let's go," Wally said. "I want to see them hand the kid off to the police."

Wally found his phone, started thumbing through a contacts list while they walked. They entered a corridor, closing the gap between them and a security team that was still in hustle mode. Wally tapped at a number and put his phone to his ear.

"Who you calling, boss?"

"Otherway Tisha was useless. I'm calling his boss to let him know what's going down. Do the guy a favor."

"You're calling Salvatore Massimo? That a good idea, boss?"

"I pay you to protect me, Magpie. I'm not asking you for your opinion."

Wally walked faster than he intended, closing the gap between him and Little Sal's forced security escort in the corridor. Soon they were right behind them, everyone's footfalls echoing except for the chubby teen who'd gone ragdoll limp, making security work harder to remove him. They all reached the exit.

No police activity yet. Wally and Magpie spilled outside behind them and moved away from the sliding glass doors. Someone answered Wally's phone call with a gravelly voice sounding worse, no doubt, because of the hour.

"Who the fuck is this?" the voice said.

"You know who this is, Massimo. Wally Lanakai. Apologies for the late call. I have some information for you. Your grandson is here at Resorts Casino in Atlantic City, in a parking garage with the casino's security. They're about to hand him off to the cops for underage gambling and for starting a riot on the floor. He's going to jail, Massimo."

"That's bullshit. I got eyes down there. I didn't hear nothing about this. Go eat some poi, you fat fuck, and spend more of your money at the casino. I'm happy to get my cut. I'm going back to sleep, asshole. And fuck you."

"You're a funny man, Massimo. Don't say I didn't warn you, *hanu peni*."

Wally hung up. "Magpie."

"Yeah, boss?"

"Get someone to send that mobster relic a Hawaiian dictionary. Next time I call him 'penis breath,' I want him to know it."

Not rock star parking, but they were close to it. Magpie opened a rear door for Wally, then sat in the driver's seat.

"Pull out of the space and put the flashers on," Wally told him. "We're not leaving yet."

Still no police car. Wally was getting impatient, watching the sliding doors for the casino open and close, cars discharging and picking up passengers near the ground floor entrance.

Their eyes fixed on one exiting patron because of the way he was dressed, in black leather from the neck down, carrying a black motorcycle helmet. Tall and blond, with a thin white face, he hesitated behind the casino's security detail, assessing them and their hostage before finding his phone and making a call.

Cars glided past, their headlights on, moving slow enough for pedestrians to weave in and out of their paths, the air near the building entrance stifling from car exhaust. The guy with the black helmet sped up his gait, crossed in between the slow traffic, and put on his helmet while he walked.

"Boss," Magpie said. "That guy—the one in the helmet—"

"What about him?"

"I don't like him. He came into the casino the same time we did. I saw him off and on while he was inside, too, by himself, him and that helmet, carrying it under his arm. Blond hair that needs a trim, all that motorcycle leather. He had dinner and drinks where we ate. I didn't see him move to any of the machines or tables. He spent a lot of time near us, boss, then he was gone."

Magpie peered over the dash to see down the aisle of slow-moving traffic approaching them, Wally's double-parked SUV worsening the flow. Magpie excused himself and exited their car. He now stood sentry, able to see deeper into the garage, locating the parking lot exit.

Wally rolled his window down. "Any cops in that line of cars, Magpie?"

"No. I'm not seeing that guy with the helmet either. Do we really need to watch that kid get hauled away? It's not like his mob grandfather even cares."

"He didn't care because he didn't believe me. His loss."

A motorcycle roared to life somewhere inside the concrete parking structure, the noise echoing. Not a throaty, heavy-metal Harley or Harley sound-alike, instead a Japanese crotch rocket with a tinny, crackling exhaust. The bike's engine revved with each twist of the handle.

"I see him, boss, far right corner. He's backing out of a space. Now he's heading for the exit."

They heard the brakes screech, and Magpie saw the rider turn his black and silver bike sharply away from the exit gate, its engine noise echoing throughout the garage, overwhelming the din. A hard left became a second hard left, and with a jolt of gasoline adrenaline it screamed past the line of cars inching their way toward the casino entrance, the bike moving like a speeding bullet toward them.

It braked on its approach. The biker's helmeted head gave Magpie and Wally a faceless look before the guy lifted a clenched hand eye level with Magpie, his finger mocking a trigger pull.

Magpie drew his handgun from his shoulder holster, targeting the biker rider as he zipped past. At the turn nearest the casino entrance, the rider's left hand now showed a short-stock semi-auto rifle. He crossed it over his right arm to point the gun at the glass double doors, his right hand staying on the throttle. "That's an Uzi, boss. Get down!"

Wally winced but stayed upright and powered down his window instead. A burst of automatic gunfire erupted, second and third bursts following it, the casino's doors shattering, people screaming and ducking for cover. The crotch rocket accelerated away from the point of attack and up the other side of the garage.

Magpie's eyes and gun tracked the motorcycle's path to the garage exit but without a clear shot. He and Wally watched it jump a curb onto a sidewalk to beat the tollgate. After a right turn out of the building and into the night traffic, the motorcycle was gone.

"Magpie. You okay, Magpie?"

"I'm good, boss." The big man reholstered his weapon, then checked the casino entrance. "But the guards, and that Massimo kid... Damn, boss, I think the kid's gone."

Magpie whipped open the SUV driver's side door and slid in behind the steering wheel. "We need to go, boss. People are on their phones. This place will be swarming soon..."

Their SUV limo accelerated to pass the cars in line, cruising past the entrance to the casino. Two casino guards lay unmoving on the concrete garage deck, draped over each other. Their teenage charge had slipped free but hadn't gotten far. Bullets had strafed him across the shoulder and the back of his head, dropping him face-first against the asphalt, his head cocked sideways, his eyes open but sightless. A third guard leaned against the front grille of a car and made gurgling noises while trying to raise himself. When he collapsed, the person trying to get him on his feet gave up.

They reached the garage exit, wholesale patron panic setting in, cars jumping a walkway to evade the toll lane, in a hurry to get the hell away from the crime scene. Magpie followed, the SUV bouncing up and over a sidewalk and out the exit. On the street now, he swiveled his head at each corner, searching.

"Maybe go after that bastard, boss? *E hookui i ka pu i kona anus?*"

"Not tonight, Magpie," Wally said. "If any weapon gets shoved up his ass when we find him, it'll be mine. Just get us back to Philly. Things will get crazy soon as this gets out."

"Boss—you think he was after us, or the kid?"

"Us. Then he saw Massimo's grandkid. He must have been a more attractive target."

Wally zeroed in on the fallout as they negotiated the late-night Atlantic City streets in search of the expressway, his mind processing the scene. A family member of Philly's mafioso—a grandbaby—had just been assassinated. Wally, the Ka Hui family "don," was right there. He'd even outted himself to the Italian mob's don as being there with a phone call. They had a personal view of the kid's execution. Wally reached back to the conversation with the elder Massimo and a comment Wally had left him with before hanging up on him.

*"Don't say I didn't warn you."*

Ripe for misinterpretation.

Their car entered the Atlantic City Expressway westbound. They'd be back in Philly in an hour.

"Boss. Maybe call Mister Massimo back? Explain what happened?"

Wally's look out the window was distant, unfocused, the night sky cloudy. A water thoroughfare on their left, and trees on the right, protecting marshland. The road had been busy on their way in but direct and uncomplicated, loaded with anxious people coming to gamble, to see shows, to drink, to eat. To experience Atlantic City and its decadence, which gave them a respite from their real lives and responsibilities. It was the same road on their way out, but things like real-world drama, personal conflicts, misunderstandings, and life's harsh realities could often become more complicated just because of the visit.

This, Wally thought, was one of those times.

"If I call Massimo, he won't believe me, Magpie, even if he says he does."

Wally needed to contact his street lieutenants, the local money launderers, his drug runners, his club in Chinatown, and the people who ran the clearinghouses for his black-market goods. They would all need to be on standby, to be prepared for retaliation.

He finished the last of his calls as Philadelphia's glistening nighttime skyline came into view. The casino incident, Little Sal Massimo's outburst, came back to him.

"Tisha," he said absently.

"I don't follow, boss."

"In the casino. That Otherway guy with the freaky eye. He ignored the Massimo kid's tantrum."

"So. What about him?"

"I don't know how he fits, but Tisha being there and not speaking up means something."

The blame would already be queuing up, Wally knew. Things around Philly and South Jersey were about to get a lot messier.

# 10

## SAFE AT HOME

Monday, December 7
Northern Liberties, Philadelphia
Number of days to the New Year's Day Parade: 25

Monday, schmonday. Philo's hangover staked its claim throughout the takeout lunch he couldn't eat, subdued by the only thing he could stomach, a quart of OJ and one piece of toast from his BLT.

He hadn't stopped at one six-pack last night while communing with the contents of his dad's steamer trunk. Now he was paying for it at a new remediation site in the middle of Philly's Northern Liberties section. He dragged his body out of the Blessid Trauma step van to face the gated community entrance. He called Rhea.

"Any insights here?" he asked her. "They've cleared the scene, so we'll be going in as soon as someone opens the gate."

In block after block of Northern Liberties, "old city" Philly industrial/commercial architecture had been leveled in favor of high-end townhouses, business offices, apartment renovations, and a few small, gated communities like the one this crime scene was in. The site was behind walls that surrounded its full-block-square footprint of courtyards and greenery not accessible to the general public. Demolition and redevelopment. New luxury homes at prices more affordable than Center City. Neighborhood gentrification had happened here virtually overnight, but now, here, also, had become the scene of a late-night murder of an out-of-towner. Another musician of color. The police said the man's wife was a person of interest, her whereabouts unknown.

"First thing, Philo," Rhea said, still on the phone, "is you need to be nice to the police team who caught this case, even if they give you a hard time. I have friends there from when I was in that district. Don't give them a reason to make your customer fire you."

A different crime scene cleaning company worked this area of the city almost exclusively, DeathClean, Inc., their offices in the neighborhood. DeathClean had a symbiotic relationship with the police district, and the district wasn't bashful about recommending them to people with homes needing hazmat scrubs from the aftermath of the loss of life. Which meant they were typically automatic as a choice when scenes in this upscale neighborhood needed remediation, except in this instance...

"I didn't chase this, Detective, the referral came to me. Teddy Cangelosi's doing. From his hospital bed. That's how important this is to him."

A New Orleans trumpeter, something-something Unser, was in Philly to perform in the New Year's Day parade with the Mummers. The Philly mayor had arranged temporary housing for him, a month in high-end digs owned by a retired bank president and his wife, snowbirds now in Florida, and friends of the city's administration. It was a place to stay while the trumpeter prepared for and marched in the holiday parade with the local club sponsoring him. Not Teddy's club, but he knew about the arrangement, all the Mummers' bands did. As soon as the news of the murder broke last night, the convalescing Teddy stepped in and referred the mayor's good friends, the townhouse owners, to Blessid Trauma Crime Scene Cleaning. The contract for the cleanup traded hands before lunch.

"I need to go, sweetie," Philo said, "the gate just opened."

Hank Blessid drove the step van into the community, Philo and Miñoso rounding out the team. The cold preserved the snow in all the right places for Christmas-card-worthy photographs throughout. A white gazebo draped in holly with red bows, a large fountain still iced over from the storm, black Victorian lampposts—even white and blue police SUVs with flashing lights rimming the common area—all of it worked as winter wonderland accessories.

They exited the truck in cleaning gear: drawstring blue hoods, purple nitrile gloves, blue pullover jumpsuits, shoe covers in blue, and handheld cleaning caddies ready for what they were told would be a simple clean, two rooms only, the living room and the first-floor bedroom off it. One person had been shot and killed. Maybe a burglary gone wrong, maybe something more. With the dead man's wife, also a person of color, missing, Philo was leaning toward the latter. One plainclothes cop met them inside the townhouse door, Philo the first to enter. Square-jawed guy, tailored pants, white shirt, tie, and a police-issue waist-length winter jacket. A detective type who looked like he relied on the rest of his team to do the heavy lifting. His hand was out. He wiggled his fingers.

"Work order," he said.

Philo accommodated him.

The cop skimmed the pages. Speaking to Philo, "And you are...?"

"Tristan Trout, Blessid Trauma's owner. Bottom of the second page."

Philo's gloved finger pointed at a signature, to speed up their exchange. The cop's no-bullshit face kept Philo from suffixing his answer with, *but my friends call me Philo.* He introduced Hank and Miñoso, their names also on the work order.

Philo asked the detective for his business card.

"You don't need it," the cop said. His hand went out again. "IDs. All of you."

Hard ass. Philo and Hank showed their driver's licenses. The cop did a doubletake with Miñoso, who earned a few more grunts than Hank and Philo got, but his Mexican Matricular Consular card and state driver's license were both in order.

The detective thumbed them through the front door. Miñoso took a wide berth around their cop host, the cop's hard look following him.

"There's expensive shit in here, Trout. Don't let any of it leave with you. The place has been photographed from top to bottom. We'll know."

Philo didn't dignify the comment. "This home have a basement, Detective?" He eyed the thick, gloppy blood splatter inside the front door. He knew what dripping blood could do to the flooring and whatever was underneath it.

"Yes, it has a basement." The detective handed the work order back. "I'll be outside in my vehicle."

In the hallway, chalk outlined where the body was found on the terrazzo tile floor near the entrance. Blood had exploded outward from the victim's head, gooey and thick enough that there was still a sheen after it dried on the tile. Philo and his assistants eyed the spray pattern, clearly a headshot, indicative, most likely, of a bullet or bullets to the face that exited the rear of the skull. Philo's first reaction was to squint at the wall at the end of the hallway. Circles around holes in the drywall outside the kitchen confirmed the headshot theory.

"Hank," Philo said. "Pictures, please, before we touch anything. The entire hallway, the entrance, all the way to the kitchen, and that drywall."

They remained near the front door while Hank snapped away with his phone as he tread lightly across the tile, around the chalk. There were no bloody footprints anywhere near the outline. Philo's first thought was the assassin might not have entered the house, maybe did the shooting from the doorway. Front door opens, bad guy fires the gun, bad guy leaves. An assassination. But there was another room they needed to remedy, a first-floor bedroom, so that theory didn't work.

"Philo."

"Yeah, Hank?"

"Check this out."

An oddity: there was more blood splatter farther into the hallway, before the kitchen. Not a kill shot, but it did indicate someone had been shot here, or suffered an injury that bled. No chalk outline, which meant the cops hadn't found a second victim there.

With the hallway chronicled, they followed the terrazzo tile to the kitchen, which was laid out to the left of its entrance from the hallway. Snacks on the counter, an open bottle of Montepulciano wine. Pet bowls in a corner. Cat photo on the fridge, a tan and black and white tabby. More photos by Hank and Philo both—evidence, on the surface at least, that there'd been no violent acts in the kitchen. Same for the dining room off the kitchen, a formal space with dark furniture and old-school colonial chair rail.

They retreated to the hallway, returning the way they came, and entered the two-story living room. Hardwood floors with random widths, knotted, with a faked distressed look, and definitely custom. Colonial-style furniture, stone hearth and fireplace, and an overlook from a second-floor landing. Hank took additional photos, Philo and Miñoso following in his footsteps. No additional damage in the living room. The last room they needed to check was the first-floor master bedroom, adjacent to the living room.

The door to the bedroom hung off one of its hinges askew of the jamb, clearly a forced entry. Philo gripped the handle and the long edge of the door, his gloved hands lifting the cockeyed door off the floor. He swiveled it out of the way by the one functional hinge and set it back down. It stayed upright, far from perpendicular to the splintered jamb.

He didn't enter, scanning the room's contents first. Much of the distressed-style hardwood was covered by an oriental rug in rose under a king-size sleigh bed, the rug large enough to surround the bed and provide soft comfort to bare feet next to it. The rug's edges greeted the legs of the furniture lining the walls: an armoire, a bureau, a makeup table, and a dresser, all of it following around the bed's perimeter. On the wall to the right hung floor-to-ceiling drapes covering a sliding glass door.

Aside from the bedroom door, did anything in here need work?

Philo waved Miñoso to proceed around him but changed his mind. He dropped a hand on Miñoso in midstride, gripping his shoulder. "Stop."

Close to his employee's right foot was a blood droplet. Philo scanned the area around his own feet. Another droplet. He retrieved his phone, snapped on the flashlight, and checked under his booties. No blood smears.

"Miñoso," Philo called, Miñoso a few feet ahead of him. "Can you see what went on in here? Anything needing work aside from these drops of blood?"

Miñoso swiveled his head to view the bedroom interior. "Blood drops only, *campeón* Philo sir, nothing else." Again with the boxing reference. To

Miñoso, student of the game, once a champ, always a champ. Philo had given up chiding him about it.

"Check the *letrina*, Philo *campeón*?"

The bathroom. "Sure. Careful where you walk. Hank, we need more pictures in here."

With the three of them now inside the bedroom, Hank snapped more photos, the sliding glass door drapes open for some of them, closed for others. Miñoso confirmed the *letrina* needed no intervention. Philo eyed those blood drops ahead of him. Not much work. They'd be done with this entire townhouse cleanup in two, three hours tops. The homeowner would need a carpenter or a handyman to replace the bedroom door.

Oops. Hold on.

The blood droplets near Philo's feet were larger than the ones in the hallway. They continued onto the rug. Three more drops near its long edge, a fourth large drop half on the rug, half on the wood floor. No blood past the fourth drop, near the end of the dresser. He looked behind him in the hall they'd just left. There just wasn't all that much blood compared to what they saw for the first victim. Not enough, he surmised, for whoever had been attacked outside the bedroom to have entered it then left again, still bleeding. And once inside the bedroom, no blood trail to the bathroom, or over to the room's sliding glass door, either, beyond which was an enclosed patio.

The bleeder had entered the bedroom, but it appeared he or she hadn't left.

Philo stepped onto the rug, followed the edge that ran past the mirrored dresser, gingerly moving around the blood spots on it. He stopped in front of the mirror to look at the wood floor, where more blood had dripped.

"Guys, help me out over here. Hank, can you lift a corner of this rug?"

It was a thin yet hearty, gorgeous rug, validating the Middle Eastern saying "Rich man, thin rug." Hank lifted the corner with one hand, then two, its binding heavy, and twisted the long edge back so Philo could look at the planks underneath. Nothing out of the ordinary for hardwood flooring like this. Gaps between planks would allow blood to drip beneath it, into whatever the underlayment was. If there were enough blood, it might drip through to the basement. There was a gap, and it ran the length of the plank. Depending on how deep the drips went, the cost of the remediation would be more if they had to remove the flooring.

Philo crouched down to get a closer look. His phone light showed the gap, wide in spots. He stuck his face and phone extra close to the floor. The blood had dripped beyond the planking into whatever material was under there.

"Hank. You still good holding the carpet up?"

"I'll live, but make it quick."

"Miñoso."

"*Si*, Philo sir?"

"Grab the other end of the rug. Hank, I want you guys to turn the long edge over a few inches and hold it in place so I can see the entire length of the plank."

They complied. Now Philo was on his knees with his phone light, crawling along the plank, checking for blood in the gap. The light reflected off something gold or brassy, about half a foot in length. A few feet farther on his knees there was more of it. Something metallic. Toward the end of the plank, another piece.

Metal hinging. There was a hatch in the floor.

"An exit leading to the basement?" Hank said. "But I don't see a way to open it."

"And there won't be," Philo said. "Probably by remote signal, like from a car fob or a signal from the internet. Gentlemen," he said, standing, "let go of the rug and pack everything up, we're not going to start cleaning. We need to check the basement. Then we'll get Detective Hardass back in here pronto."

Telling law enforcement they'd fumbled their investigation, Philo knew from experience, never went well, but that was their read after finding what they did in the basement. As soon as they left the townhouse, Hank split off and headed directly to the Blessid Trauma step van.

"Coward," Philo called, and continued his beeline to the idling unmarked car with the unnamed detective in it.

The detective powered his window down. He spoke without looking up from his phone. "What is it, Trout? You can't be done already."

It gave Philo great pleasure to say these words. "Your team missed something substantial, Detective."

If looks could kill...

"Excuse me?"

"The house has a hidden room in the basement, a trap door leading to it from the master bedroom. We'll go back in after you're done processing it, if you can figure out how to get inside. You're welcome."

Philo and company had entered the townhouse basement and found shelving that fronted walls on three sides. The false walls surrounding a small interior space were obvious once they knew what they were looking for.

Minutes later, the house was an active crime scene again. In the parking lot, the detective supposed to babysit them for the cleaning job pulled Philo aside. "You tell anyone about this, Trout?"

"About the room? Not really," Philo said.

"What the hell does that mean, 'not really?'"

There'd been two phone calls. One inbound to Philo from Teddy Cangelosi, just discharged from the hospital, one outbound to Rhea.

The call from Teddy. *"My banker buddy called me from Florida, Philo. The guy who owns the place. The house has a safe room..."*

It made sense, the owner was a bank president. Someone with access to large sums of cash and a potential as hostage material. Philo confirmed the safe room's existence for Teddy.

*"He waited for a call from the police about how to get into it, but no one called him, and he didn't know why. So he called the mayor about it, then he unlocked it remotely. I need to go, Harriet and I are late for a Christmas party."*

The second call, one Philo made to Rhea, brought her up to speed about the stall in the remediation, about Teddy and his talk with the homeowners, and about the safe room. And the owner's call to his friend, the mayor.

She'd stayed quiet until she heard the word *mayor*.

*"Shit,"* she'd said. *"He didn't. The mayor?"*

Yes, Phil told her.

Detective Hardass, hearing where the call had gone, was more direct with Philo. *"You motherfucker."*

A police forensics team was now back inside the house, the same team of cops and detectives who'd cleared it earlier, but now all of them pissed off. They hadn't chased the Blessid Trauma step van out of the community yet, but they wouldn't acknowledge them.

Should they stay or should they go? The likelihood the cops would release the scene to them again today was slim. Maybe slimmer than slim. Blessid Trauma might not get back inside the house.

The biggest question was, was there anyone in the safe room? Were security alarms tripped? With no recorded calls from inside the space, it would have been deemed empty.

"Let's pack up, Hank," Philo said from the cab of their step van. "Tomorrow's another day."

"Ah, Philo?" Hank said, pointing. "Look."

The front door to the house opened, coinciding with the quiet arrival of an ambulance. Check that, it was a medical examiner's vehicle. After a haphazard parking job, the M.E. entered the house. Under his arm—

"A body bag, campeón Philo?" Miñoso asked.

"I believe it is," Philo said.

Indeed, it was, and fifteen minutes later came the confirmation. Four cops, two on each end, carried the black vinyl bag out, the bag drooping in the middle. Behind them came a fifth cop with a smaller vinyl bag no bigger than a backpack, same color, presumed to be for the same usage.

Philo hoped the smaller bag was for a pet, not a child. A compromise, but for him, not by much.

~

"You get a one-hundred-percent, grade-A *fuck you* from me, you sonovabitch," Detective Hardass said. "I'm giving you the rest of the night to get the place cleaned up, Trout. At six a.m. tomorrow morning I'll fucking cram all that cleaning shit down your throat myself if you're still here. You are persona-non-grabass with this district going forward. Get the hell outta my face."

No sense arguing, even though it was a police forensics snafu, not the crime scene cleaners' fault, but the detective would never see it that way. All he cared about was the mayor had learned about the investigators over-looking the safe room for this higher-profile case, *his* case, from someone other than the police.

The cops gone, Philo and team reentered the master bedroom. A new smell hit them from the doorway, quite unpleasant. "Miñoso," Hank said, pointing at the bathroom. "You're low man on the team. You need to check it out. Go."

Philo and Hank stood over the open hatch leading to the safe room beneath the bedroom. Six-inch steel beams supported the trap door made of steel plate, the wood planks affixed to it serving as the bedroom floor. Not something a person could easily lift. Five feet long and three feet wide with it open, the hatch filled the space between the bed and the dresser. It exposed steel stairs with black tread on them.

"Pneumatic open-and-close hinging," Hank said, pointing at the pistons along the edge of the door hinge.

"Copy that," Philo said, and started down the steps.

"*Señor* Hank?" Miñoso called from the bathroom.

"What is it?"

"Someone left some *regalos* in the *cómoda. ¡Dios mío!* Maybe more than one someone."

"*Regalos*?" Hank said. "Oh, 'gifts.' Right. Haha. Pissed off cops, I'm sure. Take a picture, then take care of it."

Hank disappeared down the hatch, then jerked his head back up into the bedroom and called to his coworker. "Wait. Remember, Miñoso, don't—"

Too late. The fouled toilet overflowed onto the floor, Miñoso cursing in Spanish while he scrambled to turn the water shut-off valve under the tank. First rule of cleaning a toilet at a customer site: scoop before you flush.

"Rookie," Hank said.

"Contain it, then leave it," Philo called from inside the safe room. "Get down here, the both of you."

The below-deck space wasn't visible from the top of the steps, the enclosed stairs leading to it like a spout on a watering can. The black tread on the stairs was spotted crimson, from blood droplets spreading out inside the grooves. The steps at the bottom opened into a room the size of a walk-in closet. With three men standing in it, the room was tight, six-by-eight in Philo's estimation, with something less than an eight-foot ceiling. Fully self-contained, the steel walls, ceiling, and floor looked seamless, like the room had been dropped whole into the space it occupied, and it probably had. The area appeared clean except for the blood. A chalk outline on the floor at the bottom of the steps showed where a body had been found, pooled blood both inside and outside the portion of the section outlining the victim's head. A second chalk outline protruded like a thought bubble from the head of the first, smaller, pet-sized. There were paw prints in blood near it, on the floor and the walls.

Hank and Miñoso, fortified with enzyme cleaners and sponges and buckets, set about sanitizing the safe room space. Philo called Rhea while they scrubbed.

"Heard about it," Rhea said. Wherever she was, on the street somewhere, it was noisy. "Heard more than I wanted to know. Detective Reese of the Sixth wants to string you up by your balls. Tell me, how is it the mayor—"

Detective Hardass, bitching to Rhea, was looking to deflect the blame. Pathetic.

"Not my fault, Rhea, but yeah, it shouldn't have gone that way. I'll explain tonight. Listen, we're in this safe room right now, sanitizing it. Tell me what they found down here to make sure we handle it all."

Rhea broke it down for him. The good news was the missing wife had been found. The bad news was she was the one in the large body bag, her body collected from the safe room. The smaller bag the police carried out was for a dead cat.

"What did the wife die from?" he asked.

"Head trauma. Not official yet, but they think she was beat up, badly, got loose, and retreated into the bedroom. From there she entered the safe room with a remote fob, then died down there. They found her at the bottom of the steps. A cat was in there, too, dead from a bullet. Listen, I caught another case, Philo, and I'm at the scene right now. Gotta go."

"Fine. But the cat was one tough little bastard, Rhea. There were bloody paw prints everywhere, so it didn't go down easily. Wait. They didn't tell you something was written on the floor?"

"Ah, no. What?"

A pause on Philo's part. Why hadn't they told her? Was it evidence the cops didn't want to share with anyone, even other cops? To maybe help validate leads? The bloodstain from the writing was still visible, barely, on the indoor-outdoor carpet covering the floor. It might have suffered some from cop shoe leather, or maybe the cat got at it. His pause lengthened.

"Philo," she said, impatient. "You going to tell me what was on the floor or what?"

He stared at the safe room's electronic keypad at eye level, next to the steps. The digital display spelled out *ALERT* in red letters, looking fully functional. Thinking out loud: "How the hell does she make it into the safe room with their cat, then not get found? It looks like the security system sent an alert somewhere. Something no one did anything about, at least not in time."

"Sorry, I've got no feedback on it, Philo. Lead detective Reese will need to get on top of it. And they're not sure it was even their cat. Last chance, Philo—what the hell was written on the floor?"

"'*ARAB*,' Rhea. A-R-A-B, in block letters, in blood."

She went silent. Philo waited her out until he couldn't wait anymore. "What are you thinking, Detective? Hello?"

"I just learned the police commissioner's assistant, Lawrence Yonder, lives in the same community," she said. "Here we have another musician of color—another Black Mummer staying only a few doors away from him—who gets executed. Embarrassing to the department, Philo. What I'm thinking is, this is a nightmare. Arabs aren't even on the radar. We weren't thinking terrorists had anything to do with it. Or anything to do with the man's wife getting beat to death with his trumpet, either. You can't make this shit up."

"Wait. Beat with a trumpet?"

"Oh. So you didn't know. Right, no one's talking to you. A trumpet on the floor in the hallway had blood on it and was banged up, Reese said. There are cameras inside the dwelling, too. The detectives have gone to the security company to get the footage released. And now they'll have a different body they can check the blood against."

"From a victim with her head caved in," Philo said. "Or maybe the blood was from her cat. Wonderful imagery."

"They put a bullet in the cat, so the trumpet blood's not likely from him. Plus it's not definite the dead cat was theirs. No tags on him. Not even a collar."

# 11

## POSTHUMOUS

**Monday, December 7**
**Citizens Bank Park, home of the Philadelphia Phillies**
**Number of days to the New Year's Day Parade: 25**

Teddy Cangelosi and Harriet pulled into the VIP parking for the stadium, their destination the Diamond Club behind home plate. The event was the Philadelphia Phillies official executive holiday party and buffet dinner.

Teddy was beside himself. What a knockout Harriet was, dressed in a form-hugging but tasteful outfit with a vintage wide leather belt the same color red as her car. Here she was, on his arm, a spitfire of a woman with flaming orange-red hair holding him close all the way from the parking lot, shoulder to shoulder with him, to the elevators and down one floor to the Diamond Club. The elevator opened not far from the glass double doors of the club, frosted and opaque.

Harriet beamed, paying extreme mother-hen attention to him as he hobbled up to the entrance. After he stumbled once, it sank in for him: *a*, he was indeed very fortunate to have been released from the hospital in time for the team's holiday party tonight, and *b*, Harriet wasn't on his arm, he was on hers, because he needed it. It was also in direct proportion to their fondness for each other.

"Hold on," she said, and moved in front of him to look him over, letting him stand on his own. She straightened his lapels, plumped his tie with a needlepoint reindeer on it, and mock dusted off the shoulders of his long coat. She placed her hands aside each of his cheeks and drew herself in close, kissing him sweetly.

"There. You look great, honey. Enjoy yourself tonight."

With that encouragement, she opened the doors, and the two entered the club arm in arm.

"*Surprise!*"

Teddy's jaw dropped. Sure, it was the Phillies' organization's Christmas-slash-holiday party, but the party was dedicated to him, the retired stadium voice of the Phillies, on his release from the hospital today. *Get well, Teddy!* banners hung around the club as plentiful as the holiday decorations. Smiling faces, words of encouragement and best wishes, and condolences for the loss of his Mummer bandmates: Harriet streamed tears as the team's execs, their wives, their girlfriends, and current and former Phillies players moved in for handshakes, backslapping, and selfies with Teddy, as gentle as the exchanges needed to be.

But he didn't make it much past the party's hors d'oeuvres. It had been a long day, and Harriet was keen to it, at his elbow immediately when his step wobbled. She begged the indulgence of the team president soon after the exec's retelling of an infamous stadium announcement gaffe, when Teddy read the copy "the Phillies and their wives" as "the Phillies and their willies" to the glee of forty-two thousand baseball fans at a Sunday game. When the laughing relented, Teddy and Harriet began paying their respects. Their exit was interrupted when Teddy's phone rang.

The screen read *Allen Dixon*. Teddy's face lit up. It was a call from his friend, the Phillies baseball great. He pointed at the phone and mouthed the name of the caller. The small group around him quieted, smiling faces all, waiting to hear him answer it.

"Hello... Oh, hi, Richard... Yes, doing much better, thanks... Uh-huh..."

Teddy's happy expression dissipated, the color draining from his face. "I see," he said. He closed his eyes and listened. "I'm so sorry, Richard. Thank you. Bye."

Not sure what to do with his hands, or his sucker-punched emotions, he handed the phone to Harriet. Choked up, and in a small voice, he announced what he'd learned.

"That was Allen Dixon's son." His weepy eyes were joined with a deep breath. His voice quivered. "Number Fifteen is gone."

After a few gasps, the large room drifted into silence. Teddy turned to Harriet. "I'd like to go now."

People in the crowd wept openly after one of the execs announced what they'd just learned. Harriet and he left the club. One thing no one could ever take from him was his friendship with the Phillie icon, forged between a young white man who'd never had a real father, and an older Black ballplayer from the sixties and seventies who'd signed up to fill that gap.

They exited the elevator. "Teddy—" Harriet said, leaning into him, her hand in his.

"I know what you're going to say, Harriet."

Her gaze stayed riveted on his profile, her slight smile showing her admiration. "You do, do you?"

"His family called me first," he said.

Harriet's eyes filled as she nodded. Yes, it was where she was going, and yes, though hugely sad news, that aspect was wonderful. They navigated his tired, besieged body through the main concourse, pained more now by having to absorb so emotional a gut-punch. She rubbed his arm and let him continue.

"Before the execs, before any of his former teammates or managers, before any of the other team personnel, they called me. Allen's family knew it's what he would have wanted.

"What he endured in this city as a Black player... it was horrible, Harriet. He made the mistake of sticking up for himself. For a Black athlete in Philadelphia back then, that was suicide. And there's more of that prejudice still out there."

They strode outside, into the night. Teddy raised his chin, some in defiance, mostly in pride. The night air chilled them as they neared Harriet's car, her heels click-clacking in the stillness. She shuddered from a windy gust as she opened the door for him. He didn't notice the cold.

"The man had to wear a batting helmet," Teddy said, the many memories of his friend overwhelming him. "Not only at home plate, in the field, too."

For protection from what the fans threw at him. His behavior in response to the indignity and the racism—he was combative, yet righteous—caused sportswriters with long memories to say he wasn't worthy of election to the Hall of Fame. A travesty, and a wrong that had needed righting for decades.

"I'm going to get him into the Hall, Harriet. I don't care how long it takes. He and his family suffered through so much crap all their lives, waiting for his election. I swear to God, I won't let them suffer the same way after his death."

$\sim$

Six the Cat was engaged in the wilds of the neighborhood alleys, which meant Philo hadn't bothered to pull the bedroom door shut. He and Rhea lay exhausted in each other's arms, their gentle, comforting lovemaking something they'd earned after their respective long days working the unforgiving, often horrifying streets.

Rhea's head against Philo's chest, he pushed her dark hair from her face. She hadn't wanted to talk about the cases anymore tonight, but now, stretched out and relaxed, she did, pontificating. "The department, the DA—everyone—has been looking at these Mummer murders as either hate crimes or the start of a mob war, or maybe both. But that deathbed note from the trumpeter's wife..."

*ARAB.* One word at their newest crime scene, in blood, added an unexpected and more complicated layer. Homeland Security took notice and was now baring its formidable incisors, wanting in on the investigations.

A low shadow moved along the wall in the hallway outside the bedroom door, something passing through the glow from his sock monkey nightlight.

"I didn't have Islamic terrorists on the bingo card anywhere, Philo," Rhea said. "I can't be missing things like that."

The bedroom door squeaked. Philo heard it and watched the door slide open a little more. His legs girded for the inevitable.

"Look, Rhea—there's surveillance camera footage all over that community. When they get the footage from inside the house, ask for a look-see from your detective buddy, Reese."

"I already did. The perps stormed the guy when he opened the door, were masked up and in gloves and covered head to toe, no skin visible, no hints of ethnicity. No hints of gender, either. The gunshots, the dead trumpeter, the wife taking multiple blows to the head with the trumpet—no visible ethnic, or 'Arab,' indications," she said, one hand air quoting the word.

"A peculiar thing, though. One of them did a little dance near the trumpeter's body. The best description of it was, it looked like the Philly Mummers' strut."

Philo smirked. "Did he have a tiny pink parasol, too?" he said, an old-time Mummers costume accessory. It went with a strut that was slow, meandering, and exaggerated, almost a taunt.

"Large handgun, no parasol."

"That's still a tell of some kind, though, right?"

"Could be a tell, that it's someone familiar with the parade. Or at least that guy is. Could be they're just screwing with us."

"Which brings up the question, Detective, as to just how did the wife decide they were, quote, Arabs?"

"They yelled at her. No audio with the video, but you can tell they screamed at her. Did they have Middle Eastern accents? Did they invoke Allah? The detectives don't know, but they think whatever they yelled at her prompted her message."

A four-legged leap onto the bottom of the bed startled them even though Philo knew it was coming. Six the Cat scampered up Philo's body and onto his head, wanting in on the discussion.

*Meow. MEOW!*

Philo reached a hand under Six's stomach and redeposited her between their reclining bodies. She settled there, not complaining about the warm relocation, purring while he scratched her neck.

"Busy day for the district tomorrow," Rhea said. "The department's going after an illegal bookie house in South Philly."

Philo pondered the streetlight shadows on the bedroom ceiling while tending to his cat, grunting one-word answers to Rhea at appropriate times. He toyed with Six, his fingers lingering on her collar, battle-worn but still beautiful, and no worse from whatever skirmishes she'd gotten into tonight. Except...

Wait a minute.

"... A street numbers operation," Rhea continued. "It came from an anonymous tip..."

Philo dropped a hand onto his phone on the nightstand, pulled it to his face. Six the Cat's massage period was over.

The phone camera shots from today, plus the ones Hank sent him... Philo began thumbing through them. One photo in the batch showed it, he was sure.

Hallway, hallway, hallway, kitchen, kitchen, living room, living room, then photos of the door to the bedroom, then bedroom, bedroom, bedroom, safe room, safe room... No, not this picture... Not this one, either...

Back to the kitchen photos.

Rhea finished another of her thoughts. "These guys—they're ratting each other out. Why now, I don't know. Another reason we need to still work the mob-war angle. Philo. Hello? What the hell are you looking at?"

Here—he found it. A photo attached to the fridge with a magnet. He expanded the shot to get as close a look as possible at the cat in the photo.

"This," he said. "The cat at our job today—at some point, it had a collar. This photo of the townhouse's kitchen shows it. Cat and collar, with a tag hanging from it."

She took the phone, maxed out the zoom, saw what he saw.

Philo pushed. "You said, maybe as a joke, that the dead cat might not even be theirs. Have your guys enhance this photo. Zoom in on the collar. See if they can read the info on the tag."

"But the cat body they loaded up—the detectives said it had no tag on it."

"Right. Which means no collar."

"Okay. Fine. Send it to me, I'll get it to them. Do *not* send this photo anywhere else, Philo. No more Mister-Mayor-needs-to-know bullshit. No Teddy Cangelosi, no *no* one. If this amounts to anything, maybe this pulls you out of the Sixth District shithole you dug for yourself."

"You get why it's important though, right, Rhea? It's not just knowing whose cat it was, it's—"

"I get it, hotshot," she said. She stroked Philo's rooster comb of a hairline and cracked a thin smile, enjoying his eagerness in having his Spidey sense acknowledged. "We need to find out what happened to the dead cat's collar. It's odd if they took it."

# 12

## MIGHTY MOUSE

Tuesday, December 8
South on I-95 to South Philadelphia
Number of days to the New Year's Day Parade: 24

Coffee, bagels. The rising sun combining with road salt was finally doing the job after four days of a cold snap, the highway's mostly concrete paving fully visible again for the entire stretch of I-95 from Philly's Northeast into Center City, slushy even, at six-forty-one in the a.m. Philo's H2 Hummer's ample width dispatched the chunks of snow hugging the narrow shoulder in the leftmost lane, crushing them like a monster truck at a demolition car jump. At seventy miles per hour, pulverizing each ice chunk felt like riding a roller coaster full of speed bumps.

"Yo. Try getting me to the rendezvous in one piece, will you, lover?" Rhea said.

"You need to be there by seven to storm the castle, right? We're a little late."

"Slow the hell down. My team can wait a few minutes. I'd rather be late than DOA."

The topic drifted back to the home invasion. Two dead. Three, when including the cat. Inside a gated community. "A lot of good those gates did," Philo mused.

"They had the code," Rhea said. "Security video at the entrance showed the driver punching it in. The police commissioner's assistant is working the angle with one of the deputy commissioners. Commissioner Val's all over him about it. That, plus why no one responded when the safe room's alert was tripped."

"All over him who?"

"Yonder. Larry Yonder, Commissioner Val's assistant. He's a resident of the community. Other higher-profile folks and cops moving in there, too. A city judge, an assistant DA. Hell, I like the place, too. I'd move there in a heartbeat if I could afford it."

Her phone buzzed. It was a call she'd been waiting for, about the search warrant for this morning's raid. Per her sergeant boss, the warrant was now official, with probable cause relating to illegal bookmaking. Nothing like closing the deal at the last minute. "Have one of the uniforms bring it. Thanks."

The team included a few uniforms in case there were runners. Armed, wearing protective vests, the team would also be rocking a heavy-duty Ford diesel pickup in black, with intimidating law enforcement equipment inside. The team was in place, waiting on the truck, ready for the raid. Her phone buzzed again. She answered, then whispered to Philo with her hand over the phone, "*Reese*." A raised finger to her lips kept Philo quiet while she put her cellphone on speaker and dropped it into a cup holder. Out came her spiral notepad. "Go ahead, Detective."

"Enhancing that photo showed the victims' last name on the pet tag. The cat was theirs. Cat's name was J.P. Jonesy."

"Find the cat's collar yet, Detective?" she asked.

"Still looking. We done here, Ibáñez?"

"You get the Jonesy reference, Reese? The cat in one of the *Alien* movies?"

"Not how we see it, but sure, why not," Reese said. "Keying more on the 'J.P. Jones' part. You know, John Paul Jones, Navy ship captain and all that. The trumpeter was U.S. Navy."

Raised eyebrows from Rhea, and an interested glance from Philo.

"Does the Navy know, Reese? That it's another one of their guys?"

"They do now. Hanging up now, Detective."

"Wait—" she said, Philo mouthing something at her. She got it. "Was the guy a Navy SEAL?"

"Not a SEAL," Reese said. "Adios."

Off I-95 at the Columbus Boulevard exit—"No, I don't know the guy," Philo said before she could ask the question—they turned right onto Columbus, right onto Washington Avenue, then left onto 2 Street at the Mummers Museum.

"What do you think?" Rhea said. "A coincidence he was Navy?"

"No such things as coincidences in police work, right?" he said.

"Right."

"For my money, I'm thinking this time it is a coincidence," Philo said. "But not a coincidence that he was Black and would be performing with a Mummers string band."

"Agreed."

After driving block after block south, they reached McClellan Street. They pulled behind a column of unmarked vehicles double-parked before the intersection, a practice in South Philly as common as cheesesteaks. Rhea made another call. The doors for the gathered vehicles opened and shut, her team meeting at the corner to wait for her.

"After we clear the intersection, you can backfill it if you want to watch," she said to Philo. "But stay at the corner. Don't enter McClellan, we'll be busy up there. And no gun."

"Copy that," he said. He put his Sig in the Hummer's glove box to prove his cooperation.

"Not sure how long I'll be," she said. "If you get bored, just go, I'll hitch a ride."

In helmets and flak jackets, Rhea and her team of three waited, their eyes searching north on 2 Street. A call between her and the two uniforms in position in the alleyway behind the house confirmed everyone was a go. A Ford four-door pickup dieseled into view, maintaining a slow, lumbering speed as it neared the intersection, then wheeling sharply onto McClellan. Rhea and her team filled in behind it, walking briskly. Midway up the street, the pickup stopped. Two cops exited, moving quickly to the rear where Rhea met them.

"Ready for the mouse?" one cop said.

"Copy that," Rhea said.

The cop dropped the tailgate and dragged out their police-issue breaching device, a forty-two-pound, two-foot-long handheld steel battering ram nicknamed Mighty Mouse. One cop banged on the front door of the brick house, the second stood behind him on the door's stoop with the battering ram in both hands.

"Police! Search warrant! Open the door!"

Guns drawn, with eyes trained on the front door and the windows on both floors, they didn't wait for an answer and demolished the door's lock and handle with two thrusts from the ram.

"The mouse is in the house," Rhea said into the phone, alerting the cops in the alleyway that the police team had breached the front door.

Philo observed from a distance, hands in his coat pockets outside his Hummer, shoulders hunched because of the cold. How long would executing a search warrant on a bookie house take? Fifteen minutes? Thirty?

At the ten-minute mark, his phone buzzed. Teddy Cangelosi. Philo answered. "You're up early, Teddy. How the hell was your party?" It was Harriet's doing that Philo knew about it.

"Mixed." Teddy talked about the Phillies team execs' surprise for him, but he moved quickly to the phone call he got about Allen Dixon's passing. He was still broken up about it.

"But that's not why I called. I just got some weird news from Harriet. Her aunt lives on McClellan Street in South Philly, just off 2 Street. You'll never believe what's going down at her aunt's house *right now...*"

Teddy went into a short primer on Harriet's Aunt Yvonne, something Philo could hear Harriet delivering in the background, because Aunt Yvonne, caught up in the middle of the raid, was relaying it on the phone to Harriet in real time. From the aunt to Harriet to Teddy to Philo.

"Harriet's ex, Nicky, bought the rowhome for her aunt for a hundred thousand bucks in the nineties," Teddy began.

The ex was Nicky Bricks Broglio. This information now had Philo's full attention.

"Nicky brought the entire amount in cash. Handed it to the previous owners in brown paper bags. Harriet's aunt moved in. Then"—Teddy paused, listening to what Harriet was feeding him—"then Nicky had a proposition for her aunt."

Let a Massimo numbers guy use her house for their illegal bookie business, Philo was hearing. She could pocket an extra five hundred a month just to let him sit in her upstairs bedroom with a separate phone line. Take bets, make bets, do football pools, record daily street number activity, all with the aunt looking the other way. The aunt kept the arrangement even after Harriet and Nicky divorced. With Aunt Yvonne liking, needing the money, the deal stayed in place after Nicky's death.

Philo listened, conveying appropriate disdain for this invasion of poor Aunt Yvonne's privacy, but damn if it wasn't surreal hearing it happen third and fourth hand while it was still in progress right up the street from him. Philo relayed his sympathy for poor Aunt Yvonne's inconvenience, and oh my, what about the destruction of her front door...

"They've got one guy in cuffs," Teddy said, pausing, gathering more info. "Yvonne says he's a sweet guy from the neighborhood. They've got the trash can from Yvonne's front bedroom. It was where he worked. There was water in it with dissolving rice paper. They took her aunt's address book from a nightstand. Harriet says her phone number is in there. Now the cops will take another look at her, just like they did while she was married to Nicky."

They'll sort it all out, Philo told him. Harriet will be fine, Aunt Yvonne will be fine, they won't do anything to the aunt because she's ancient, tell Harriet to relax, etcetera, etcetera.

"It's not working, Philo, she's flipping out. Yvonne just told her there's a false wall in the basement. Drywall with shelving on it. It slides out of the way, covering a hole that opens into the house next door."

Philo, in processing mode, could hear Harriet cursing a blue streak in the background. It wasn't just a one-house operation, it was two, connected by their basements.

Did the cops know this going into the raid? Did they know it now?

"Gotta go, Teddy." Philo might tell him later he saw the raid go down in real time, but not now. "Yes, I'll talk to Rhea. Nothing will happen to Harriet's aunt. Calling Rhea right now."

He rang Rhea on her phone, walked briskly to the end of the back alley that ran the length of the block behind the rear of the houses, waiting for her to answer.

*C'mon, c'mon, Rhea, take the call...*

The alley was bricked in at each end of the block, a nice touch for the street, the brick walls having some height, nothing visible beyond them except through a black wrought-iron gate, the entrance/exit for the alley, the latched gate shorter than the walls. He peered down the alley through the gate, shielding his eyes. Still no answer from Rhea. He texted her instead. The two uniforms in the back alley stood in the ready if someone took a powder out the back door of the raided house.

But they wouldn't be concerned about people leaving the houses on either side of it.

Philo's phone rang.

"You called," Rhea said, her voice barking into his ear. "What is it? I'm kinda busy here."

"Rhea. Long story, but you need to know the house you're raiding has false drywall in the basement. It leads to the house next door. They're connected."

Rhea ended the call abruptly, Philo watching the city block's back alley from outside the gate, empty of anyone except for the cops, and quiet except for one barking dog, then another, plus a chattering squirrel bouncing from fencepost to fencepost above each dog's reach. Philo backed away from the gate and stuffed his hands into his pockets.

Someone entered the alley from a backyard. Philly Eagles football jacket, waist length, earbuds, gym clothes, sneakers. He ignored the cops, they ignored him back.

Philo shielded his eyes again, checking the bearings. Which backyard did the guy exit from, three houses away from the numbers house or two?

Neither. He'd left the backyard for the house next door.

Philo girded for a confrontation, big man, ample shoulders, white, his hands in his jacket pockets. The gate opened. The guy nodded, gave Philo a single "'S'up" comment, then turned his back to him and headed up the street.

Notify the cops, or make it happen himself?

"Citizen's arrest," Philo called. "Stop right there."

The target kept walking, raised one hand, then one finger on it.

"Not fucking around, asshole. Stop and turn around. Citizen's arrest, and there'll be no hard feelings about you flipping me off."

Philo went for the holstered Sig on his hip, except—

His gun was in the SUV glove box, his holster naked.

The guy slowed his pace, both hands back in his coat pockets, and stopped. The mark capped off an about-face with a handful of currency, dropping it onto the sidewalk. Misdirection meant to distract. His second hand now showed a raised handgun, Philo's face the target. Right about now, Philo regretted not yelling to the cops.

"Be a good little neighborhood watch guy"—the gun was inches from Philo's forehead, full-on mobster style, no sideways gangsta bullshit—"pick up the money, and maybe get some takeout coffee and a danish for yourself instead of making this mistake."

He ground the barrel into Philo's forehead hard enough it was going to leave a mark, damn it.

Philo reached up, a lightning-fast move, and backhanded the barrel from his forehead. His other hand gripped the guy's wrist, twisting it to disarm him. No go. Philo slammed him hard face-first into the sidewalk, dazing him, then wrapped his legs around his neck and shoulder in a submission move, squeezing the breath out of him with his thighs. The resistance continued, Philo staying attached to him like an octopus until he wrestled the gun free and stuck the barrel into the top of the man's head, pressing it into his scalp, his finger on the trigger.

"Take the nap, hotshot," Philo grunted, breathing heavy, "or a bullet puts you to sleep permanently."

The two uniforms exited the alley on the run and arrived behind them, Philo's hostage no longer squirming. Philo placed the gun on the sidewalk.

"Let go of his head," one cop said, "and stay where you are. You need to show me some ID."

Philo disengaged, remained seated on the ground, and went for his wallet. He produced his ID plus his license to carry permit. "My piece is in my glove compartment, Officer."

The cop glanced at the Hummer, then checked Philo's ID more closely. "You came with Detective Ibáñez."

"Yes."

"Okay then. Nice chokehold. Thanks for the assist. You're good to go." Their prisoner groaned and gagged, shaking his head to clear the cobwebs.

"You come out of that numbers house?" the cop's partner said to their person of interest. "Sure you did. We're arresting you for illegal gambling and bookmaking. You have the right to remain silent..."

Across town in a suite at The Rittenhouse Hotel in Center City Philly, a call came in to Wally Lanakai's personal cellphone. He didn't recognize the number, hesitated, then tapped the speaker button in between bites of his room service breakfast. He was still in his robe. "Who is this?"

"Listen, you fat Hawaiian prick—" came back at him in a voice as leathery as a barber's razor strop.

"Old man Massimo," Wally said. His eyebrows tented, entertained by this senile Italian fathead's attitude. Magpie Papahani got up from a sofa, put away his phone, and came closer to listen.

"I've had enough of your shit, Lonnie Cannoli, or whatever the hell your name is."

"Wally Lanakai."

"Shut up! Two things. First, someone executed my grandson in Atlantic City. My people tell me to forget about it, Little Sal was a pain in the ass, was dealing drugs on the side and was into the product, but I can't forget about it, and I won't. You were there, Cannoli. Second, I just lost two of my best numbers houses in a raid. Big producers. The houses, plus the guys who worked them. I don't get it. I'm not in your face on the streets, and you're not in mine. Why make a phone call about my operation? It's revenue I figure you now owe me. I know where you live, Cannoli..."

Wally tossed his napkin onto the table and stood. Magpie produced his own cell while Wally ranted.

"Sorry about your grandkid, Massimo. It wasn't me. And I don't know what numbers houses you're talking about, and best of all, I don't fucking care. Again, not me. Not before, and not now. Cram that tough guy mobster veneer up your wrinkled ass, you senile bastard. You come anywhere near my place, I'll personally cut your scrotum off and feed your ancient balls to the rats. I'm going now."

Massimo was still yelling threats into the phone when Wally hung up on him.

"Magpie. His numbers houses. Tell me it wasn't something we did."

"Texts are out, people are working it. Far as I know, we're clean, boss," Magpie said. His phone jolted him, a text coming in. "This is from one of our guys. A shop owner near the Mummers Museum—"

Autobody shop-slash-chop shop-slash-illegal high-stakes Pai Gow dominoes. "His overnight game was breaking up. He says 'Heavy police activity came in hard on Second Street. House raid nearby, people in custody...'"

Wally had no illegal numbers operations in the States, nothing close to that shit anywhere, not even in the Asian communities. His Ka Hui family meant no harm to the Italian mob, but the old mobster still knew how to press Wally's buttons. Wally gritted his teeth, his blood pressure rising, his temper working him into a rage.

"I—didn't—fucking—do this, damn it..."

Nothing good could come of this. The mafia's misplaced blame, two crime bosses trading threats. Both enterprises stood to lose big. Neither was interested in the other's businesses, yet both were plenty ready to finger point, the offenders misidentified. Escalation, regardless of who or what had started it, would slam everything together: the streets, the different crime families, everyone. The cops too, who'd be busy as hell trying to sort things out.

Wally could feel it. Massimo's call was a warning shot, but he'd fired it at the wrong person.

He exploded, flipping the breakfast cart over, jettisoning dishes and carafes of orange juice and coffee, the OJ smashing against a hanging art piece, soaking the drapes and a corner window, the coffee leaking onto an oriental rug. His chest heaved until he calmed himself. He steeled his voice.

"We need to be ready, Magpie. Massimo won't be sitting on his hands. Thinking what he's thinking, where his senile mind is right now—we'll get the brunt of it."

He stood at the window peering at the buildings surrounding Rittenhouse Square. Below him, holiday-themed ice sculptures anchored the greenery now poking through receding snow piles, the park decorated warmly, cheerfully, the tree lights glowing in the daylight. His jaw unclenched and he took slow breaths, further calming himself. The therapeutic view was having a positive effect.

"I swear to the island gods, Magpie," he said, his temper subdued, "something else is going on here, and if we don't figure out what it is..."

He finished the outlook in his head.

... *this city will become a bloodbath.*

# 13

## TIT FOR TAT

Wednesday, December 9
Chinatown section of Philadelphia
Number of days to the New Year's Day Parade: 23

The padlock snapped open, the heavy galvanized chain dropping against the gate. Business suit, white shirt, black tie, shiny patent leathers, that was how Ka Hui's onsite manager Bernard dressed daily, to serve those invited into a social club that was part bar, part restaurant, and part social hangout. Behind the scenes, the club was also part-time speakeasy and full-time home base for Wally Lanakai's Hawaiian syndicate. He pushed the scissored, accordion-style gate back to expose the entrance to the club. The carved front door painted in a black gloss was deeply inset, the gate protecting the space from vagrants and drunk partiers looking to empty their bladders on the Chinatown streets late at night.

Bernard produced a key from a stylish flat box that fit neatly inside his suit jacket vest pocket. It was one of the many keys needed to get the operation going daily, and he was able to fit them all into a stylish pill box, preferable to hanging them on a keychain. Bernard had class, and he wouldn't be caught dead with a ring of keys hanging gauchely from his waist like an effing janitor.

Early morning, seven-ish. The bold nighttime splendor that was the bright marquee lights and neon attraction of Philadelphia's Chinatown quieted each day when the sun came up. Bernard appeared Asian enough to fit into the neighborhood as a local businessman, the reason Mr. Lanakai chose him to manage their space. Chinese, Japanese, Thai, Korean, all were at home in Chinatown's melting pot. A Pacific Islander, Bernard had a pleasant, welcoming disposition, except for those times when a different disposition was warranted. Inside the club, he closed the front door behind him and locked it again. He flipped on a row of lights and spoke to his alter-ego, the club, his home away from home.

"Wakey-wakey, my pretty."

A long wooden bar spanned the left wall well into the interior, with black high-backed bar stools. Blue-flowered chinaware and copper utensils covered tables pre-set for today's guests whose eyes would also feast on bright, blooming wall murals of frondy-palmed Hawaiian sunsets from the front to the rear of the main room, where dart boards and pool tables sat with other felt-covered heavy tables. All were in place for friendly Asian and American games of chance and skill, officially never for money, but they always were.

The Chinese New Year, beginning mid-February, was a comfortable two months away. Mr. Lanakai expected Bernard to handle Ka Hui's anonymous participation in the community celebration. A lot to do, daily and weekly, but Bernard was on top of it. He pushed through the doors into the kitchen, switched on the lights, the wall-to-wall stainless-steel blinding him, spotless and sparkly as a shipboard galley. A package sat front and center on a butcher block table, a small bakery box. Was it here last night? He doubted it was. He opened the box.

In it were four massive stuffed cannoli from Termini Brothers Bakery, from the store's original location on 8th Street, with a hand-printed note that read *Mangiare*, "Eat."

He tripped on something, needing to stutter-step over it, something soft and furry. He wheeled to get a look.

There was nothing there, but he knew what had been there. Attila, the club's massive mouser cat. Bernard stared into a corner of the room wrapped by shadows.

*Meow.*

Attila crept out slowly, like he was on a hunt, except he was returning from one. A bloodied rat corpse, his teeth in the rat's stomach, filled Attila's closed jaws. He hissed, then he scampered forward and rested in his Sphinx pose, poised for a delivery. He pushed the dead rat out of his mouth with his rear claws. It landed at Bernard's feet.

"Out, you thug! Gah! Thank you, but get—*out!*" Bernard shouted. Attila retreated, skulking to the rear of the building and entering the bathroom that the kitchen help used. Bernard clanged his way through the kitchen's steel drawers until he found a plastic trash bag and a pair of disposable gloves. He gagged when he lifted the dead rat by its tail and shuddered after dropping it into the bag. Now to thread his way through the vegetable supplies storage area, to the back door that led outside to the large trash bins. Something stopped him short.

Eyes right. Another rat tail, protruding from the fresh eggplant bin on a shelf.

What the hell? The club hadn't seen any vermin in months, ever since Attila was on the job. Now an infestation?

The tail didn't move. Closer inspection answered why: it wasn't a tail, it was a gray cord. He stepped back, eyed the other veggie bins on the shelves. The lower bins of fresh squash, banana peppers, and cucumbers had similar cords leading into the piles of vegetable stores. He moved aside the eggplants, uncovering an olive-colored block of cheese.

Not rat tails, and the block wasn't cheese. Detonation wiring led from what looked to be blocks of improvised plastic explosives used for building demolition. Or terror attacks. The cords led nowhere.

Wireless detonation.

A double take preceded his quick stride to the kitchen's rear door that was already ajar. Bernard hopped onto the concrete landing serving as a back step and loading dock. Across the narrow street, a parked motorcycle suddenly sprang to life, its tinny engine revving, the rider's tinted helmet visor down. He pointed at Bernard, pressed a button on his phone, and waved a good-bye. Bernard launched himself behind the iron trash bin in the alley and covered his head. The back of the building exploded, upward and outward, blasts coming from all three floors, the rear of the club now ablaze.

Jettisoned bricks and dust and glass and window framing showered the bin and the alley. Bernard emerged from behind the bin and coughed through the dust, squinting at the taillights of the motorcycle speeding away, then recoiled from and released the trash bag full of dead rat he still held. He called Wally Lanakai. A call to 911 would have to wait.

"Mister Lanakai! Bernard here," he said, holding back tears. "I have some terrible news. There's been an explosion..."

The flames in the rear of the building rose higher with the back wall gone, reaching through the top floor to the roof, beginning to consume it. Distant sirens gathered, coalescing toward a crescendo, all of them descending on Chinatown.

He'd been the only person in the club, and he was safe, he told his boss, then he mentioned the four cannoli in the Termini Brothers pastries box, and the message in Italian.

"What about Attila?" Mr. Lanakai said.

Poor Atilla. "Sorry, Mister Lanakai, but I don't see how he could have survi—"

A ball of fur sprang from the trash bin. Same arrogant cat, his mouth again full, this time with a live rat. Attila landed at Bernard's feet and lumbered off, keeping this gift for himself. Bernard gushed the good news into the phone, that Attila had survived.

"Thank you, Bernard. I'm relieved you and Attila are safe," Mr. Lanakai said. "Stay on with me a minute, I'm in the car with Magpie. Magpie—pull up our accounts receivable on your phone. I decided to call in some debt."

Debts owed to Ka Hui were chronicled two ways, Bernard knew: those payable in cash and other instruments, and favors returned with other favors.

A fire truck arrived, its siren winding down, with another fire truck approaching from the other direction. Philly's Bravest had its work cut out, the fire threatening to spread to adjacent buildings.

"Bernard?"

"Yes, Mister Lanakai?"

"Cooperate with the authorities, then you should go home. I know how much the club means to you. To me, as well. Get some rest and keep your head down. Ka Hui is proud of you. But tonight, after you're refreshed—"

Mr. Lanakai laid it out for him. *I will give you a list. You will call every person who owes Ka Hui a favor. They will help us locate Salvatore Massimo. If they refuse, we will make it so they wish they hadn't.*

"We will sort this mess out, Bernard. When we find old man Massimo, I'm going to kill him."

~

"Detective Rhea Ibáñez?"

"Speaking." With the phone receiver against her ear, Rhea was tucked behind her Third District desk. She shuffled paper, and instead of an uninspired *how can I help you* follow up, she exhaled an expletive when the papers didn't cooperate.

"This is Lawrence Yonder, Detective."

She sat straighter in her chair to refocus herself, said nothing while she cleared her head of images from the crime scene photos on her desk. Blanking her mind took too long for the caller.

"You know, assistant to the commissioner of the Philadelphia Police Department? Hello?"

"Sorry, Lieutenant, yes, I got that, I'm just surprised by the call. What do you need?"

"A deputy commissioner had me call you. He wants you and your partner at a new scene right away. Not your district, but because there's a good chance it's related to a case you're working on inside the Third—the Dominion case—he wants you in the loop."

The armored car murders. Three dead, all people of color, the case now five days old. If there was a connection, she wanted to learn what she could about it. "Sure, Lieutenant. Where?"

"Chinatown. That two-alarm fire this morning. Preliminary indications are arson caused the explosions."

"I don't understand. Why do we think it's connected to a hate crime?"

"Wrong tree you're barking up, Detective. Still not enough evidence to consider those three hits hate crimes. The connection you should be going for is to organized crime. One of the mob families. The building is—was—a hangout for the new players in Philly, the Hawaiians."

She didn't argue, but she thought Lieutenant Yonder was full of shit. Not a hate crime? Kiss my ass.

"We're headed for a mob war, Detective, just accept it. See the fire chiefs working the Chinatown scene and talk to the club's manager. He survived the explosion. Something about a gift box of cannoli. You need to get on board with this."

Mob war or not, that didn't guarantee the motivation for each event was mutually exclusive.

"I'm good, Lieutenant," she said, but she wasn't. While she had Lieutenant Yonder on the phone: "Sir, anything on the Northern Liberties case?" The police lieutenant was a resident of the gated community.

"Anything as in what, Detective?"

"The safe room. One victim, the wife, made it into the room with their cat. What did the security company say about the alarm? Why didn't the alert register? Why no response?"

"Oh. That. Do you know that house is the only one in the community with a safe room? I didn't know it was there, and I run the community's homeowners association."

Interesting, but she didn't care. "No, sir."

"Well, it is. Yes, let me see, the detective working that case is..."

"Detective Reese has it, sir."

"Yes. You'll need to follow up, Detective, I don't know what the outcome was. I don't think we yet know what caused the malfunction."

"The alarm for the room was either sent to the security company and received or it wasn't, sir. I don't see the issue. Is the security company not making the response a priority?"

"Water over the dam, Detective. Like I said, follow up with Reese."

# 14

## THISCLOSE

Wednesday, December 10
South Philadelphia
Number of days to the New Year's Day Parade: 22

It took the rest of yesterday and today for Ka Hui to track him down. Wally had Salvatore Massimo's cell number but had no residence and no hangout information to go with it, only news of occasional sightings around the South Philly streets. Whenever the crazy don made an appearance in his robe and slippers, word got around, but after the fact.

The street corner bodega owners, the Center City restaurants, and a few Chinese businessmen on Bernard's list all coughed up what they knew, or were willing to admit to, about the Massimo crime family. "They see him, they talk to him, they think he's compromised mentally," Bernard said to Wally when he called for some follow-up, "but no one knows where he lives."

Then a substantial lead. A Korean store owner gave up an address for where the Massimo family did some of its business, a facility very close to the Termini Brothers Bakery on South 8th.

Dickenson Street near South 8th, nine-thirty p.m. Wally with Magpie as his chauffeur cruised past the address in an SUV. Three garages, two stories, a non-descript red brick front with no noticeable markings on the outside, and one nicely kept large rowhome residence next door—facades that were all clearly visible, even in the shadows. They were within walking distance from the bakery, although Wally doubted old man Massimo regularly trekked the distance himself. He doubted Massimo could find anything on his own nowadays, considering the bullshit that seemed to occupy the old man's head.

"Show me the route again, from their place to the bakery," Wally said.

Wally sipped from a bottle of organic fruit juice in the back seat of the heavily tinted Tahoe SUV rental he'd gotten specifically for this gig. Bright street lighting highlighted the melting snow piled high on the sidewalks, the piles refrozen for the night, crusty and gray and ugly. Nothing was happening on Dickenson, quiet as they drove it, followed by light traffic on South 8th. Magpie circled the route in full, Dickenson, South 8th, west on Cross Street onto South 9th, and ending back on Dickenson, where they started. He double-parked half a block from the location they were surveilling.

"I want this bastard," Wally said.

"Boss..."

"He ordered the hit on my club, Magpie. I'm going to annihilate him."

"You know that for sure, boss? This is a big step, killing a crime family head, and you're basing it on a box of pastries. We'll be at war..."

Wally's teeth clenched. "He thinks I had his grandson hit. He also thinks I dropped a dime on one of his numbers houses. It makes perfect sense he'd go after our space."

"Sure, boss, but"—a cop car blew past, flashing lights, no siren, kept moving, no interest in them—"we didn't do any of it, remember? Now you decide he's retaliated based on some cannoli left at our club? I dunno, maybe confront him first?"

"Magpie—" Wally had heard him, but he was preoccupied. "That garage—"

One of the three garage doors opened. A nineties silver Lincoln Town Car crept out, long, an old-school livery type the length of a limo. It held fast at the curb. Clear window glass, the street well lit. Unlike Wally and Magpie in their tinted SUV, the Lincoln's three occupants were visible.

"Back seat, boss. Massimo."

A tense moment, both cars in view of each other. The unease ended when the Lincoln entered Dickenson Street four, maybe six car lengths ahead of where the Tahoe was double-parked.

"Soon as they turn," Wally said, "follow him."

"Sure, boss, but are we—?"

"I don't plan on killing him. Not tonight at least. But he's going to hear from me up close before the night is over."

East on Dickenson took the Lincoln limo under I-95 before its first turn, a right. Magpie closed the distance to that turn in a hurry, no cars between them, and their SUV made the same turn.

They stayed almost a full city block back. The Lincoln found the first entrance to the interstate and took the fork leading to the ramp. Magpie's heavy foot brought the Tahoe to the entrance quickly.

Except it had started snowing. Not heavy, but persistent, and the streets were cold enough to get slick from it.

The Lincoln eased its way up the ramp. Magpie tossed a comment over his shoulder as they closed the gap.

"Boss, this weather's bothering me." Magpie looked skyward, the snowflakes getting larger. The Ka Hui mob had been away from the tropics for almost a decade, but with them both being Hawaiian trans-plants, Magpie still wasn't comfortable driving in snow. Philly had already had a season's worth of it this crazy-weather year, and it wasn't even Christmas.

"Your seatbelt's on, we've got airbags, this is a four-wheel drive," Wally said, "and their limo isn't. That sumo body of yours will be fine. Stay with them."

Magpie followed them, was now directly behind the Lincoln as both vehicles threaded their way onto light interstate traffic. The snow came down harder, the flakes larger. Magpie engaged the wipers. The Town Car sped up but topped out at forty-five miles per hour, driving what was now the middle lane, the right lane of the four-lane highway closed for construction. Magpie stayed a few car lengths behind. Snowflakes swirled in the headlights, cars passing them on the left, the road narrowing from four lanes to three because of the roadwork.

Wally produced his phone and called a number in the address book. The male voice that answered wasn't who he expected. Not Massimo's raspy voice, and the hello was too business-like. Wally got direct.

"Put Mister Massimo on the phone. This is Wally Lanakai. It's about some Termini's cannoli that one of your guys left at my club, just before he blew it up yesterday."

"He's got nothing to say," the man said, and hung up.

Wally redialed, the call ringing multiple times then went through, the same man answering. "We're not interested in—"

"Listen, prick, I'm in the car right behind you, traveling south on 95. Magpie, let them know we're here."

Magpie flashed the brights twice. One man in the back seat straightened up and labored to twist his gray head around to see what was following them. His thick black glasses told Wally it was Salvatore Massimo. The headlights blinded Massimo, making him turn forward again.

"I see I've got your boss's attention," Wally said into the phone.

The second backseat passenger glanced once at the Tahoe. He was a younger guy, a phone attached to his ear.

"This is a big mistake, Lanakai," the younger mobster said. "Back off." Still talking, the guy now showed a large handgun as an FYI, the long silver barrel raised skyward. Magpie clicked on the high beams, kept them on. The gun stayed raised, gleaming in the headlights.

"Ahhh, big gun, little dick, right?" Wally said. "But you're not my problem. Find space between the traffic cones and move into the right lane. Well-lit highway, plus there's traffic... it's only me and my driver back here, and there's three of you. No one needs to shoot anybody tonight. Put your dick away, have your driver stop the car, and your boss and I will have a chat."

The Massimo car maintained its speed while whoever Wally had been talking to ended their conversation. The phone, visible in their headlights, returned to the man's ear again.

"He's calling for reinforcements," Magpie said.

"Probably," Wally said, "but they won't be necessary. We're not staying long."

Massimo's car signaled a right, Magpie signaling as well. When the Massimo car drifted into the construction lane and stopped, its flashers came on. Magpie passed them, then did likewise a hundred feet ahead. He put the Tahoe into reverse and tightened up the separation. Their positions now reversed, Wally acknowledged the headlights, now high beams, on the back of his head by raising both hands to show they were empty. A few minutes of wind and swirling snow passed, but there was no other movement between them, into or out of their respective cars.

"Boss, you sure—?" Magpie said.

"I'm doing this with or without you, Magpie. He and I need to talk. I'm going to show good faith here." Wally called the number back. "Tell your boss we're getting out of our car and walking back. Is there room in that limo for us?"

A moment before an answer, then, "Yes."

Magpie exited the SUV and held the door open for Wally. Two Hawaiians, one larger than the other, their hands empty, held their dark suit jackets closed in the windy snow as they tread on the slick, snowy pavement to the silver limo, its door held open by the driver. They piled inside the back seat of the limo, the overhead light on, and sat across from underdressed old man Massimo and his business-suited employee, the four men facing each other. All hands visible, all eyes vigilant, the new back seat occupants sat in silence. Stoic, gray, and godfatherly, Big Sal Massimo looked underwhelming, dressed in pajamas, a robe, and slippers. The guy in the suit opened his mouth to speak but Massimo raised his hand to shut him up.

"I didn't do it," Massimo said.

"I don't believe you," Wally said. His eyes spent too long absorbing Massimo's choice of clothing for his limo ride. Wally regretted it immediately.

Massimo rebutted him. "First, Lanakai, I'll correct one misconception you have about me. Something I won't hold against you, because it's an image I've been cultivating for decades."

The business suit next to him interrupted. "Mister Massimo—don't, he doesn't need to know. As your lawyer..."

"Shut the fuck up. He doesn't need to know, but I'm telling him anyway. Here's the deal, Lanakai.

"I'm old, but I'm far from senile. You remember Vincent Gigante, the New York 'Oddfather?' Vinnie the Chin? 'The Walking Robe Don?' The Genovese family boss tried to make 'crazy'—as in an insanity plea—work for him as a legal defense in case the Feds went at him again. That was *my* schtick, damn it. A Philly thing, and that New York guinea bastard stole it.

"Second, I had people run down some info on you, checking up on your connections to the rackets, here and overseas. I know who the hell you are, Mister Walinika Lanakai, Hawaiian 'businessman,'" he scoffed, air-quoting the word. "The Feds kicked you off your own island and you went to prison with a bunch of your associates. You resurrected yourself here on the East Coast when you got out. You're named after your maternal grandmother Walinika, a woman's name. You embraced it and never hid from it, even though it makes you look weak.

"Third, you carry a machete or a freakin' dagger or a straight edge of some kind. Handguns bore you. Because of some native Hawaiian island practice, or another bullshit reason.

"Fourth"—he leaned forward on creaky knees to emphasize his words —"do you have any idea how many Italian bakeries there are near my house? Termini's isn't the only good cannoli in South Philly. I didn't leave no cannoli for you at your club.

"Last, I'm out for a ride tonight because I want a quart of Rita's Wild Black Cherry water ice, and there's only one Rita's walk-up open around here during the winter. I called my order in, and we're on our way to pick it up before they run out of the flavor.

"So one last time, Wal-i-ni-ka," Massimo said, emphasizing each syllable, "I didn't order a hit on your club, even though I have my doubts about you and what happened to my grandson. Me and my family had nothing to do with it."

Wally held back a beat before answering, wanting to clap at the performance. He wagged his finger and cracked a smile instead. "I have to admit, old man, I'm this close"—he pressed his thumb and forefinger together—

"to believing you. But what remains is this. I don't know what triggered it, but we're closer than even that, now, to an all-out war."

Magpie stiffened, poked Wally in the ribs, and chin-pointed out the back window of the limo. A set of car headlights stopped abruptly behind the limo, shining in their faces. No rooftop flashing lights on the car, so it wasn't a cop. Magpie followed the path of another car as it slowly passed the limo, watching it over his shoulder. It veered into their lane and stopped beyond their Tahoe SUV where it shifted into reverse, its rear wheels spinning until they grabbed and moved in close, blocking their vehicle in. The righthand lane of I-95 now looked like the front end of a gathering funeral procession.

Massimo spoke while he tightened his robe. "You thought you'd be confronting an old man with dementia and his pencil-necked lawyer, so you figured you wouldn't need your soldiers."

Doors opened and closed, and men assembled on both sides of the limo, limiting visibility outside-in and inside-out. Wally counted six of them, each with one hand tucked inside their jackets.

"You just made it a whole lot worse, old man," Wally said. "I'm here because I thought we could have a polite chat out in the open like this. Guess I was wrong. Magpie?"

"I already took care of it, boss."

More activity queued up behind the limo. Headlights moved into place at the end of the line of cars, then came more slamming doors. It wouldn't take much for Massimo's men, ready for confrontation outside the limo, to draw their handguns.

Wally spoke. "Goodness, Magpie. Bravo. Some of my associates have arrived in a Ford heavy-duty diesel, a really nice pickup, to check on my wellbeing, Massimo. I'd say we have a standoff. So why don't we do this, before someone kills someone out there? Or inside here. No one shoots any more people, no one blows anything else up. Let's try getting through the end of the year, and then we reassess."

"And no one kills any more Mummers," Massimo said, his stare icy.

Wally tsk-tsked his head. "Not me. Never was me. Easy for me to say yes, because I'm not from around here. Just let it go. Let law enforcement figure it out."

"Easy for you," Massimo repeated the words, sneering, "because your type probably doesn't care about Philly traditions."

"*My type*? You goddamn racist. Tell you what. I'll see myself out, and you and your racist, wrinkled white ass will let me see myself out, or I'll reach over there and cut your fucking throat. How's that sound? Magpie, get the door."

They exited the limo, Magpie parting the gathering of well-dressed goons all striking poses, Wally in his wake. A trickle of cars flowed past in the lanes next to them, traffic at a near standstill. Wally saw flashing lights from police cars in the distance gathering on both sides of the highway, closing as fast as the backed-up traffic would allow them, their sirens wailing.

"Magpie, I'd say we need to hustle ourselves out of here."

"With you, boss."

They traveled the roadwork lane, Magpie finding a seam in traffic that slowed from a whiteout squall blowing up. Their SUV disappeared in the swirling snow.

Old man Massimo exited his limo in the heated three-car garage holding a quart of water ice, the top of the waxed container off, a plastic spoon tending to it. His driver closed the car door behind him. A small freight elevator at the rear of the garages was already open, waiting for him. He scooped out another spoonful of the maroon ice, his mouth and the elevator doors closing at the same time with him, his driver Enzo, and his lawyer inside. He savored the melting sweetness, his dentures chewing a piece of the black cherry fruit that the spoon had mined from the container.

They exited on the second floor where young and old mob associates were chilling, the din low. Enzo put the second quart of Rita's in the fridge in the galley kitchen. Two stories of warehouse spread out around and above them, comfortably furnished with leather sectionals, a vented kitchen, a bar, conference tables, card tables, desks, and phones, and walled space sectioned off as a bunkroom for soldiers called to stay on site, or any mobster who'd had too much to drink. The building wasn't a residence, was more like a clubhouse. Big Sal found a plush side chair with an ottoman. He sat, continued slurping and spooning his treat, his lips reddish purple, his feet up, his focus on the half-empty quart container.

"When does he get here?" he asked his lawyer.

"Twenty minutes. Your diabetes, boss, that water ice, you really ought to..."

"You my doctor now, too? I already overpay you as my lawyer. Indian chief next?" Massimo turned off his scowl to return to the business at hand. "What about Dizzy? He coming?"

"They're picking him up now. Separate cars."

"Good. Does he know why I want him here?"

"He thinks he's getting his Christmas bonus tonight," the lawyer said.

The comment Lanakai had made—"*I don't know what triggered it*"—put a Massimo capo on the phone immediately with Dizzy Punzitore, the family's numbers guy who had grilled Otherway Tisha about the armored car murders. It took a little longer to find Tisha. They found him at Parx Casino in Bensalem just outside Philly, chilling at a blackjack table.

"Otherway's spending a lot of time at the casinos," Big Sal said. "Who died and made him wealthy?"

A rhetorical question, yet the shoulder shrugs and shaking heads circled the room like The Wave at a sports stadium. Men playing cards, drinking beer, on the phones, eating sandwiches, they all knew Otherway Tisha, knew his work ethic, knew his loyalty, also knew him when he was a truck driver, and knew he quit gambling. Massimo intended to revisit the armored car event with the dynamic numbers-running duo of Dizzy and Tisha. Have them answer a few questions. When the two arrived, he'd send everyone home except for the lawyer and Enzo, Massimo's neckless, waistless, brick wall of a driver with Andre the Giant hands.

The elevator door opened to Dizzy Punzitore, smiling large and laughing, impressed with the joke the soldier who retrieved him had told. His smile dissipated when he saw Big Sal across the room. Dizzy said something under his breath to no one in particular. Big Sal lip-read it: "*Shit.*" He also lip-read the Italian curses Dizzy then directed at the joke-telling soldier who'd chauffeured him here.

Big Sal Massimo waved Dizzy to the leather chaise near him and directed the chauffeur to leave the room. When Dizzy sat, his host offered him a cup of water ice and a plastic spoon. Dizzy declined. Big Sal pursed his reddish lips and stared him down. Dizzy accepted.

"Eat. You got diabetes, I got diabetes. Maybe we check outta here together, eating some Rita's tonight. Wouldn't be so bad, right?" Big Sal said, blessing himself with his spoon. "C'mon, Diz, eat, it's good."

Dizzy sampled the water ice but kept his eyes on his boss. After a few moments of silence, Dizzy planted his spoon firmly into the cup and made his stand.

"Salvatore. Big Sal. What the fuck. What did I do wrong? Why am I here?"

"Good, Dizzy, good. You're not feeling it, so that's good. My guess is"— Salvatore nodded to himself, still interested in his water ice—"you believe you did nothing wrong, so we're halfway there. Maybe you didn't. Sit tight."

The elevator door opened and coughed up another driver-soldier type accompanied by the man he'd been sent to retrieve, Frank Tisha. Frank's expression didn't change when he read the room, was calm, unassuming, and with no tells. He took off his winter coat and draped it over his arm.

"Sit on the sofa, Frank," Big Sal said.

Soon as he sat, he was joined by Enzo. Adding the bodyguard to the full-sized sofa turned it into a love seat. Frank didn't flinch with the addition. He wasn't offered any water ice.

"Here's why I'm having you fellas join me tonight," Big Sal said. "I could talk to you separately, so you wouldn't have a chance to get your stories straight, the way the cops like to do it. Or I could interview you together with Enzo, to referee, to make sure what you tell me is true. So here we are. First question goes to Otherway. Why the fuck didn't you ever get your eye fixed?"

"I ask him that all the time, Salvatore," Dizzy said, "that fucking thing is unnerv—"

"Am I talking to you, Dizzy? Shut the fuck up. Otherway—Frank— answer my question."

Frank stayed focused on Big Sal, wouldn't lose eye contact, his good one at least, and would speak directly to him. He would tell it like it is, or was.

"The family had no money. It was something someone should have taken care of when I was a kid, but it never happened. I fought my way through high school with it, washed dishes afterward, lots of different restaurants. They always had me stay in the back, away from the customers. I never even bussed tables. Kept to myself, stayed out of the bars, and saved all my money, then I started driving for the trucking companies. Saved even more money, retirement money and shit, always looking to make a buck. I became a Teamster. I met my Teresa at a church bake sale. She loved me despite the lazy eye, so I never thought any more about it. I stopped all my gambling. It was taking too much food from my family. Now that I'm retired, I'm spending some of it, no second-guessing, no looking back."

The last line hung out there, about not looking back, his audience assessing it. Frank went for cute, filling the dead air with the obvious. "I look sideways at things, because, you know, that's my thing, but no looking back."

Another bit of dead air, then the room erupted in Goodfellas' guffaws, the small audience joining Big Sal in giving the humor its due.

"Now"—the mob don finished clearing his tears of laughter and set his nearly empty quart of water ice on the coffee table—"about that night in the snowstorm, Frank. That armored truck and those dead guards. Tell me what you saw."

"Sure."

Frank crossed his legs. He never talked with his hands, had trained himself that way, always thought it looked amateurish, like the person doing the talking was nervous. He stated his business with his hands folded in his lap, straight eye contact and minimal gesturing, tonight as always. One, maybe two glances at Dizzy max, the looks neither for validation nor for coaxing. He got through the entire scene, finishing with the banjo, the smiley face drawn on the banjo head, and his disgust at realizing the third victim was headless.

"It took around ten minutes for it to play out, Mister Massimo..."

"Salvatore. Call me Salvatore."

"Sure, Salvatore. I called Dizzy from the scene, then I met up with him the next day for lunch to spell it out for him, too."

"I didn't hear you mention anything about money, Frank," Salvatore said. "An armored car and all, and no money fell out the back of the truck? No Joey Coyle, Purolator moment for you?"

"No money, sir—Salvatore. Just those bodies. Two dead guards, both Black, and one headless guy, Black, too, but I didn't notice it then because, you know, no head. All pushed out of the truck by a guy in a camo jumpsuit."

Big Sal picked up his quart container, started prospecting with his spoon again. "The guy in the camo outfit. Hawaiian, you think?"

"See, about that, Mister—Salvatore—here's the thing. It was snowing and all. I couldn't really tell. Not necessarily my first impression. Just seemed like a white guy with dark eyes and dark facial hair. Maybe Hawaiian, maybe not, same as I told Dizzy when he suggested it. My opinion? No, not Hawaiian."

Dizzy's face blanched. One phrase Frank used had caused it to lose its color: "*when Dizzy suggested it.*"

Big Sal crinkled his eyebrows while he chewed through another piece of frozen black cherry. He directed his interest to Dizzy.

"Tell me, Diz, what made you decide it was the Hawaiians? Why'd you tell me that?"

Dizzy puffed up. "I seen too much of them douchebags lately. Making collections, running chink card games in Chinatown, doing weird shit on people. I got a cousin who came in from Brooklyn wanting to sell a kidney to them to make some money. They arranged for the surgery. He was sick for weeks after the operation. Some kind of illegal zombie organ shit."

"Did he get paid for the organ donation?"

"What?"

"Listen when I talk to you, Diz. I said, did the Hawaiians pay him what they said they would pay him?"

"Well, yeah."

"And did he live? No major issues?"

"He couldn't work for days afterward, and he had a scar."

Big Sal stopped chewing his fruity water ice, placed the plastic spoon on a napkin, sat back, and folded his hands.

"Tell your cousin he's a pussy. What did he expect? It sounds like a valid business deal the Hawaiians made good on. Answer me this, Dizzy. Are they taking money from us? You told me they were."

"Well, see, I don't really know—"

"Goddamn it, Diz. I'm guessing, then, that you also don't know if they had my grandson croaked in Atlantic City, now do you? That maybe it wasn't them..."

Dizzy shrugged, then searched Frank's face. Frank was about to get tossed under the bus.

"Frank told me about the hit afterward. Said he seen a coupla them at Resorts just before it happened. Ain't that right, Frank?"

Frank nodded, still calm. "I did. I saw them on the floor playing dominos at one of the tables. But I never noticed when they left. Could still be there, for all I know."

Massimo tented his fingers in his lap. "Little Sal was killed in the parking garage, near the entrance to the casino, and you didn't see the helmeted guy on the bike take him out? You also didn't see the Hawaiians out there? Do I have that right, Frank?"

"Yes. I was inside, playing blackjack."

"Okay then. Dizzy."

"Yes, Salvatore?"

"What I'm getting here, Diz, you motherless asshole, is that what I thought was a sure thing about the Hawaiians, because *you* said it was, is maybe just a house of cards."

"But—"

Big Sal gripped the rim of the water ice quart and flung it at Dizzy's chest. "We're persecuting them, you bastard, and they're calling us on it, and it's because you've got a hard-on for them. This is one big circle jerk, goddamn it. Enzo!"

The hulk sitting on the sofa next to Frank nodded.

"Find a rag so this fool can clean himself up, then I want you to take him home. And about that guy I told you to get a hold of, about that job? Call him back. We need to call it off."

Dizzy fidgeted in his seat. "But boss—please—"

"No worries, Dizzy," Big Sal said, "we'll straighten this mess out and make it right. Go home, we'll talk about it later. But this is gonna affect your bonus this year. Get the hell out of my face. Frank, not you. You stay."

Salvatore had the room cleared, no Enzo, Dizzy, no lawyer who thought he was also Salvatore's doctor. Which left it with considerably less hostility and testosterone. Salvatore found a new bottle of Scotch at the bar, opened it, and splashed some into two glasses, one for himself, one for Frank, the only two people left in the cavernous space that Salvatore "Big Sal" Massimo considered his headquarters.

"*Saluti*," Salvatore said, and raised his glass. Frank responded in kind.

"Here." Salvatore reached inside a pocket in his robe. "I have a present for you. Put your drink down."

For a moment the world stood still, Big Sal's robe pocket potentially holding anything from a cup of melted water ice to a handgun. Frank tensed, was close to wetting himself.

Salvatore recoiled from Frank's discomfort. "What's wrong? Oh. No, Frank, hell no, it's not like that. Just take this. You earned it. For your work this year, and your loyalty."

He handed Frank a long white business envelope, thick and heavy with cash, the flap not able to close on it, then he handed him a second one, equally heavy.

"Your Christmas bonus this year. Yours and Dizzy's both, actually, because that stupid dago fucked up this whole thing with the Hawaiians. There's more than enough in there for you to get your eye done, Frank. It's good to hear when a man fights his way through adversity, stays frugal with his money, prepares himself and his family for his retirement. But stay clear of the casinos. Those places will rob you blind."

"I don't know what to say to this, other than thank you," Frank said, pausing. "Salvatore. But about Dizzy, with Enzo—"

"Relax, Frank, drink up. Dizzy's fine." Salvatore downed his Scotch. "For now."

Frank was a bit overwhelmed and partly giddy for having pulled this off. He not only would leave the clubhouse alive after having lied to Salvatore Massimo's face, he was also leaving with a ton of money, his other money cache still safely secret.

# 15

## A LATINO WALKS INTO A BAR...

**Thursday, December 10**
**Alive Alive-O Pub, Northeast Philadelphia**
**Number of days to the New Year's Day Parade: 22**

A Northeast Philly cleaning job had filled their day. Philo, Hank, and Miñoso were physically drained from handling the scrub-down of a rowhouse basement with a cat litter problem. Rather than put the cat litter in the trash, the senior citizen homeowner who lived alone had been tossing it into an old coal bin in the basement. For months, maybe years. Enter the Philadelphia Board of Health after a complaint filed by a neighbor about the smell, then the homeowner's Catholic church clergy trying to reason with him, and then late yesterday, the Philadelphia police, responding to an armed standoff between neighbors, the home-owner with the litter problem eventually leaving peacefully. Philo and his team had loaded twenty-seven heavy-duty bags full of hazardous waste into a city trash truck, and there was still more. Unfortunately some of the referrals the police gave to potential Blessid Trauma customers, in this instance from the nephew of the homeowner, were far from "blessed." But hey, they were making good money on the gig—five figures, the homeowner needing to tap into his insurance policy—and Philo decided to celebrate by decompressing at a local pub afterward. Hank had headed home to check on the ever-convalescing Grace, his wife. Tonight, in a pub that Philo hadn't frequented in years, it was Philo and Miñoso only, the two men expecting to eat, drink, and then, maybe—

"You play darts, Miñoso?" Philo asked.

"No, *señor*, never played. Never been in an Irlandés bar before either, Philo *campeón*."

They seated themselves near the dart boards at a highboy table with two barstools. Philo checked his watch. 10:42 p.m. An observation about late-night barhopping from his experience: male territorialism in bars usually took an hour or so to manifest and resolve itself after entry. He expected he and Miñoso would be through their dinners and a quick game of darts before then.

Philo ordered for them both: draft stouts, one medium-well cheeseburger with a side of onion rings, and one corned beef and cabbage dinner.

A handful of patrons were at the dart boards near them. "We'll play one game before we leave. Good eye-hand coordination is all you need. Same as throwing a punch."

"*Si, señor*, good. I am good at that."

Philo clapped him on the shoulder. Not a hollow boast, Philo knew. Miñoso was maybe five-eight, maybe one-fifty, and had boxed as an amateur in Mexico. He'd sparred with his boss—prep for a bareknuckle fight Philo was cornered into taking last year. A good outcome for the fight for Philo personally, and good money earned, with Miñoso giving a decent account of himself during their sparring session.

Elapsed time inside the bar, three minutes.

Alive Alive-O as a corner pub was walking distance up Frankford Avenue from Philo's Northeast Philly house. Full-on Irish décor, it was filled with knotty wood paneling, shamrock neon lighting, leprechaun napkins, a fiddle music background, more than one redheaded waitress, and loud, opinionated drunks. Plus a few blokes who weren't drunk yet, their opinions on everything and anything forthcoming. Philo hadn't taken notice of this at first, so it was a surprise to him when he realized it: there were no ethnic minorities in the bar except for Miñoso.

They'd set themselves up near a dart board, one of three regulation boards the pub boasted. They were there to chill after spending a full day in that asphyxiating rowhouse basement full of cat shit. Tonight was Philo's treat. Their draft glasses of Guinness arrived.

Elapsed time in the bar, five minutes.

"Can you smell the cats on me, Philo *campeón*, sir?" Miñoso asked.

"No. No worries, Miñoso, we should be good. The hazmat suits took care of it." They'd also needed oxygen concentrator backpacks for the job, otherwise they'd each have suffered the same fate as the health department inspector who'd been overcome by the cat litter fumes and needed EMTs to revive her.

Their food arrived. The waitress got it wrong, as Philo knew she would, when she placed the corned beef and cabbage dinner in front of Philo. "Not mine, his," he said.

"Really?" She looked more closely at Miñoso, a dark-skinned Latino. "You're just messing with me, aren't you?" she said.

"Cross my heart, no," Philo said.

About now, Miñoso became self-conscious, but he kept his head down and sipped his Guinness. When she left the table, they started in at their food.

Elapsed time, eleven minutes.

Philo chomped on an onion ring and gulped his Guinness. Umm-umm-*umm*, what a great combo.

Knife and fork in hand, Miñoso went to work on his slab of corned beef, carving it up.

Philo eyed his eager employee-slash-friend. "Hard to believe you've never been to an Irish bar, Miñoso, with you ordering the most Irish thing on the menu."

"*Si,* Philo *campeón*. I like the corned beef."

By the time they'd finished their meals, all the dart boards were open. Their dinners cleared, their Guinness drafts replenished, Philo marched up to a board and snagged the board's six darts. "We'll play something called

'Round the World.' I'll go first. Three darts. Watch me. Keep your toes behind this line on the floor..."

Philo followed his own advice, set his right foot forward and leaned onto it, spreading his legs for balance. "You want to put it into that sliver with the number one at the end. Anywhere inside it. Or the bullseye, if you're adventurous. Then go for the sliver for number two, then the three, then four, one dart at a time."

He leaned into his first dart and let it fly. At least it hit the board.

"Huh. I haven't played in a while. We might be evenly matched tonight, bud."

Elapsed time for them in the bar, twenty-six minutes.

"Okay, Miñoso, you're up. Balance on the ball of your right foot, then..."

"Excuse me." The male voice came from the corner nearest to the dart boards. Miñoso held up his throw, and Philo shielded his eyes to get a better look. The corner held a rectangular table with chairs for six. Five seats were taken, and in the dim lighting the occupants were only silhouettes, their faces nearly invisible, not like in the better-lit space where the dart boards hung. Philo squinted. Four men, one woman.

He checked his watch. Elapsed time, twenty-eight minutes.

"That's our board," the "Excuse me" guy said. The man was in an end chair, a longneck beer bottle in his hand. The other people around the table sipped at their bottles or their drink glasses. No one had anything to add to the comment.

Philo raised an eyebrow. What the hell, no big deal, he'd acquiesce.

"Sure. No problem."

He moved one dart board over, nearer the table of five. He had Miñoso set himself up and get comfortable behind the line. "Ready, bud? Don't tense up, stay loose, visualize the dart hitting the board where you want it to hit, raise it, then—"

"That one is ours, too."

Miñoso lowered his arm and backed away from the line. Philo's shoulders drooped. Same man, same table, the rest of the table's occupants again showing an interest in the exchange, bottles and glasses rising and falling in the shadows, no one else at the table speaking.

Philo smiled this time, smoothed back his hair. An urge rose inside his gut along with a rush of adrenaline. He felt his blood pressure rising. Give in to the urge, or give this guy the benefit of the doubt?

"Okay. Sure," Philo said, acquiescing. "But let me go with a question here, sport." He directed the comment at the faceless objector. "Just out of curiosity, I'm wondering—"

"Yeah, the third one is ours, too," the guy said. Philo could hear him smiling through the interruption. "Guess you won't be playing darts here tonight, cowboy."

Philo squared his shoulders up. "That wasn't what I was going to ask." He took a few steps toward the table that contained the guy professing ownership of this corner of the bar.

"What I was going to ask was—and I'm taking a wild-ass guess here that you're not the pub owner—who is it, exactly, who owns these dart boards? And why is it that this person let other people use them while we ate our dinner, but we can't?"

The one communicating with Philo stood. He entered a cone of recessed ceiling light when he moved away from his table. Same height as Philo, a little broader at the shoulders, with a smooth, creaseless face and light hair, the lighting showing a cleft in his chin that some might have considered sexy. Tattoos and symbols with bold coloring were attempting to escape the neckline of his tight black T-shirt, crawling north, up his throat. Expensive artwork, Philo surmised, expressing views on topics that in the colder months would stay suppressed under his clothing, but in the warmer months, with his shirt off, would most probably offend all non-Caucasians. When Philo arrived at the loudmouth's table, the guardian of the dart boards and he were nearly chest to chest. The talker puffed up as he spoke, the visible parts of his tats puffing up as well.

"This corner of the bar is what we like to think of as community outreach for the Philly chapter of The Real Proper Punks. That name ring a bell? Irish Jack Maguire and all that? I expect it does. That's who owns these dart boards, cowboy. This here is a minority-free zone."

"Interesting. I know about Maguire," Philo said. He spoke so the entire table heard him. "Ex-Navy. They discharged him—"

Philo knew the "Punks" were here in the city. A primetime white supremacy group. A disease that was a national embarrassment, and here they were, one of its chapters laying down roots in his backyard, within walking distance of his house. Irish Jack Maguire's Navy discharge wasn't common knowledge, with the Navy typically keeping its dirty laundry secret. His white supremacist leanings had played a large part in it. But furthermore...

"It was because he couldn't measure up," Philo said, a truth Philo felt really good being able to tell one of Maguire's followers. "He was a washout."

This Real Proper Punk took offense.

"Maguire quit, asshole. He couldn't deal with all the political correctness bullshit. Something we won't deal with, either. We let other people use the boards tonight because none of them were wetbacks."

The Alive Alive-O Pub began buzzing like a hornets' nest. Patrons sitting at the bar swiveled in their stools to watch. At nearby tables, people resettled in their chairs to better face the action.

"You march in here with frickin' Guadalajara Gomez, and we see him eating corned beef and cabbage just like a mick, and then he wants to play darts. Darts is a white person's game, Gonzo. An *Irishman's* game. I'm not letting no wetback disgrace these boards. Get the fuck out"—he moved close enough for a pre-fight stare-down with Philo—"or we'll throw the two of you out on your heads."

"Neal Egan," Philo said, not budging, instead returning the stare.

"*What*?"

"You know who he is?" Philo asked.

"World darts champion, asshole. From Ireland."

"You know, then. Good for you. Egan's middle initial is S. For Sabado, his mother's maiden name. She's Mexican. Would you let him play here?"

The room bristled, heads leaning closer to each other, the buzz getting louder. His Proper Punk aggressor laughed, glanced back at his table, looking for guidance or permission, or maybe just an explanation behind WTF this guy was telling him.

"*Sesenta y ocho*," Philo said discreetly to Miñoso, "*mabe más.*" *Sixty-eight, maybe more* was the translation, as in this was Philo's prediction that this man would be his sixty-eighth knockout.

"*Si*," Miñoso said, totally on board. Miñoso put down his beer and his darts, and he pushed the long sleeves of his shirt up to his elbows.

Philo checked his watch. Elapsed time, thirty-three minutes.

A short fuse. That's where Philo's was, attitude-wise. A day spent removing a basement's worth of kitty litter could do this to a person. Maybe the fumes had introduced a chemical imbalance in his nervous system, or maybe it triggered a latent inner anger about having to clean up other people's shit for a living. Or maybe Philo just needed to use a bathroom really bad and had to leave asap, because once he knocked the hornets' nest out of this pub's tree, he wouldn't get to use theirs.

"Is that surprising, sport?" Philo said. "It should be, because I made that up. I have no idea what Egan's middle initial is. Or if he's one hundred percent Irish or not. Probably isn't. But who in the country is really one hundred percent anything, know what I'm saying? And you know what else is surprising?"

"Listen, dickhead," the Punk said while squaring up, impatient, "quit the bullshit. I said you need to get the fu—"

Philo's lightning quick open hand was big enough to close around the grandstander's crotch. His grip of the man's testicles forced the air out of his chest and a squeal from his mouth, with Philo then delivering a short right cross that snapped the lower half of the guy's jaw sideways. Mr. Proper Punk number one and his cute, clefted, glass chin dropped face-first and unconscious to the floor, hard enough to break his nose.

Another check of his watch. Elapsed time, thirty-six minutes.

Let the games begin, Philo mused, waiting for the other men in the group to express their intentions. No one at the table moved, but a few homie hornets at the bar got out of their chairs and were thinking about it. Behind him there was one he didn't notice.

"*Señor* Philo!"

Philo needed to wheel around but was too late to see someone with a dart in his hand raise it over his head, ready to jam it into the back of Philo's neck. The man's hand came down with authority but never connected. Miñoso's combination started with a head-jarring right that overwhelmed the man's temple, was followed with a left uppercut, and ended with a right cross, dropping another body to the floor.

"I guess we'll go now," Philo said to the waitress, loud enough for everyone to hear. He slapped a hundred bucks in cash in her hand. "This should cover it. The food was good..."

He kept his eyes on the two groggy men trying to roust themselves from the floor, neither in any condition to fight back.

"... and the entertainment was outstanding."

The buzz in the room tailed off. The audience gave him and Miñoso a wide path to exit.

"We need to go *now*, Miñoso, or I'm going to wet my pants."

"*Si,* Philo *campeón.*"

Philo was feeling damn good about having given into his urges, able to right at least one wrong tonight. One more check of his watch. 11:26 p.m. Total elapsed time, entry to exit at the Alive Alive-O Irish Pub, Northeast Philly, forty-four minutes.

# 16

## MARLINS AND PEABERRIES AND LUPARAS, OH MY

Saturday, December 12
11<sup>th</sup> and Christian Streets, South Philadelphia
Number of days to the New Year's Day Parade: 20

Wally Lanakai exited his townhouse into a brisk, chilly wind. He held his upturned coat collar closed around his neck and descended the steps to the sidewalk. It was daybreak, the early morning sun hiding behind the urban skyline, brightening the soft blue sky with a faint orange glow. Magpie would be here to pick him up after Wally had his coffee in the shop across the street. The corner store stocked costly "estate reserve" Peaberry coffees from Kauai after Wally's suggestion that the owner stock it, just so Wally could have his large cup of freshly ground, heavenly hometown brew every morning. He'd leave an outrageous tip like he always did, enough to cover the owner's loss for carrying the expensive blend, might have even been enough to pay for the shop's electric bill. He sat at the counter, sipped, and schmoozed with the waitress. His second cup would be to-go, timed for when Magpie arrived out front with his SUV.

Wally knew the history of this street corner. It was why he bought one of the townhouses when he brought Ka Hui to Philadelphia after serving his time in the Federal Department of Corrections prison in Honolulu, Hawaii. If it could be said he put down roots anywhere inside Philadelphia, this was where these roots were, on this street corner, where Angelo Bruno, the "Gentle Don," ate his last meal at Cous' Little Italy Italian restaurant. The restaurant was gone, replaced by townhouses on two of the four corners. Wally owned one of those townhouses and lived in it by himself whenever he wasn't operating out of different luxury hotel suites around the city. It wasn't the way he saw himself, as single, at this point in his life. He'd found who he wanted to spend the rest of his days with, one of his contractors, but she hadn't seen things the same way. Now she was gone, a casualty of the thug life in which the two of them toiled.

There was no lengthy history for the Ka Hui crime family. No generation-to-generation transfer of mob family power. Ka Hui sprung into existence in the Islands when Wally and his young relatives created their persona in the mid-eighties. They were kids back then, known simply as *nā kamali'i hewa* in Hawaiian. Translation, juvenile delinquents. But the Hawaiian cops called them *iole alanui*, or "street rats," and had shown them absolutely no respect, considering them nuisances like the feral chickens the Islands couldn't eradicate. Smash and grab at the luxury storefronts, shoplifting, tourist pickpocketing... petty crimes to the nth degree. Then Wally organized them, and they grew from children to young men. Ruthless, fearless, enterprising young crooks, the media called them. Wally liked the "enterprising" label. Ka Hui, or "The Enterprise," was born, and it flourished for more than ten years in the Islands. Until the Feds killed some of them in an ambush, tried and convicted Wally and others, and put them in prison. It destroyed his mob "family" at its source, the Hawaiian Islands. When Wally was released, he resurrected his beloved Ka Hui team on the east coast of the mainland, where crime families had survived generations beyond their emigration.

History. The Cosa Nostra had it, and Wally as the boss of the Hawaiian mob coveted it, so he followed in some of the Mafia's footsteps, mimicking his way into it. His first two property purchases were the townhouse across from the coffee shop and Philly mob boss Angelo Bruno's rowhome at 10<sup>th</sup> and Snyder, where the Gentle Don was assassinated in a car at a curb in 1980.

Wally wanted his mob family to belong, so he'd shoehorned his organization into this city, whether the city wanted him here or not. There was enough room for multiple crime families if they stayed out of each other's business. Lately, there'd been difficulty in maintaining the distance, but not all this difficulty was Big Sal Massimo's fault.

"Sugar, you seem preoccupied," the counter waitress said to him.

Wally picked at a danish with a fork and offered a wan smile. No reason to dump his worries on this coffee-shop drill sergeant, a wizened sixtyish woman whose earthy demeanor Wally cherished each time he stopped in.

"It's always something, isn't it?" was all he gave her. She didn't need to know about the mob war that was brewing.

"Ain't that the truth," she said, then she moved down the counter to another customer.

He left his tip, a coupla fifties, as usual large enough to generate attention. Also as usual, it was something that would sit under the saucer for as long as the waitress took to clear it, because no other customer would dare mess with it, the regulars knowing who Wally was. A situation he relished, the respect that his station in life had garnered in this part of Philly. He retrieved his long winter coat from the rack, shrugged it over his dark suit, thanked his server for the second cup to go, and found the exit. He stepped outside.

No Magpie SUV at the curb yet. He checked his watch. Magpie wasn't late with the car, Wally was early leaving the shop.

There it was, Magpie in the Escalade, stopped at the red traffic light half a block away. Wally sipped his takeout.

It went down in slow motion for him, a guy in a ski mask leaving the protection of the covered bus stop fifteen feet away, his menace building stride after lanky stride in his long, gray winter coat. Put a fedora on him, he'd have been straight out of a 1940s movie's central casting. The coat opened, the hand reached inside and emerged with a lupara, a single-hand, double-barreled, sawed-off shotgun, as traditional a Mafia weapon as the Tommy Gun. Wally tossed his coffee as the guy raised the gun's double barrel head high, at Wally's face. On reflex, Wally's protection came from a vest pocket, a knife with the tip of a marlin bill as its blade, out of its sheath in an instant.

Except he was too late.

The lupara flashed, but not from the end aimed at Wally. It misfired, the blast snapping the gun in two where the barrels met the stock. The weapon exploded out of the surprised assassin's hand. Before the gun's pieces hit the ground Wally was at him, wielding his marlin-billed knife. The knife sliced off the last two fingers of the hand the man raised in defense just short of the knuckle, the severed fingers tumbling to the sidewalk, then off the curb. The moaning gunman sprinted up the street to an idling sedan. With him inside, its tires spun in place, the car fishtailing from the curb before careening out of sight around the corner.

The Escalade screeched next to Wally at the street corner. Magpie emerged with a drawn handgun. "Boss! BOSS! You hit, boss?"

Magpie's words were no better than whispered echoes to Wally, his eardrums still smarting from the blast the shotgun made. A distraught Magpie circled him, patted him down, and opened Wally's coat looking for wounds. The coffee shop's customers had spilled outside, and the drill sergeant waitress sidled up to Wally and escorted him by an elbow to a bench. No wounds surfaced from the cleanup, no blood visible.

Wally shook loose from the waitress and rose from the bench light-headed. He regained his equilibrium and lowered himself into a crouch close to the sidewalk. He picked up the shotgun. In one barrel was a shell that hadn't fired. The barrel that had exploded was still hot, the metal compromised by a crack, the pellets in the cartridge only partly expelled.

Sirens kicked in. Cops on the horizon, probably EMS vehicles, too.

Wally slapped the damaged lupara into Magpie's chest. "This goes with us. We need to leave now, Magpie." Wally wobbled to the rear door of the Escalade.

"What about those, boss?" Magpie said.

Reflexive glances by them both at the sidewalk, then at the muck in the street, where a severed ring finger and a pinky oozed blood next to candy wrappers in the gutter.

"No," Wally said, taking deep breaths, calming himself. The shock from the attack was setting in. "Leave them. Gifts for the cops. I already know who did this. Get me the hell out of here."

# 17

## AN ARSENAL

**Sunday, December 13**
**Northeast Philadelphia**
**Number of days to the New Year's Day Parade: 19**

For some god-forsaken reason, the theme from a sixties Saturday morning kids' show, *The Banana Splits*, was in his head. Worse yet, he was singing it.

"*La la la, la-la-la-la...*"

An earworm. Morning TV Land fare, and a show Philo had never seen as a kid because it was before his time. The earworm morphed into humming, Philo leaning over his old man's homemade workbench in the basement, a heavy lumber and bolt-laden relic from the fifties. On the bench in a state of disassembly was handgun number four of the eight he owned, another semi-auto P226 Sig Sauer. Laid out next to it were cloths, sprays, swabs, brushes, bore cleaner, a cleaning rod, lubricant, miscellaneous rags, and cleaning patches. His laptop was open on a shelf above the bench, a slideshow on the screen on how to disassemble and reassemble his handgun. His hands were busy, his eyes moving back and forth between the laptop, the disassembled gun parts, and the cleaning supplies.

Spending time at this bench doing this task, and whatever else around the house that needed a repair, he could forever feel his dad's presence here. The organization of the tools, the labels printed in perfect block lettering on drawers, the pegboards on the walls, the vise bolted onto one end, the bench's user-friendly, lived-in nature—down to the holes in the wood planks from hand drills that had gotten away from both him and his father—this part of the basement was his dad personified. Left of center on the wall behind the bench hung a framed black-and-white picture of his pop as a young man in his USN uniform, a head-to-toe photograph circa 1944, begging the question how many visits to the bench were necessary for Philo to keep his home arsenal of weapons in working order, and how many were needed simply because he wanted to commune with his old man's spirit?

"*La la la, la-la-la-la...*"

His time at the workbench was always therapeutic unless Six the Cat involved herself.

Six hopped onto the bench. First it was a stare-down at Philo, then it was a shove of a can of cleaning spray overboard, onto the floor. Just because she could.

Freakin' cats. "You little brat."

She leaped down, squatted in a litter box, left some parting gifts, and padded to the back of the basement.

"Swear to God, Six, when the flights get cheap enough, you wiseass little bastard..."

... but he'd never send her back there, back overseas to the Pakistan streets, ever. He and Six were buds, and his was the bluster of an ornery cat owner trying to get some work done when his calico wanted him to pay attention to her instead. Philo heard the pet door that led out of the house and into the alley behind it, the small door inside a door, as it flapped open then shut.

Back to work on the gun. He picked up the loose gun barrel and reached for a brush. Another interruption: his phone's ringtone, with the phone jitterbugging at the end of the bench. He checked the display.

No phone number, just a name. Someone he should have removed from his contacts list after his most recent near-death experience with the guy last year.

*Wally Lanakai.*

He let it ring through, then he listened to the message:

*Trout. I need a favor. I'll make it worth your while. Call me.*

Philo shook his head. It was a slow shake that reiterated his distaste for this guy, but at the same time it was reminiscent of their history together, a history that wasn't all bad. So, against his better judgment:

The phone connection went through.

"It's Philo, Wally. You're on speaker. I'm in my basement, alone. What do you want?"

"That package I sent you means we're even now, correct?"

The $400K. "Yes."

"Good. You owe me nothing, I owe you nothing. No need to comment on that, just know that I was happy to pay off my debt. But there's something else you need to do for me. Something that will save lives."

"Really," he deadpanned. "Whose?"

"Mine, for starters, and the lives of people who work for me. And most of the Italian mob in South Philly. I just survived a hit. It was retribution for something I didn't do. But there's going to be a war because of it. Before that happens, I want someone as a go-between. Someone who might be able to stop it from materializing. You."

Philo picked up the loose gun barrel from the bench and stuck a wire brush and a patch cloth inside it, working it from both ends, checking to see what came out with each pass. It wasn't that he wasn't focusing on the conversation. He already knew Wally's request was insane.

"What do you say, Trout? Hello?"

"Look, Wally, I'm flattered you have so high an opinion of me, but you're way off base here. I'm of no use to you, so it's not going to happen. My advice is you wear a flak jacket from here on in."

"Ten grand," Wally said. "For a meeting with Salvatore Massimo, representing me. Just a quick meeting where you'll tell him I want an official sit-down with him to clear the air. He can pick the venue."

"That's nuts. *Me*, represent *you*? How do you figure that? If anything, I had a longer relationship with Massimo and his guys than I did with you, back when I was young and crazy. I could see him asking *me* to be the conduit to *you*."

"And therein lies my point, Trout," Wally said. "You've worked for both sides. You're trustworthy. I like you, and chances are Massimo still likes you, too, and he probably won't try to kill you as the messenger. Did I say probably? Sorry, what I meant to say was he won't croak someone he likes. It has to be you."

Even Wally had his doubts, Philo took from that "probably" slip. It just kept getting better and better. And yet, Philo decided, there was something to be gained from all of this.

"Here's what I want, Wally," Philo said. "I want your bodyguard Magellan with me."

"Magpie," Wally said.

"Whatever. Him. I can hide behind him if you're wrong about that probably-won't-try-to-kill-the-messenger thing you just mentioned. He's a monster."

"Deal."

"Second, you and Massimo need to compare notes about these Mummer murders when you meet." Philo would not endear himself with Rhea by making this request, which was why he planned to say nothing to her about any of this. "A little birdie told me the Italian mob is working those attacks as tightly as the cops are. To sweeten things a little more, let me tell Massimo your guys are on the case, too."

"Deal."

Philo was on a roll. He went for broke.

"Those things, and I want thirty thousand bucks."

He could almost hear Wally clenching his teeth through the phone. Philo wasn't greedy, he just liked pulling a mobster's chain when he could, bad as these thugs made it on the street for Rhea and the rest of the Philly police force. Bad as whoever was killing the Mummers was making it, for them and for everybody else.

Philo was liking the dead air while Wally held his temper.

"Deal, you opportunistic bastard."

"Super. Pleasure doing business with you, Wally."

"Hold on. This needs to happen quickly, Philo. When will you make the connection?"

"Give me two days, so I can figure out my way in. Have your guy Magnum—"

"It's Magpie, Trout. Remember his name and get it right. Do not disrespect this man. He can crush you like a coconut with his bare hands. And he *can* crush a coconut."

Again, this was Philo pulling Wally's chain. He knew exactly who Magpie Papahani was. That was why he wanted him. The man would lay his life down for Wally, and for whomever Wally told him to protect. Magpie was his best bet for getting in to see Massimo and getting out in one piece.

"Magpie, Wally, sure, I won't forget. Have a good rest of your day. I'll be in touch."

~

One cleaned and oiled and re-assembled Sig Sauer handgun, check. A bottle of beer in hand, Philo relaxing in the recliner in the quiet of his empty basement, check. Thoughts on how to play this Wally Lanakai request, pending.

A call from Teddy Cangelosi's girlfriend Harriet, Nicky Bricks' widow, to a Massimo goombah, that would be the ticket.

The pet door flapped open and shut. Cat eyes glowed, moving through the darkness in the narrow hallway near the back door. "Six," Philo called.

His calico sauntered forward like a model on a runway. "Have a seat, old girl."

He patted the arm of the recliner. Six sprung onto his lap with the invitation, her digestive system growling, and she soon horked up something from its depths, Philo slipping out from under her before it could ruin his jeans. On the seat of the chair was a small, undigested animal ear, from a kill that was maybe no more than fifteen minutes old, a little bloody thing with a rip in it, plus other cat stomach juices. Whatever the hell else was inside Six—Philo guessed squirrel—he scolded her for her stomach being the vessel that brought it inside his house.

He gathered up Six's gift with a cloth rag, bitched about the stain, and marched it out to the alley to a garbage pail. Back inside, he side-eyed her in the recliner and double-stepped his way up to the first floor, closing the basement door before she could catch him. Better that she regurgitate her kill in the basement than to have him find similar gifts on the other floors.

A phone call to Rhea to see how her night had gone went unanswered. Hell, it was better this way that she hadn't picked up, plus it was easier on his conscience not needing to lie, dodging how his night had included a request that involved hooking up with two crime families from his past.

*Babe*, he texted. *Ignore my call, I'm going to bed. We'll catch up in the morning.*

He needed a day or two to decide how to play this.

# 18

## SOFT PRETZELS

Tuesday, December 15
Washington Avenue, Philadelphia
Number of days to the New Year's Day Parade: 17

"*Not a factory, a bakery,*" the website said.

Philo knew about this soft pretzel bakery but had never been there, inside or out. Washington Avenue was a busy mid-Philly thoroughfare that still had a few sets of trolley tracks along parts of the street's wide, commercial swath running east-west south of the city's — the nation's — premier historic district. So far, the gig with Magpie was working out fine. It was four-forty-five a.m., fifteen minutes before the rendezvous at the factory—check that, "bakery"—between them and Big Sal Massimo's people. They were making good time going cross-city this early, and at Wally's behest, Philo was enjoying a great cup of Kona-blend coffee bean takeout in the back seat of an Escalade SUV with an old acquaintance. Magpie Papahani, his dark suit the size of a circus tent, was his chauffeur and bodyguard for the morning.

"Where does he get the coffee?" Philo said. He sipped and watched the early morning commerce move along the street, fruit and produce trucks, refrigerated vehicles, step vans, blue collar beater cars. This was small talk from Philo to take the edge off where they were going, but he did want an answer, to maybe order some of those beans.

"He's got a guy," Magpie said.

"What, that's all you're gonna give me? '*He's got a guy*?'"

"A breakfast shop near his house. He has a deal with the owner. Very expensive coffee, flown in from Hawaii. The boss subsidizes it." Magpie stopped the SUV at a red traffic light and changed the subject. "What are you carrying, Trout?"

They'd already established they were both armed, but Magpie was going for specifics.

"My Sig's a .45 caliber. My derringer has two barrels and works in a pinch. You?"

"A Dirty Harry special."

A Smith and Wesson .44 Magnum. Sweet.

"... and the SUV's got a semi-automatic long gun under this seat."

"You know they won't let us take any of these weapons in there with us, right?" Philo said.

"We'll get inside the door with what we're carrying," Magpie said, "but we won't get to keep them." He looked left out his window. "Here we are." He stopped the SUV across the street from their destination, double-parked, and put on the flashers.

They surveilled the commercial building that housed the pretzel bakery. Brown brick all the way up, from the sidewalk to the roofline of its two stories. A one-vehicle garage entry on the left, the garage door closed, and a metal single-door entry on the right for walk-ins, no glass. The place would open for business at six a.m. with a short line of customers at the entrance, there to pick up their orders.

Magpie did a U-turn and pulled into the tiny parking lot next to the building, inside chain link fencing. Spaces for ten vehicles, the first space open. He steered the SUV into it but had to stop short. The spot was occupied by a guy sitting in a lawn chair with a thermos. Short, broad, dark, and bald, with ear coverings to handle the twenty-eight-degree weather. He gestured for Magpie to turn off his high beams. The man got out of the chair to approach them.

"You Trout?" he said, his mouth wide, eager, and toad-like, like he was about to catch a fly with his tongue.

"No. Him," Magpie said, gesturing.

The toad leaned down, looked past Magpie at Philo in the passenger seat. "Trout. This is your space for this visit. Prime real estate around here. Lemme move the chair. But before you lock up, I suggest you leave your weapons inside your vehicle."

"Nope, not a chance," Magpie said.

"Suit yourself," the toad said.

By the time they got out, the toad had hopped away somewhere. Philo took the lead out of the lot and pulled open the pretzel factory's heavy front door. They entered the building, Magpie looming over his shoulder. Moist, oven-y baking smells permeated the interior space. A guy with a scarred lip at the walk-in customer counter greeted them. He held out both hands, his fingers beckoning. A second interesting and larger character stood behind him.

"Your weapons. I'm still gonna pat you both down, but if you give me what you're carrying now, we can avoid any misunderstanding."

"No issue," Philo said, removing his two firearms and placing them on the counter. Magpie begrudgingly surrendered his .44.

"I have a favor," Philo said to the gatekeeper. "Can I place a pretzel order to go, for when we're done?"

"I don't work here, wiseass," the guy with the scarred lip said. "The boss loves these pretzels, but he doesn't own the place. Raise your arms and spread your legs, Trout. You too, Sasquatch," he said to Magpie.

When he finished the pat downs, the counter guy made a call and received the go-ahead. "We're good to go back."

Past the assembly line of ovens, dough-cutting machinery, and dough prep and mixers, all in motion, and past the sacks of salt and flour and stacked cardboard, they reached eight chairs arranged in a circle in the rear of the bakery. All but two were occupied, the men eating soft pretzels.

"Mister Trout. Wonderful to see you again. My, my, you are still looking fit. We saved two seats, for you and your associate."

Here was old and supposedly senile Big Sal Massimo, in his eighties now, speaking above the din of the bakery. The bathrobe was still there, and the slippers, but the senility for sure wasn't, because it never was. Philo knew it was an act from their dealings together fifteen plus years ago. The building was overly warm from the ovens, which allowed Big Sal the mob don the luxury of wearing his signature garb with no winter coat. Philo was tempted to remove his coat but didn't. He took the seat offered. Magpie hovered, leaving the one next to Philo empty.

"Nice to see you again, too, Mister Massimo," Philo said. "This is Magpie Papahani, Wally Lanakai's second in command. No disrespect intended, but he'd rather stand."

"Call me Salvatore. I'll go with 'Philo,' if you don't mind." Salvatore gnawed at the last nub of a soft pretzel, needing to adjust his upper dentures to accommodate it, then he wiped his thumb clean of stray mustard. "We'll have a box of pretzels ready for you when you and your associate leave. Does that work?"

"Much appreciated."

"I'll forgo other introductions. These guys with me here are window dressing. The guys you should worry about are here and there around the bakery and outside, in case things were to get crazy, which I'm sure they won't. Tell me, Philo, why are you here?"

Philo's hands were on his knees, which seemed the best place for them because they were fully visible. A quick, contorted glance behind him showed Magpie taking the same approach, his large hands by his sides, exposed.

"Three reasons. One, Wally Lanakai asked me to represent him today, to deliver a request. He'd like a serious meeting with you. To discuss the tragedies each of your families have experienced this holiday season. To clear up misconceptions about them, and to reassure you of his complete lack of involvement with them. Second reason, like you, he's now looking for whoever is murdering all these Mummers. He'd like to compare notes when you meet."

Philo expected an acknowledgment, a nod or headshake yay or nay, not the blank stare he was getting. Were they even on the same page with this? Old Man Massimo didn't budge, stayed stoic. The din of the soft pretzel assembly line seemed overbearing as background noise, until—

"That's only two, Philo. Your third reason?"

"Sorry. Right. Okay, full disclosure, he's paying me to be here, banking that whatever goodwill I might still have with you and your family will get me in and out of here alive. I tell you this only because you should know how serious he is." A pause. "Too many people will die if you guys can't clear up these misunderstandings and return things to an equilibrium."

Massimo eyed his own lap, brushing crumbs off his robe. He re-crossed his legs. "I appreciate the candor about the appearance fee, Philo. Was it good money?"

Philo's turn for nonchalance. He brushed his crumb-less lap off, re-folded his legs, and leaned back. "Not going there, Salvatore."

"Okay. I have an observation, Philo. You look like you could still throw hands with the best of them. If you ever want to get back into it..." Massimo let the comment hang.

"I'm done with that. I'd really like to stay on topic here."

"Fine. My search, plus the cops' search, your female detective friend's case—all those Black people murdered, Philo—the community, my beloved South Philly, is taking this very badly. It pains me to see it. I love the Mummers."

Philo ignored the Rhea reference, had half expected her name to come up. He didn't doubt the sincerity. "Yes. Wally intends to help the same way you're helping. Shake some trees, see what falls out. He'll compare notes when anything materializes. Can he meet with you to do that?"

Salvatore slapped his hands against his boney knees and stood, signifying their meeting was ending. "I have the request, Philo, and I will consider it. Thank your boss for having you stop by. Don't read anything into the brevity of our discussion. Enzo will see you out."

A hulk of a man left the shadows and was on the move. Massimo's version of Wally's Magpie.

"To clarify, he's not my boss," Philo said. "I'm not happy being near either one of you guys. The problem is..."

Enzo arrived in Philo's face, obstructing his sightline to Massimo.

Philo stepped around him. "I'm not done talking with Salvatore, big guy, so back the hell off."

Enzo dropped a hand onto his forearm. It felt like an iron clamp, the grip tightening.

"Go," Enzo said. "Now."

Magpie shoved a chair out of the way, and the two ultra-large men were now close enough for a kiss, both in posture mode, scowls a-blazing.

"Enzo!" Salvatore Massimo chided. "Let him speak. What is it, Trout?"

Enzo's grip relaxed. Philo shrugged free of it, Magpie and Enzo still within reach of each other.

"The problem is, Salvatore, there's someone else out there with even less scruples than the two of you feuding bastards, with an agenda that has put the entire Philly police force and other agencies on notice, and that scares the hell out of me. It should scare you, too.

"*Now* we will leave, Enzo. Soon as we get our weapons back. And my soft pretzels."

$\sim$

"You what?" Rhea said.

7:15 a.m. Philo had parked near Wally's townhouse. He was driving the Center City streets feeling pret-ty proud of himself. Rhea was on Bluetooth and harshing his positive energy.

"You're missing the point," he said. "I delivered Lanakai's request, so maybe these guys will stop fighting with each other and nobody else gets killed. I got out of there without any issues. I even got a full box of fresh Philly soft pretzels you can hand out to your detective friends this morning. With mustard. How about I stop in at the precinct—"

"I... I can't even begin to tell you how pissed I am, Philo. You met with crime boss Big Sal Massimo? I can't tell anyone about any of this. You *asshole*."

Far from the hero's welcome he was expecting. Unbelievable. "Okay then. Guess I won't be stopping by."

"Shut up, just... hold on. Damn it, what am I going to do with you? I'll wait for you outside the precinct, on the street. Bring the pretzels. I do *not* want to hear any more about it today. Swear to God, Philo…"

"Love you, too, sweetie."

# 19

## THE LIST

Sunday, December 20
Lincoln Financial Field, South Philadelphia
Number of days to the New Year's Day Parade: 12

Halftime, Eagles versus the New York Giants, the late afternoon game, Philo and Miñoso at the fifty-yard line.

"Enjoying your first game in person, Miñoso?"

"*Si. Gracias*, Philo *campeón*. Great seats."

"Not my doing, bud. I'll pass the thank-you along."

Teddy Cangelosi gave Philo the tickets, two fifty-yard-line beauties. Rhea had to back out at the last minute, needing to work a case. Fifteen rows up, the seats had a great view of the field and the players' benches. An Eagles fan's dream. Philo brought Miñoso with him as a reward for all his hard work, plus he felt responsible for the crap Miñoso took during that racist incident and brawl at the Northeast Philly bar. But an even more exciting event was on tap for halftime.

Teddy's connection to the seats was his girlfriend Harriet Broglio, because today she was being feted at an Eagles football game for her heroic efforts after the Mummers massacre under I-95. The seats now occupied by Philo and Miñoso came with the celebration.

"And now... here to present the Mayor's City of Philadelphia Hero Award to Miz Broglio is"—the stadium announcer held out for a few extra beats to milk the drama, then milked it some more—"the mayor... of the city... of Philadelphia!"

Teddy stood with a cane next to Harriet on the field. The mayor placed a medallion with a ribbon around her neck and Teddy handed her a large bouquet of flowers. Instead of getting ticketed for speeding 82 miles per hour through the South Philly neighborhoods to the hospital, Harriet was being feted for her bravery and quick thinking. Both endzone screens captured, with great clarity, a close-up of a smiling Harriet and her smelling the bouquet, then Harriet moving in for a passionate assault on her boyfriend Teddy, planting kiss after red kiss on his cheeks and mouth. The stadium erupted, couples following the Teddy-and-Harriet lead. The large woman in the seat next to Miñoso grabbed him by the shoulders and dipped him into a VJ-Day kiss that he just let happen, Miñoso weak-kneed when it ended.

Halftime over, Philo's phone buzzed in his pocket. He let the call go through to voicemail, except no voicemail showed up. A text followed.

*It's Captain Zorn, you ape. Call me.*

Angus Zorn. Someone Philo expected to never hear from again, never take orders from again after he left the Navy. A call that, now that he had heard from him, had to be returned. He excused himself from Miñoso and headed up the stairs to the concessions area. He pressed return call. Zorn picked up.

"Trout?"

"Yeah."

"'Yeah, *sir*,' to you, or do you still not like me?"

Captain Zorn was a fiftyish U.S. Navy lifer when he retired. Or maybe the Navy retired his Black ass for him. The man was legendary, his methods for completing missions as subtle as freshwater fishing with quarter sticks of dynamite. Philo hadn't heard from or about him since Philo had turned in his own retirement papers.

"Not 'sir' anymore, Zorn. What do you want? I'm busy."

"They've got the list."

Philo looked for privacy somewhere. He stepped off some distance from the crowd and headed to a railing overlooking a parking lot.

"That's funny, Zorn. There is no list."

"*You* say there's no list, and *I* will say there's no list, but apparently *they* don't know, and won't buy, that there's no list, and that screws up our shit big time. I'm hearing a lot of chatter out there, overseas and domestic, and I can't contact my men about it because you guys are all redeployed or witness-protected or whatever around the planet."

"Not Kase Winslow."

"Forget Winslow. He's never met a TV camera he didn't like. Poster boy for how not to be a retired SEAL. He's got a death wish, you don't. Which means I'll never understand why you've still got a landline, and the number for your white ass is in the phone book."

"Yeah, how about that. Are you going to tell me what happened or what?"

"Ogden's gone, Trout. He ate a gun, but it went down different than that sounds, bless Hughie's hoo-yah heart. May his soul rest in peace. Some people witnessed the assault. They saw the abduction squad and the take-down, saw him muscling the barrel of an abductor's gun into his own mouth, then saw him take care of business so they couldn't haul him off alive. Parts of him are now showing up at different news agencies around the country tonight, but the Feds are pushing back, warning the media to keep it quiet because they were working an angle."

Hugh Ogden. Damn. On many missions with Philo.

"Where was this?" Philo asked.

"Rehoboth Beach."

In Delaware, only a few hours' drive from his Philadelphia digs. If a list had surfaced, the two dozen or so people on it would be compromised no matter where they were, resettled or not. Philo had already accepted this as a potential outcome for himself ever since that final SEAL assignment, knowing this day might eventually come, which made him cavalier about the inevitability. But he'd never understand the direction Kase Winslow had gone. National media type, Winslow was cashing in on his celebrity.

"Look, Trout, if you want some help, I'll get someone to bring you in."

"The timing's not good, so no. We done here?"

"What the fuck, your death wish kicking in now, too? I can get someone down there to extract you..."

*Down there* meant down from Massachusetts. Philo had recognized the 978 area code. It could have been faked but he knew it wasn't. Zorn's hometown of Rockport. It seemed his captain hadn't taken himself that far off the radar either.

"You took a chance calling me, Zorn. I appreciate it. I've got some good things going on here, so I need to pass."

"Good gig, good woman, or both? Never mind, forget I asked, not my business. But listen to me, Trout..."

There was no use extending the call. "I appreciate your concern, Zorn," he said, talking over his former superior. "Thank you, but let's shut this call down."

Philo heard a frustrated grunt on the other end.

"Still not taking orders. Fine, Trout. And you're welcome. But if I were you, I'd wear something heavy around my neck, like maybe chainmail. Or better yet, get one of them medieval knight's helmets."

"Because?"

"Because they took Ogden's head. Decapitated him. Even after Hughie croaked himself. They masked up, paraded around the internet with it before the social media heavies realized what was happening. They left his head on Pentagon property, in a cat carrier."

Philo noticed only now that on reflex he'd slipped his hand behind his back to feel for his Sig. But a football stadium would not have been a good place for a civilian to show a piece, and that was why he didn't have it with him. He dropped his hand back down to his side. "Not changing my mind, Zorn."

"Then I guess we're done. You know how to contact me. Good luck, Trout."

Respect for authority. Tradition. Discipline. The best damn military training in the world. Philo owed a lot to the Navy, his different SEAL team members, and especially his captain, who'd helped him turn his life around. A lot to be said for all of it, and at this moment, this maudlin sentiment was grabbing him by the shorthairs.

He swallowed hard. "A pleasure serving with you," Philo said into his phone, his pride stoked, genuine and heartfelt, "Captain, sir."

Some throat clearing preceded his captain's cracked-voice response. "A pleasure knowing and serving with you too, Philo. No one better than you, son."

Game over, the Eagles won. Philo bought Miñoso a Nick Foles midnight green Eagles football jersey from a parking lot vendor outside the stadium. For sure it was an unauthorized knockoff, and the NFL and the former Super Bowl MVP wouldn't get a dime from it, but the thrilled recipient didn't care. Philo didn't miss the long look Miñoso gave the Latino vendor after the transaction and the man's nod in return, unspoken words acknowledging hardscrabble lives here in the States, and perhaps from similar origins as well.

He dropped Miñoso at his North Philly apartment in front of two of his roommates on the front porch drinking something from coffee cups that was probably not coffee. They both cracked wise at him—Philo could tell from their body English, not knowing their Spanish slang—as Miñoso ascended the steps. Philo left and headed home.

He waited up past midnight for Rhea. When she arrived, she stripped down to her skivvies on her way to the bedroom and confided about her exhaustion when she got there. She fell asleep in Philo's arms soon after she laid her head on his shoulder.

His mind raced. He had Zorn's call to thank for it. At one a.m. he slipped out from under Rhea's draped, beautiful body, checked the doors and windows on all the floors, and went down to the basement. He started in on another load of "laundry."

Rhea needed to know about those thirty-eight minutes in Pakistan. She already knew about Ed Bounce's background, but he'd need to also tell her about Zorn, Winslow, Ogden, and Geronimo. Not tomorrow, that was too early, because he was still sorting this all out, but soon.

How long the Navy and the Feds would keep quiet about what happened to Hugh Ogden in Rehoboth Beach, he couldn't know.

# 20

## DRIPPING WATER

**Wednesday, December 23**
**Columbus Boulevard, South Philadelphia**
**Number of days to the New Year's Day Parade: 9**

They were at the Best Buy on Columbus Boulevard, mid-afternoon, two days before Christmas. The gray skies reached east, beyond the docks visible from the parking lot and across the Delaware.

Philo had a few free hours, as did Rhea. He'd closed out a project near the Navy Yard this morning, a hazmat dump in an open landfill from a trash truck labeled "Recycling Mavens" that contained untreated hospital waste. The balls on these guys, the mob paying people to look the other way while they illegally dumped hazardous materials for the recycling company. Rhea and her Philly brass management had met with Homeland Security at the Roundhouse in the morning, going over where they were regarding the Mummer murders. The teams were now investigating a potential connection to another gruesome death, this one in Rehoboth Beach, she told Philo.

"Another Navy guy," she said, preoccupied.

"We do get around," Philo said.

They found the Xbox gaming display near the widescreen TVs. Rhea's nephew wanted the newest console, and Rhea was going to spoil him with it. "The guy was Black, Philo. He was also beheaded, but it was post-mortem. Too much of a coincidence to ignore."

"Yep," he said, still studying the Xbox display.

Philo wanted this topic to go nowhere. He'd decided not to ante up what he knew, his connection to Zorn, Zorn's phone call, none of it. The authorities were piecing it together. If it happened organically, great, no reason for him to get more particular with Rhea about... things. No reason for her to worry about him.

They'd gone from one stressful situation to another, from the professional to the more immediately personal, trying to find last-minute gifts for relatives. Holiday stress sucked.

Rhea was with a sales associate. Philo stayed out of her way by getting lost among the large-screen TVs. He watched a news story that the forty or more display models on the walls and floor were running. The crawl at the bottom of the screen boasted "Breaking News."

"Whoa," he said under his breath.

"*Here is former Navy SEAL Kase Winslow in a clip from his press conference yesterday,*" the reporter said.

The piece began rolling, and Philo moved in closer to the screen. The resolution was incredible—the blackheads on Winslow's pretty face had no place to hide.

Winslow was a grandstander. The U.S. military preferred their current and former combatants be "quiet professionals" when they were deployed, also wanted them to remain that way after their military service ended. The unspoken code was to put your mission and your team's accomplishments before your individual goals and recognition: get the job done, credit your team, and move on. One of the SEAL mottos was *The deed is all, not the glory.* Kase Winslow would never be mistaken for a quiet professional, flashing medals and awards for the public to see at every juncture of his post-Navy career as a perpetual, unsuccessful political candidate. The Navy made a point of distancing itself from him. But why release footage of a press conference from a few days ago that, from what Philo could tell, only a few people and one reporter attended? Winslow was back in the news today, but for what?

Philo exuded a growing hatred for the man while he listened to him.

"*The threatened U.S. military pullout... more American and Afghan deaths are now on the horizon, home and abroad. I do support the pullout, but just because we're not at war with someone any longer doesn't mean they're not still at war with us, wherever they can find us.*"

The story took a turn, the TV anchor blanking his face at the camera then starting in again with a still photo of what appeared to be Kase Winslow on his knees on a patch of dirt, his head lowered. "*What you see here is disturbing, but it gets extremely disturbing further in. We can't show you what happened during the entire sequence because a, we no longer have access to the video, and b, if we did, it is too gruesome for public viewing.*"

"What the hell...?" Philo said much too loudly. His glances darted from one TV screen to another.

His outburst got Rhea's attention. She steered her shopping cart over to him from the cashier, and the two watched as news footage ran in slow motion until it stopped midframe, the image blurred. The news anchor started in again.

"*News organizations around the world received this today. The timestamp has yesterday's date. It was recorded outdoors, the location believed to be somewhere in western Maryland, in the Appalachian Mountains.*"

Kase Winslow's comment about "wherever they can find us" was in the process of being validated. Shirtless, his breath visible, he struggled against the white plastic zip ties that held his hands together behind his back, but the struggle was weak, the man exhausted, defeated. A person in a dark hood with a large machete entered the footage, spoke to him, then raised the weapon in both hands. The film blurred, then stopped.

Whatever "angle" the Feds were working—Captain Zorn's words to Philo on the phone—this execution proved it wasn't happening fast enough.

Rhea grabbed Philo's arm. "Let's go. Out of here. Now."

In Philo's SUV, she shared a text with him, one she'd received while in line at the cashier. "Carl says they have a print match for the fingers."

"Fingers?" Philo said. "What fingers?"

"Sorry, I thought I told you. The two severed fingers found near your Hawaiian buddy's house, outside a coffee shop where witnesses said there'd been an assault. No one gave up who the assault victim was. But the prints from the fingers are in a military database. They belong to a discharged U.S. Marine." She shared a name.

"No idea who that is," Philo said. "They picking him up?"

"Not yet, and they're not hopeful. He seems to be moving around. The thing is, Carl says, his discharge from the Navy was a sham. The NCIS administrator on the phone spoke off the record about it. The guy was discharged, quietly, but it was for acting on anti-minority impulses."

Not a surprise. Philo knew the Navy often rid itself of bad apples with attitude problems this way.

"You're saying he's a white supremacist, Rhea. Sure. The military's got them, just like on the outside. I'm guessing the discharge was honorable, too."

"Right. A sham. I don't get it. Why not—"

"Court-martial him? Hit him with a dishonorable discharge? Too much negative publicity. Plus there's no section in the Navy criminal code that addresses extremism. Easiest to just kick him out."

Her phone made a noise. She read a text, lingered over it, then keyed a quick response. She put the phone back in her coat. Philo waited on her, expecting her to share, except she didn't.

He pried. "What was that?"

Her "nothing, forget about it" response had an edge to it.

"What, you pissed or something, Rhea?"

"Oh, I dunno, Philo, maybe I don't like hearing how little the U.S. military cares about white supremacists and extremism. Not doing more with that bigot to make his life miserable. In case you haven't noticed, I'm not white. So yeah, it pisses me off."

Philo felt helpless here, and guilty by association. Yes, the military was wrong. It was too passive-aggressive a position for the Navy to take.

"Look, how about we head back, I cook you a nice meal, we have some wine, relax in front of my fake fireplace, and I give you a fantastic backrub as a way of apologizing for something that isn't my fault?"

Another text came through before she could respond. She read it, exasperated. "We can't. The cop brass wants me to come in today. With you." The "sorry" she added should have had a "not" with it.

They were inside Rhea's precinct, seated next to each other at a table in a large conference room. Also at the table were the police commissioner, her assistant Lawrence Yonder, Rhea's partner Carl, and two men in civilian suits, both on the job with Homeland Security.

"Lights," Commissioner Val said. The conference room lights dimmed, and the footage began to roll on a drop-down screen.

What had been blurred on the TV screens in Best Buy and mercifully cut short by the news agencies ran until the footage was exhausted. Philo was unimpressed by the gore of the beheading and the multiple hacks the masked executioner took to fully separate the head from the body. Carl flinched during it, but no one in the room looked away. Winslow's severed head was dropped into a waxed cardboard box, the phone camera moving in close, above the box's open end. The lens zoomed in on Winslow's star-struck face. The video ended.

Rhea spoke first. "Commissioner, may I?"

"Go for it, Detective."

"With all due respect," she addressed the Homeland Security guys, "why show us this? Shock value? Why did I need to bring Mister Trout with me? I don't doubt that the full weight of your agency will come down on these Islamic terrorists, but unless you connect some of the dots for us—"

Commissioner Val raised her hand at Rhea, a stop sign. "Detective, Homeland Security believes this guy—these executioners—are working with domestic extremists. Not sure how, or why, but that's the assessment. Homegrown domestic terrorists who have joined forces with a U.S.-based Al Qaeda group. No ideological commonalities other than paranoia about the U.S. government, far as Homeland can ascertain." The agent nodded when Rhea looked his way. "But that gives them some similar enemies, and they're willing to work with one another to murder common foes.

"Al Qaeda's using white supremacists because they move more easily around these parts. They supply Al Qaeda with guns and intel. Did I get that right?"

One of the unnamed Homeland agents nodded. "The enemy of my enemy is my friend," he said. "That's what we're dealing with."

"Sorry, Commissioner," Rhea said. She leaned onto her elbows. "Not enough info. Similar enemies? Like who? And you haven't answered my question. Why have me bring Philo here?"

"We'll get to Mister Trout in a moment," the agent said, barely a nod in Philo's direction. "The Mummer murders, Detective—all African Americans, right?"

"Yes."

"Easy dot to connect. So many domestic terrorists are white supremacists. Why go after Black Mummers? Because the New Year's Day parade pushed the people of color envelope on a grander scale. The Mummers have been all white for so long. *Change*, Detective. Not everyone wants it. Good exposure to intimidate the Mummers. It helps with recruiting. Now" —the agent locked eyes with Philo—"we get to the Mister Trout perspective. You want to tell her, Trout, since it seems you haven't, or should I?"

Rhea's turn toward Philo was abrupt. "Tell me what?"

"About Mister Trout's thirty-eight minutes in Pakistan, Detective," the agent said. "In 2011. Trout, you're up."

Philo's scowl said the agent was out of line. "That's classified."

"*Was* classified, then it leaked. There's relevance here. Law enforcement needs to know. Tell her, Trout."

Philo gritted his teeth at being cornered, could so easily punch this bastard in the face for not giving him a heads up beforehand. He wanted to take Rhea's hands in his while he explained, but this wasn't the place for that. He also knew she wouldn't abide by his touch right now.

"Ed Bounce, Hugh Ogden at Rehoboth Beach, and now Kase Winslow," Philo said. "All three were part of SEAL Team Six with me. Twenty-two of us on that mission together."

And all three beheaded, Philo internalized.

"SEAL Team Six," Rhea said, "was the team that assassinated Bin Laden. *That* SEAL Team Six?"

"Yes."

The revelation stunned her, Philo seeing the disappointment in her eyes. She recovered by turning away, leaving him with a cold shoulder. When she spoke, she split her looks among the other people around the table, excluding Philo. "What about the Black trumpeter in Northern Liberties? The home invasion victim, and his wife in that safe room? SEAL Team Six?"

"Not him," the agent said. "He wasn't military. He also wasn't beheaded. But his death indicates the nature of their cooperating agreement. The execution comes from the white supremacist playbook, the beheading comes from Al Qaeda's. Again, *the friends of my enemies...*"

"Yeah, yeah," Rhea said, "we got all that the first time, Agent...?"

"Smith."

"Sure, why not," she said, dismissing him. All eyes were on her, now that these cards had been played. She finally acknowledged Philo. "So I'm the last to hear about this."

"It was classified, then it wasn't," Philo said by way of excuse. By way of personal explanation, "I didn't want you to worry."

Rhea straightened up and gave Philo the death stare he knew he had coming. She cleared her throat and resumed her questioning with anyone other than Philo. "Where do we go from here, Agent Smith?"

Philo reached for her hand under the table. Her sharp nails made him retreat.

～

Back in Philo's vehicle.

"Goddamn it, Philo, you embarrassed me," Rhea said. "You not trusting me is unacceptable. It makes me out as someone who can't be objective. Someone who couldn't be entrusted with that information. Take me home. I'm done for today."

"I'm sorry," he said, "but I think you know why I didn't tell you, and it's scaring you."

He wouldn't say more about it, it would only make today's revelation worse. He wanted to protect her, his girlfriend, his confidante, his most significant other, all the time. This was where they were in their relationship. He—they—had grown that close.

"Shut up," she said. "Just get me home."

But there was one aspect of the visit to the precinct, and his viewing of the video, that he needed her to hear before she shut him out for however long it was going to be, hours, days, whatever. "Did you notice the water, Rhea?"

"Stop. We're done talking today."

"I'll take that as a no. Water was dripping from Winslow's nose and mouth in the video, and there was a puddle of water in the box with his severed head."

"Maybe they gave him a shower before they hacked it off," she said, her sarcasm dismissive. "Save it, Philo."

Her stare out the passenger window stayed blank, unfocused, the epitome of a deflated human being.

"Look. No one said this back at the precinct—maybe because Homeland Security doesn't know, isn't sure about it yet, or doesn't want it broadcast," he said, "but I'm thinking the man was waterboarded. Like we did to Al Qaeda prisoners held in Guantanamo. Ed Bounce, too, if you remember the ice the coroner found in his nose."

His assessment was info she might use to impress her management. Something she could suggest that the authorities could run down. His olive branch, if she chose to take it.

Her apartment building was half a block away. Philo slowed the SUV to a crawl, to check for parking.

"Don't park," she said. "Leave me off at the door. You're not coming up."

# 21

## UNSENT TEXT

**Wednesday, December 23**
**Neshaminy State Park Marina, North of Philadelphia**
**Number of days to the New Year's Day Parade: 9**

The Delaware River had large, bobbing ice chunks close to the shore. Rhea and Carl were on foot next to it, peering down the marina boat ramp that led into the river's black depths. At 9:10 p.m. the lights affixed to the marina's utility poles illuminated the trail from the parking lot blacktop and down the ramp, onto the water's surface. Her first impression was they could have filmed the miniatures work here for *Titanic*, the movie, the river's ice chunks afloat as far out as she could see from the shoreline.

Partying teens had found the submerged vehicle, the park open but the marina closed during the off-season. The marina parking lot was gated and off limits, accessible now because of the police activity, but also because the gate had been compromised and swung freely.

"Up here," Rhea said, and she started into a break in the trees.

Thirty yards upstream their flashlights showed a shoreline graced with empty beer cans and pint liquor bottles and a dead bonfire, the partyers super diehards in such cold weather. Here was their vantage point, granting them a full view of the end of the marina ramp. The rear corner of a commercial vehicle protruded above the river surface a short distance from the ramp, a police car searchlight illuminating it.

Two police divers poked their heads above water in their scuba gear, high-lumens safety lights affixed to their shoulders. One diver removed his scuba mouthpiece to speak.

"It's a Dominion Security armored car," he called to the gathering of cops. "All the doors are closed."

Back at the ramp, Rhea high-fived Carl. They were outside their Center City Philly jurisdiction and had gambled this would be the vehicle from the armored car murders, the case nearing twenty days old. So far, so good. The local district detectives and the two uniforms sent with them had been sweethearts, letting Rhea and Carl call the shots.

"Pretty freakin' convenient, Ibáñez, don'tcha think," Carl said, "dumping the truck near a boat ramp?"

"Don't overthink it," she said, "but yeah, as an easy find, convenient as hell."

The truck was under fifteen feet of water. The divers finished hooking the frame to two steel cables connected to a winch of an industrial strength tow truck. A few hand signals by a diver and the winch went into action, the cable snapping taut, the wrecker laboring. The submerged vehicle emerged rear first. It moved up the ramp, the wrecker dragging it forward until it reached the marina's empty parking lot, under the lot's bright nighttime lighting.

A sight for their sore eyes. The large, black, steel-encased box was recognizable as the cash-in-transit vehicle, or armored car, they were looking for, its doors closed, its glass intact. The tow truck braked, the submerged vehicle drifting a few more feet before coming to rest, water streaming out the edges of the doors. A police diver unhooked the cables from the frame. The diver called Rhea and Carl over.

"All yours. Been a pleasure, Detectives."

Rhea nodded. Now to process its interior. If they could get inside.

Three heavy, armor-plated doors. The side and rear doors of the carriage bed were either locked or frozen shut. Rhea pulled at the driver's side door. When it unlatched and opened, a gush of water poured out, with water dripping from the saturated ceiling. Rhea and Carl slipped on rubber footies and nitrile gloves and climbed under heavy-duty rain ponchos.

"After you, miss," Carl said, gesturing.

"How magnanimous of you, you scaredy cat."

"Am not. Seriously, I can do this. Just—"

"Shut up, Carl, I'm good with it. Let's go."

Rhea pulled herself into the cab and slid into the driver's wet pleather seat. She checked out the cab from behind the steering wheel.

"They destroyed the dashboard, the instruments... A lot of the wiring is ripped out. Why the hell do that?"

"Might explain why the GPS tracking cut out."

"Ahhh. Yes. Very good, Carl."

She slipped out of the seat for a check of the interior. Diagonally behind the driver was a jump seat for the armored vehicle's "hopper"—the guard who hopped into and out of customer establishments, doing cash collection or delivery. Above the jump seat, head high, the interior wall showed tiny holes in it. The partition behind the driver's seat showed similar holes.

"We'll need to dig inside these walls, Carl, to see what's in there," Rhea said. "Looks like buckshot from a shotgun."

"Copy that. Forensics will rip it apart when it gets downtown. Am I allowed in, partner?"

"Sure. I'm on the move."

Carl climbed into the cab behind her. When she moved past a partition to look in the back, she didn't get far. "We're going to need the coroner, Carl."

The body was in a camo jumpsuit on the floor, against the rear wall in a half-foot of water still draining out, the body bloated, the jumpsuit barely containing it. Leather boots on the feet, the laces straining. A black beard and mustache, both thick. Was probably Caucasian, but waterlogging did strange things to dead people. A black watch cap was still on his head, black gloves on the floor, not near the body, resting wherever the streaming water had left them. Carl joined Rhea, the two of them in a crouch over the body.

"Look at his left hand," Carl said. "He's missing two fingers. Probably our Marine. The one discharged on grounds."

"Okay then. Wow. So the guess is he turned into a liability, which meant *whack*, goodbye. Your turn for pictures, Carl."

Rhea adjusted her nitrile gloves to pat down the body's legs, waist, and chest, to see what the multiple pockets of the jumpsuit held. Maybe an ID, or a weapon, or keys, or maybe—

Hanging from a belt loop was a small rectangular pouch, same camo print, and stamped *Waterproof*. She felt its contents. Something flat and rectangular. She fumbled with the top of the bag, closed with a Ziploc-like seal, her gloves a pain in the ass to work with, but she got the bag open and slid out its contents. Not a surprise: a phone, and it was dry.

"A prepaid. With a camera," she said.

"As good a place to start as any," Carl said.

Rhea turned the phone over in her hand. Her push at a button didn't turn it on. A second push at a different button rectified that. "Battery's still good. Still has juice," she said when it came to life. She started poking, looking for whatever the phone could tell her.

"It's juiced because it hasn't had much use in the last nineteen days," Carl said.

"Maybe, or maybe less than that. We don't know how long this truck has been in the water. Or how long this guy's been dead."

The phone beeped, which caught them both by surprise. Carl leaned over her shoulder to see.

It beeped again. Rhea now realized she'd made a huge mistake.

A third beep. Was it another text, or were the beeps indicating something had been activated? An IED?

"Shit! Get out, Carl, now!"

She pushed Carl out the driver's side door, dove out the door behind him, and came up running, Carl beside her, the two of them yelling for everyone in the parking lot to take cover. They ran behind the wrecker, their rapid foggy breaths surrounding them. They peeked back at the waterlogged truck. The other detectives and uniforms were behind their own vehicles giving Rhea and Carl curious looks.

They waited, then waited some more. Rhea produced her phone, ready to call in whatever happened, whenever it did, but the marina, the armored truck, and the parking lot stayed eerily silent, the lapping of the river against the boat ramp the only sounds. They straightened up and slowly left their cover, retracing their steps back toward the armored car, tentative in their approach until—

*POP!*

They all dropped to the blacktop, their eyes on the armored car. The noise had come from inside. She got to her feet and was the first to reenter the truck.

The good news was Rhea was wrong about the vehicle being booby-trapped. The bad news was the body had exploded from the chest cavity outward, muck everywhere inside, the walls, the ceiling...

"False alarm, Ibáñez. No IED, but *yuck*," Carl said.

Bodies sometimes exploded, just ask a funeral director. She'd now have to hear about this from Carl forever and ever. "Let's finish up our preliminary work so we can get the hell back outside. The coroner will be here any minute. The flatbed, too."

She searched the floor and found the jettisoned prepaid phone. After a few touches she realized what had happened. The beeping came from a received text, more than one. Nothing, no security thumbprint or code, stopped her from pulling the text up to read it.

*Who is this?* the text read. It was ten minutes old. A second text had followed. *Who the fuck is this?* And a third, this one more graphic. *When I find out who the hell this is I'll stick a shotgun up your ass and*—

Carl, looking over her shoulder, verbalized what she was thinking. "Who the hell is that from, and where's the text that prompted it?"

Paging up on the screen, they learned the text out was a photo of a hatless man in a snowstorm, by all bets Caucasian, standing in the middle of a street, his coat collar pulled tightly against his neck, his facial features and hair not discernible because of the blizzard conditions. Between him and the camera was a Dominion Security canvas satchel the size of a gym bag, yellow-white in color, with brown handles. Behind him, bodies.

She pushed the *Photos* button on the camera. There was only one, the man in the snowstorm, creation date 12/5—the night the bodies were discovered and the armored car went missing. She pulled up the text trail again. Only one text: this photo, plus a one-word greeting to go with it. *Aloha.*

The true nature of her mistake hit her. The message, and this picture, had been queued up on 12/5 per a timestamp, but it hadn't been sent until tonight. When she manhandled the phone.

"Sonovabitch." She'd have an interesting time explaining this to her superiors.

They settled on a few things. One, someone in addition to the camera person—someone in the street—had witnessed the bodies dropping from the armored car and a cash bag tossed or accidentally dropped out as well. Two, the picture that was now nineteen days old had been sent via text to an unknown recipient only moments ago, by her, a detective assigned to the case. Fucking wonderful. Three, the person it went to did not know who it came from.

And four, that person would now look to track down the sender.

A doable thing, tracing it back, on the part of the recipient, unless it had come from a burner phone, which this phone was, so sorry, Mister gun-up-your-ass, she internalized, you are S-O-L. Which meant that for whoever had composed the text, with the photo, its delivery was all that mattered, not necessarily who it came from.

The coroner arrived, then the flatbed. Things swirled in Rhea's head, the repercussions starting to coalesce. She and Carl talked at length about them as they followed the flatbed down I-95, on their way back to a department forensics unit with their armored car prize.

Frank Tisha sipped a cup of hot chocolate in his recliner, watching a late-night talk show in his living room. He'd finished up his street numbers pickups quickly tonight and was home early. His cellphone rang.

"Tisha," Frank said.

"Hi, Frank."

A woman's voice that he recognized. He was surprised to hear from her. "Nancy?"

"The one and only. Listen—"

"Hey," he said, his voice low, "um, I'm thinking this isn't a good idea, you calling me like this." He cast a reflexive glance at the stairs to the second floor. His wife Teresa was up there in bed, also watching TV, a different late-night talk show. "I mean, it's not like we're still, you know..."

"Yeah, your loss, Frank, but listen, I don't have much time. He's here, but he's in the bathroom. You need to know something. He—"

"He who? Dizzy?"

"Yeah. He stopped by. I called to tell you he just got a text. It's a picture of an armored truck and some bodies. From the snowstorm the other night on 2 Street. The truck, the bodies, and you."

"Calm down, Nancy, no worries. I already talked with him about it. Big Sal Massimo, too. We're good. Everything's good, honey, relax."

"Frank," Nancy said, whispering now. Frank heard a toilet flush on her end. "There's a Dominion money bag in the picture, on the ground with the bodies, and you're standing right behind it. I gotta go."

## 22

# PLAN B

Friday, Christmas Day
Frank "Otherway" Tisha's residence, South Philadelphia
Number of days to the New Year's Day Parade: 7

Frank and Teresa attended Midnight Mass at Our Lady of Mount Carmel, which meant the empty nesters could sleep in on Christmas morning. He'd have a major surprise for her when they finally got downstairs to open gifts. But it had to wait until after the Christmas-morning lovemaking Teresa decided to initiate and was in the process of delivering. Frank had been so on edge the past forty-eight hours. The straddling, grinding Teresa worked her slim and trim body extra hard to get him to the release point, cooing his name until it happened.

Teresa talked to him from the bathroom through a mouthful of toothpaste. "Feeling better now, Frankie? A little less stressed?" She and her sweet, white-lathered grin leaned out the doorway to smile at her man, who was still prone from their lovemaking.

"A wonderful present. Thank you." The sexually spent Frank, in pajamas and slippers, climbed out of bed to get downstairs before she did.

The lovemaking barely qualified as a diversion for him, not the stress-reliever Teresa had been going for, and initially, it had been a non-starter. Preoccupied, he'd struggled through the sexual machinations until he'd found the visual he needed.

Nancy. Sweet, sexy Nancy.

The warning that streetwise Nancy had given him was still on his mind. She'd taken a chance delivering it to him, her occasional lover, one of a few he knew she had. There had to be feelings there to do that, and Frank bathed in the thought of them this Christmas morning while his enthusiastic wife Teresa made love to him. Visualizing sexy, bouncy, slightly overweight Nancy was what he'd needed to bring him to the finish line.

Downstairs, he placed a brown envelope behind the other presents, all of them under the tiny ceramic Christmas tree on the mantel, their lone decoration for the holidays. In the envelope were downloaded tickets and receipts and an itinerary arranged through a travel agency, changed to move their departure date up by a few days. Today they'd spend visiting their son and daughter and their families including, most importantly, their two grandkids, one per couple, opening gifts, having some laughs. Then they'd catch their flight to Miami on Monday and leave from there for a tropical cruise of the Caribbean, his Christmas gift to his wife. New Year's Eve in St. Lucia, a cruise ship spin around the tropical islands, a final stop in Belize. Dizzy Punzitore told him to go ahead, take the time off, he'd have someone else do the collections during Christmas week.

"Spend time with your family this holiday, Otherway," Diz told him. "At our age, you never know when it will be your last one, capisce?"

Teresa's face lit up when she opened the card in the envelope. It listed the flight info, the dates, and their cruise stops. She hugged him extra tight, the glimmer in her eye insinuating she'd maybe give him another dose of Christmas seduction later that morning.

But he was such an imposter. A failure. When Teresa learned what was ahead, she might not ever forgive him.

He would not be coming back from Belize, the last stop on the cruise, and he hoped his wife would agree to do the same. On Monday he'd confess to her at the airport. She'd have time to think about it while they were in the air then on the water over the next seven days, soaking up the sun, living the life he'd always dreamed of. The life that the money he'd found inside the bag could now afford him. The life he would now be forced to live, somewhere outside of Philly, outside of the U.S., outside the reach of Big Sal Massimo and his crime family, all because Frank had lied. First to Dizzy, and when given a second chance, he committed the most mortal sin of sins out there: he told the same story about the money, or its lack thereof, to Big Sal Massimo. If he'd told the truth about it from the beginning, he'd have gotten to keep some of it. But keeping some of it would not have been the life-altering decision that keeping all of it was. And now, with the truth about it out there ricocheting around the Massimo crime family by way of a photo of him in a snowstorm, that choice could turn into a life-ending one.

He'd worked the pitch in his head all day yesterday, playing it back while he went from bank to bank, moving money around.

"*The danger I put our family in, Teresa honey, I... I didn't know what I was doing...*"

Oh, but he did know what he was doing. His selfishness had gotten the better of him.

The cash he'd kept in his car trunk he deposited into different banks yesterday. He moved some of it from the Philly banks to one in Belize, then converted a ton of it into cryptocurrencies. Digital money. His son was always talking about it and Frank had finally listened. He'd convert all of it back when he would need it, after he dropped anchor down there.

"*But it was for you and me, Teresa baby, so we could finally enjoy our dreams...*"

His dream, not hers. Wanting to live on a beach somewhere in a tropical environment, that was all him. She was content with her life as it was, she'd often said, seeing her kids and grandbabies nearly every day in good ol', close-knit South Philly.

"*You'll love it after we're settled, sweetie. If you don't, you can come back, but I won't. I can't. I'd be a dead man if I did.*"

True.

And if she did come back, she might well suffer the same fate.

What the fuck had he done?

"What a wonderful Christmas, darling," Teresa said, beaming, the two of them sitting in their living room on the floor, sipping hot chocolate with marshmallows, their unwrapped presents surrounding them.

"I love you so much, Frankie. But we need to get a move on. Let's get dressed and see what Santa brought our grandkids at their houses, and we can deliver what Santa left here for them."

His final Christmas in Philadelphia. He intended to savor it.

An Uber Eats car stopped in front of the middle of three adjacent garages on Dickenson Street, its flashers on. The driver exited, grunting while lifting a Styrofoam container the size of a hope chest out of the back seat, leaving it in the front of the garage. He reached back inside the car for a second package, an open-top carton with a brown paper bag in it. When he turned to place the carton on top of the Styrofoam, he bumped into a large man with a dour look and his hand in his pocket. The driver had to look up to talk to him.

"Whoa. I don't want no trouble, sir..."

Enzo, his hair a wavy black, his jowls and chin covered in white stubble, stood over him. "What's in these fuckin' deliveries?"

"I dunno. Food, I guess, addressed to Salvatore Massimo. The Styrofoam's got dry ice in it, the carton I think has something wrapped in foil."

"Who sent it?" Enzo said.

"Um, let me check. Just... don't get crazy, okay?" His arms were raised to keep the monster at bay. "I need to check something on my phone." The driver's eyes flitted from his phone to this monster's face.

"Here it is. It says it's from a 'Ka Hui.' That's all I've got."

"Fine, get the fuck out of here. And Merry Christmas."

Enzo dragged the deliveries inside the garage and called his boss.

"Who the hell sends an Uber out on Christmas Day?" Salvatore said. "Doesn't the driver have a family? Stay there, don't open it, let me get my slippers, I'm coming over."

Salvatore Massimo shuffled into the garage from his house next door wearing a new robe with tacky red and green Santa Clauses on it, a present from one of his great-grandkids. Enzo stood guard over the packages.

"Okay, Enzo, let's do this." Big Sal moved behind a car for safety, leaned his old white head below the hood, his eyes visible above it.

Enzo took out a knife, broke the seal of the Styrofoam lid, and slowly lifted it out of the way. A cold mist drifted north. Dry ice.

"What's the verdict, Enzo?"

Enzo lifted two white quarts of Rita's water ice out of the package and showed his boss. "There's another six quarts of it in here, boss."

"What's the flavor?" Big Sal said.

Enzo squinted at each of the two he held up. "Wild Black Cherry."

Big Sal smiled. "Sonovabitch. Nice. How about the paper bag inside the carton?"

Enzo ripped the paper away, saw aluminum foil underneath. He turned back a corner of the foil.

"Soft pretzels, boss. They look fresh."

"They can't be fresh, no soft pretzel bakeries are open today. It's Christmas."

Enzo peeled off a pretzel, held it up, then pulled it apart. Soft and stringy as saltwater taffy. There was steam coming off them. "They look fresh to me, boss."

"Damn," his boss said, impressed.

When he had Enzo bring over the printed card included in the Styrofoam container, he gritted his teeth while he read it, then opened his mouth wider to enjoy a fresh piece of soft pretzel.

*"I'm glad we're talking, Mr. Massimo. Merry Christmas. – Wally Lanakai."*

Could he be bought with water ice and soft pretzels? No, he could never be bought by anybody, but he could be persuaded to listen.

His cellphone rang. A call from Dizzy Punzitore. Dizzy was still on his shit list. He didn't want to hear Dizzy wish him a Merry Christmas and Salvatore didn't want to wish him one in return. He'd let Dizzy stew a few days, to teach the lying SOB a lesson.

∽

Lucky for Philo, Rhea hadn't held out. She'd spent Christmas Eve with him at his house. Her mood had changed. Finding the submerged armored car, and another dead body that was likely one of the perpetrators from the car heist, most probably the owner of the severed fingers, plus a live Tracfone with an interesting text with responses to it while it was in her hand—all had improved her outlook, making her feel relevant again. They awoke together Christmas morning, made love, then wandered downstairs to find the gifts under Philo's artificial tree compromised by yet another organic present from Six the Cat, something she'd regurgitated on the jewelry box Philo had for Rhea. The nose of a vole or a mole, he wasn't sure which. He quick-cleaned the gift box, flushed the animal part, and presented Rhea with a diamond bracelet that had set him back a few grand.

Yes, he'd decided to try buying his way back into her affections, but it hadn't been necessary, Rhea coming around on her own, the discovery of the submerged armored car the clincher. He didn't care, all's well that ended well, and he was excited and gratified when he saw her face light up. Such a good feeling seeing her happy.

He had to know, so he asked her: "Did you tell the commissioner what I told you about Winslow, that he was probably waterboarded?"

"Yes. It went over well. Homeland Security knows now, but we think they knew already. The commissioner said it was tough to read them when she passed the info along."

She reached over, cupped his head in her hands. "Philo, baby, I'm worried. It would appear you are a marked man." She kissed him, not a passionate kiss, a kiss rather more out of concern, her eyes drilling his.

"Hold that thought," he said. "Let me make some 'Merry Christmas' phone calls before we head out to see your family. We'll come back to that."

"You're making calls on that thing?" she said, pointing to his phone.

"Um, yeah," he said. "What about it?"

"That's a Tracfone. Why are you using a burner?"

"I'll get to that."

On the phone with Hank and Grace:

"Merry Christmas. Look for a large box in the mail from me, Grace. Sorry it's late. My only hint is, your new lungs are going to get some great exercise."

His gift: a karaoke machine. Rhea's suggestion, but he'd take the credit for it.

On with Miñoso:

"Feliz Navidad, bud. I hope you find the cards useful." Miñoso cried through his thank you. Five hundred bucks in gift cards could do that to someone barely scraping by. "Spend some of it on yourself, okay?" Miñoso agreed, but Philo knew his employee would figure a way to get most of it to his family in Mexico.

On the phone with Teddy, his convalescing Mummer buddy, Teddy thanking him:

"I don't know how you did it, Philo, but getting those replacement drummers... that's the best Plan B for the parade that I could have ever imagined. Me and the rest of the band owe you big time. Make sure you're there to watch it, my friend."

Philo said he would, how could he not, but knowing the state of things, that was now a huge stretch. "I hope you and Harriet have an extra special holiday, Ted."

Finished with Teddy, he had one more call, but he needed to talk with Rhea first. It would be the toughest talk he'd ever have with a girlfriend. Except she was more than a girlfriend, they both knew, which would make this discussion even more difficult.

He'd been faced with a life-and-death decision, about his own life, but maybe hers, too, if he stayed as accessible as he'd been.

"It has to be this way, Rhea. I need to disappear. For how long, I don't know. Today we'll do the Christmas thing with your family, but tomorrow I'll need to split."

She melted into his chest, then lifted her head to search his eyes. She understood, but—

"There'll be none of this good-bye shit, Philo. And no hero shit, either. Assess what needs to be done, tell the right people, and get back here, or I'll come looking for you. And give me your burner phone number."

"Copy that, Ibáñez. Feed and water Six, and sleep with your gun." His hands went to her hips, pulling her closer. "I like it when you put your hard-ass face on. It makes me want to, you know—"

"Yeah, well, no," she said, and pecked him on the lips before pushing away from his hug. "Make your phone call, then we go. My nieces and nephews await their Christmas loot."

His last call would be to Angus Zorn, and he went into the basement to make it. Strength in numbers, something he hoped to get from his pop's spirit while he multi-tasked, packing his gear into two duffle bags large enough to handle his entire home arsenal, plus ammunition.

Zorn didn't answer the call. Sure, that made sense, he wouldn't recognize the burner number. Philo left a voice message that got him a call back within thirty seconds.

"You in trouble, son?" was Zorn's greeting.

"Negatory. Merry Christmas, Captain. Unless you're holed up in a bomb shelter, I expect you know why I'm calling you." A comment that was really a question.

"The beheading on U.S. soil heard 'round the world. Kase Winslow."

"Affirmative, Captain. I'm wrapping some things up where I am, then I'm going on a road trip. I think it's best. Winslow was easy for them. I expect the targets now on our backs all measure the same way, about the size of a city block. I can't have innocent lives on my conscience should someone take indirect fire."

Zorn suggested he head north until the Feds and the Navy and Homeland Security were able to sort things out. Canada, maybe. Yes, Philo said, maybe Canada, but that really wasn't what he'd planned.

"You'll stay in touch," Zorn said, "until more of this gets fleshed out?"

"Affirmative, Captain."

But he planned to do more than stay in touch.

## 23

## TILT

Saturday, December 26
the Massachusetts Turnpike
Number of days to the New Year's Day Parade: 5

The first part of his road trip: north and east to Massachusetts to see Angus Zorn, unannounced. Anything after that would be unscripted. Calls to employees Hank and Miñoso gave them the keys, password-wise and security-code-wise, to the Blessid Trauma kingdom in his absence.

All Philo had on his former SEAL captain's location was a town in Massachusetts. Rockport, a fishing community on the Atlantic Ocean above Cape Cod about an hour north of Boston. In recent decades Rockport had become a thriving artists and writers community. A place people could go to get away from it all. Or in Zorn's case, to disappear. Coveted real estate because of its scenic seaside location. Philo had visited there with a former girlfriend years ago, a free spirit still in art school. Picturesque, the seaport boasted the most photographed and painted harborside fishing shack in the world, the iconic "Motif No. 1" on Bearskin Neck Wharf.

But he wasn't going for the scenery, the ambiance, or the quaintness. He was looking for Zorn. He had a phone number, and he'd contact him with it once he got inside the town limits, to tell Zorn they should meet in person to map out a plan, rather than do what Zorn had suggested for him, which was go to Canada. Never a consideration, because he'd never run from a fight. It wasn't in his father's DNA, it wasn't in his own. Deciding to get proactive had liberated him.

He stayed within five miles per hour of the speed limit, considering the firepower he had on the floor behind his seat. His phone rang. No name came up with the call, and the phone number didn't register with him. No voicemail, or at least none he knew how to get at, and no Bluetooth connection, so if he wanted to know who was calling, he'd need to answer it old school. The phone to his ear, he was skeptical of who the hell this was.

"Hello."

"*Twist and Shout,*" the male voice said.

He hadn't heard that phrase in years. It was SEAL code, a nickname for him, U.S. Navy SEAL Tristan Trout, when he was active. Still, he wasn't sure about this: should he trust this contact, or should he hang up? Friend or foe?

He kept quiet, let the air between them stay empty while his nerves danced. A second attempt at engaging him came through.

"*And let me know that you're mine.*"

The last line of the iconic rock 'n' roll song, before the final chorus. That had been the agreement with his superiors, with Captain Zorn and those above him. Philo's silence had meant the caller needed to go directly there, to that last line, to confirm authenticity, and he had.

"*Shake it up, baby, now,*" Philo said. The correct response. "Who am I talking to, and how the hell did you get this burner number?"

The freakin' phone had been in Philo's possession less than two days. Only a handful of people—his short Christmas greetings list—had received a call from him with it. Sure, this call had started in code, but still, how did this guy get this number?

"I was A2Z's boss," the caller said. "Let's keep the identifiers to a minimum. I need to pass along some info. You're not going to like it."

*A2Z.* Angus Zorn. That needed no explanation for him. Captain Zorn's boss would have been a one-star Rear Admiral or above. Philo stiffened in his SUV seat, straightened to attention, a force of habit when speaking to a superior, even though he couldn't now recall who any of the people in place above Zorn were during his multiple deployments. Protocol, as far as he remembered, was to answer him without mentioning any rank, and with no chitchat, and no "sirs."

"Go ahead," Philo said.

"A2Z has hung up his cleats," the Rear Admiral or higher said. "We were surprised, too. I'm sorry, son."

Philo went silent until he could compose himself. Translation, Zorn was dead. "Do you know, ah, any of the particulars... bud?"

"Yes and no," Philo's boss's boss said. "Here's how this needs to go. When you get to where you're going—tomorrow—stop into Sam's Canoe Club. They're waiting for you. They'll give you more details on A2Z's party. We're sorry to see him go, son, really sorry. We knew he was fond of you. If we get more info on who was working on his surprise retirement party, we'll pass it along. Unless, that is, you find out more about it first. Then I'd love it if you would get a hold of me at this number. Thanks." The call ended.

By another phrasing, "retirement party" meant Zorn's murder.

His caller had Philo's phone's GPS coordinates, so he apparently knew where he was, and it wouldn't have taken much to figure out where he was going. He'd prepared Philo for what he would find when he got there, although "there" wasn't yet fully identified. *Sam's Canoe Club* was Navy slang for the U.S. Coast Guard. Once Philo located them in the Rockport area, he'd learn more about what had happened and where.

So there it was. The guy Philo hoped would help him go deeper into this terrorism situation, to cut out the cancer that was spreading, had been eliminated. Philo thumbed his way around his other phone while he drove, his personal one, and found a picture of a Black man with a drunk, goofy grin posing with a small swordfish on a dock somewhere. He cursed out this man, his captain, for getting his ass killed and leaving him with no partner in finding answers to this mess.

He breezed by highway exits for Manchester-by-the-Sea and Glouces-ter, home of the Gorton Fisherman, and followed Route 127 into Rockport.

He dropped anchor in a free parking lot, Motif No. 1 jutting from a wharf inside Rockport Harbor, his windshield framing it.

A phone internet search for the U.S. Coast Guard Auxiliary brought him to the contact info for the nearest unit, located in Gloucester. He made a cold call, not sure of the reception he'd get, and led with "I'm in Rockport for A2Z's party." Two transfers later, he had the right person.

"Commander Quinlan," a woman's voice said, announcing herself. "Twist and Shout?"

"Speaking. Where and when can I meet you?"

"Tomorrow, zero six hundred, at our Coast Guard installation in Gloucester. Our home base. That's where we have his trawler."

"I didn't know he had a trawler."

"You don't know much about this, do you? He lived on it. We're twenty minutes south of Rockport. See you tomorrow."

∽

The smell was what Philo remembered about Gloucester. A combination of fish guts, salt air, and seagull excrement. The locals said families got used to it after a few generations. Comingled with the fish markets, seafood restaurants, and commercial fishermen and lobstermen outbuildings, the Coast Guard's facility jutted into Gloucester's calm, cold Inner Harbor. Zorn's houseboat was dockside, surrounded by the Coast Guard's flotilla. Commander Quinlan read to Philo from a tablet on her clipboard. Under the tablet, the clipboard held manila envelopes.

"What I have on you, Mister Trout, is you're a Navy SEAL, Chief Petty Officer Second Class, retired."

"Correct."

Zorn's trawler. What a beautiful boat. Sapphire blue hull, cream cabin, gleaming railings. The commander rattled off some of the vessel's other particulars from her clipboard before they boarded. Philo listened while he walked alongside the vessel. Painted in cursive across the stern, above the water line, was the trawler's moniker, *Geronimo at Sea*. The name gave Philo a chill. It came from a momentous day from their shared past, May 2, 2011. Zorn apparently reveled in it. Philo did not.

*Geronimo* was the military's code name for Osama Bin Laden. The Navy dispatched his body in the North Arabian Sea within twenty-four hours of his execution. No country wanted his remains. By not burying him on land, they prevented his grave from becoming a shrine.

The commander droned on. "A Lyman Morse trawler, built in 1980. Fifty-three-foot diesel. Fiberglass hull. Beam, thirteen and a half feet. Four-foot draft. Cruising speed ten knots, maximum of fourteen. Three state-rooms retrofitted into two..."

Philo raised his hand to make her stop. He wasn't interested in buying it, he just wanted to know what happened with it, or on it, and how it related to Zorn's death. "And the Coast Guard has his boat why?" he asked.

"It was found adrift in the Atlantic, outside Cape Ann. A family on a Christmas Day cruise called it in. We towed it back here."

Two days ago. He'd spoken to Zorn on Christmas. Zorn had mentioned nothing about his boat, so it couldn't have been missing at that point. Commander Quinlan hopped aboard *Geronimo at Sea* and waited for Philo. He followed, then he saw the crime scene tape blocking the door to the front cabin.

"He was found onboard?" Philo asked.

"Affirmative. The police processed the entire boat. I don't need to tell you not to touch anything, Chief. I also don't know who you are to merit this inspection, but this is a special deal the police extended to the Navy to let you board it. Here we go."

Well-appointed with polished hardwood in the first cabin, the compartment he'd entered was gorgeous, the walnut extending overhead onto the deckhead and surrounding the windows. Two long benches, port and starboard, stretched beneath windows that ran nearly the length of the front cabin, each bench's seat covered with long, royal blue seat cushions with white piping. A built-in wooden table, finished to a bright luster, was attached to the deck floor between the benches. The table was hinged. The table's two sides were up, making the path around it, to the rear of the boat, tighter. White pillows with blue dolphin silhouettes accented the bench cushions, showing as lean, crisp, and orderly, like someone had straightened up their living room. All except for the blood.

"It happened here," the commander said.

The table was central to whatever this scene was telling them per the way the blood had splattered. Ceiling, bench, cushions, and deck, it all spread out from the table, and no one could miss the yellow chalk outline of the body taking up most of the table's surface.

"Guns onboard?"

"Yes. Four. Ballistics will determine if they were fired. The detectives ran down ownership. They were Mister Zorn's. No bullet holes or bullets were found, no shell casings. The assumption is they weren't used, by or against him."

Philo stepped away, toward the front of the cabin, to stand next to the boat's helm. As a steering wheel, the helm was nothing special other than oversized. His new vantage point gave him an expanded view of the room. At that moment the boat rose and fell from the wake of a passing vessel in the harbor, a gentle wave rocking them. A speck of blue rolled a few inches out from beneath the entry hatch, something tiny and plastic. As the wave rolled under the boat and another wave replaced it, the blue speck rolled back under the hatch.

"That's a syringe cap," Philo said.

"Yes. Leave it," the commander said. "One of a few the police found on the deck when they processed the scene."

"Syringes, too?"

"Yes. But in this compartment only, and out in the open. Nowhere else onboard, the police said."

Captain Zorn was not a drug user in Philo's book, was actually militant anti-drug from what Philo remembered. Which made it difficult to accept that he'd gone in that direction. Commander Quinlan volunteered what she knew.

"Someone jabbed him with syringes. That's the detectives' take on it."

"Copy that. About the table, Commander. You notice the tilt?"

As the boat settled back in place, the table's lean from starboard-to-port was noticeable. It took his eyes directly to the legs supporting its center section. The two starboard legs were clamped to the deck, the two port legs were not.

"Yes. Easier to notice when the harbor is calm," she said. "Two table legs were cut. They put it on a slant."

He kneeled in close to where the legs met the deck. The cuts were not uniform, the ends jagged and splintered. Not a carpenter's work.

"Any idea if Zorn modified the table this way?" he asked.

"The police are interviewing people in Rockport about him and his boat. Short answer is, I don't know."

"What was the condition of the body?"

"Yes, about the body." She rearranged her clipboard to retrieve a manila envelope. She opened the envelope's clasp. "Are you ready?"

"Never, but go for it, Commander."

She removed a stack of prints. Zorn's torso was on the galley table, shirtless, on its back. A muscular Black man in excellent physical condition in his boxer briefs. Three canvas straps held him in place, at the chest, waist, and feet, extending under the table. At the neckline was a pulpy stump, no head above it.

"The police cut the straps to remove the body. His head was there," she said, and pointed. A chalk circle on a ledge in front of the ship's front window surrounded the base of a small Jesus statue affixed to the dashboard. Philo recognized the figurine as the irreverent "Buddy Christ" version of Jesus, with a smiling, winking face, a thumbs up, and the other hand pointing at onlookers. Dried blood covered the base of the figurine, the blood trail running down an instrument panel.

"Our pilot said he'll have nightmares. Captain Zorn's head was jammed up there, looking out across the bow before our seamen were about to board. Here, look."

She produced the second photo. Zorn's head, above the dash, a NAVY baseball cap snugged in place on him, the photo taken from the Coast Guard vessel. From the front of Zorn's boat, at the right angle it might have looked like he was piloting his vessel, the cap shielding half-opened, sightless dark eyes.

He flipped through prints of the crime scene from other angles, gruesome and disgusting, all telling the same story: a restrained torso, its severed head jammed onto the trawler's dash, and blood.

Philo wandered the rest of the vessel filming with his camera, investigating the staterooms, the galley, the bathroom, the engine, seeing how Zorn lived. An orderly, disciplined existence on the water, a way to enjoy an

ocean view for someone who might not have been able to afford it otherwise. Zorn was living the dream in his retirement after serving his country,
willing to serve his country again by contacting his former team to help
with their protection.

Until the enemy found him and ripped him apart.

"I've seen enough, Commander."

Hotel room, internet connection, a to-go cheeseburger from a Rockport
eatery, in a paper bag he split open to get at fries that were way too salty.
Canned soda from a machine, no beer, Rockport a dry town. His loaded Sig
Sauer sat as close to him on the coffee table as the food and his laptop. On
his mind was a meeting with the local police scheduled for tomorrow
morning, arranged by Team Six's code-talking benefactor, the "Rear
Admiral."

His second session with the R-A was in progress online inside the darknet, the deep web links, cryptic passwords, servers, protocols, and a secure
chat window all provided by his host.

First chat entry, R-A to Philo: *Sending four videos. Confirm your receipt.
Refrain from opening until I finish sending all of this, son.*

First files sent were videos with titles EB, HO, KW, AZ.

Ed Bounce, Hugh Ogden, Kase Winslow, Angus Zorn. Four of the
SEALS from the team of at least twenty-two, all dead. Three beheaded, the
fourth a suicide before what would have been the same outcome as the
other three. The beheadings were an Al Qaeda signature, but in these
instances none of them were performed in far-off places that most Americans couldn't pronounce. All were executed on American soil, or close to it.

Philo's response: *Received all four.*

Next entry: *Sending additional photo files taken by persons of interest from
domestic & foreign Al Qaeda sites & chatrooms & domestic extremist sites &
rooms.*

An avalanche of files came tumbling across the internet embedded in
the next few chat entries, with long random names consisting of alphas,
numerals, and symbols.

He counted the files. Fifty-six.

Per Philo, *Received fifty-six files.*

*Now you're up to speed, son. A lot of night ahead of you, so have fun. Put on your glasses, work some magic with the zoom button, absorb. Your Gloucester police visit tomorrow might be worth it, might not. Probably not, but do it anyway. Ask to see the corpse. See Homeland Security when you get home.*

While the photos uploaded, Philo talked to himself, the file percentages advancing onscreen.

"Twenty-two of us," he said.

Neptune Spear was an expected kill operation, the trident image of the spear a good fit for the SEALS on land, air, and sea. Headgear that night included night vision goggles, the compound's electricity cut by U.S. operators on the ground.

A planned fast-rope descent from a Black Hawk into the compound. His copter's rotor clipped a compound wall, spinning out of control, crashing. The SEALS were able to deploy with no serious injuries.

A second Black Hawk touching down outside the compound, its SEALS scaling the wall.

Entering the building. On the third floor, Bin Laden using a woman as a shield. The woman lived, Bin Laden didn't.

Thirty-eight minutes in hell. Five kills, one from Philo's weapon.

Computers, thumb drives, other Bin Laden evidentiary detritus including uploaded pornography and funny viral videos, of babies and of cats—it all came back with them.

They destroyed the crashed copter with explosives, eliminating the salvage of classified equipment.

A third copter, a Chinook, gave them a ride out with the one dead body that mattered, the rest of the compound's occupants left behind for the Pakistanis to discover.

A SEAL raid that had PTSD written all over it. Usually the images were only late-night infrequent visitors to Philo in his sleep, but tonight, anticipating these videos, PTSD reigned.

The anxiety subsided. He opened the first video from the Rear Admiral.

A hotel room, bright, daytime. A dark-hooded man retrieved a Gideon's Bible from an end table, then read from it in accented English. A squirming man in a gym suit, a person of color. Ed Bounce, spread-eagle across a coffee table. *Whack,* then *whack* again, a different hooded person separating his head from his body with a machete, then stuffing the head inside a plastic bag, its new contents swirling with blood and water.

Second video, Kase Winslow, Caucasian. His Appalachian Mountain wilderness beheading. Footage he'd seen already, but like it or not, now he had his own copy.

The third compilation, Hughie Ogden, another person of color, making the ultimate sacrifice. Videos from people on the street saw him struggle with his attackers, then eat a terrorist's gun. The video was compiled from social media posts taken down by internet providers, but not before they could be reassembled in the dirty corners of the internet, where tasteless subject matter reigned.

Final video, Captain Angus Zorn. Footage that was new to Philo, starting with a disoriented Zorn dragged into his boat's forecastle—the forward berth—by two men with face coverings, the film then picking up with the semi-naked victim strapped to the table and the boat underway, fighting a rough sea. The footage continued: a shaky sword lowering slowly to the victim's throat, to measure the distance, then multiple angry hacks at the front of the neck. The executioner jammed the severed head onto the dashboard Jesus statuette, Arabic chatter ridiculing their victim after the placement of the ball cap. The final footage lingered on Zorn's hacked head on the dash, his expression serene above a jagged neckline, blood on the ledge running down the instruments, and water leaking from his mouth, nose, and ears.

Three out of four heads had abnormal amounts of water in them.

The legal name, per the documents reviewed at the U.S. presidential level, was Enhanced Interrogation Technique. The common name was waterboarding.

Tilt the table. Cover the mouth with plastic wrap to prevent water from escaping. Pour water into the upturned nose. It stayed in the head, filling the mouth, the throat, and the sinus cavities, but it never got to the lungs, so the victim didn't drown, it only felt like drowning, prolonging the torture.

That was what this was all about. Retributional torture, then murder.

He opened each of the stills, file after file of single photographs, studied them, their locations, camera angles, each subject unaware that the photos were being taken. Men he hadn't seen or heard from, or about, in over ten years, all domesticated and living their best lives post-Navy. Some places were identifiable as Boston, Rockport, and Philly, and others in western Maryland. Most locations were not. All, in Philo's mind, were surveillance photos. Preparations for strikes.

Then the shocker, as in one of these things was not like the other: photos of Teddy Cangelosi's Old Time Philly string band in full strut, surrounded by piles of snow, including stills of the band's drumline, may they rest in peace.

"Whoa."

What the hell was the connection? None of the drummers could be Navy, they were too young. But all were Black, and all were dead.

The last few photos made him bolt upright in his chair.

A cat preening itself in a weedy, trash-filled urban lot surrounded by chain link fencing, behind a retail business.

The second photo, a cat with a discarded water ice cup in its mouth, crossing a street from between parked cars.

The same cat was in both photos: Six, his beloved calico.

And a photo of Philo getting out of his Hummer at a Dunkin' Donuts within walking distance of his Philly rowhome.

Overnight bags, duffels with guns, stowed laptop, a thermos with stale hot coffee from the hotel lobby, he couldn't stuff it all into the back seat of the Hummer fast enough. He backed his vehicle out of its space, its large tires kicking up gravel from being in a hurry, and he sped out of the parking lot.

Rhea was staying at his house in Northeast Philly, alone, watching Six. Sure, she was a cop, and sure, she was armed, but his beheaded SEAL team members had been armed, too.

~

After midnight. His long night would need to be longer—five and a half hours longer, spent on the road back to Philadelphia.

He gave his regrets to the Gloucester police via a phone call, burner phone speaker on, driving south on a winding road out of Rockport:

Thanks for the invitation, gentlemen, but he wouldn't be seeing them in the morning.

He then reported in to his Rear Admiral, sharing his take that *a*, waterboarding was a common denominator in three of the four executions, *b*, three of those four were people of color, and *c*, there were multiple photos of pets in the files he'd sent to Philo, not only surreptitious shots of Six the Cat. Cats, dogs, a friggin' ferret, and one of what looked like a macaque monkey on a leash. He didn't know what the hell to make of these, other than guessing that all were pets of his former SEAL Team Six members.

Last, he gave his final regrets, minimal and impromptu, to Captain Zorn as he drove past the Coast Guard base in Gloucester's Inner Harbor. Past *Geronimo at Sea*, the last place his captain had called home. "No one better than you, sir."

He called Rhea. After bitching about the late hour, she listened. He didn't pull any punches and was graphic where it was needed. She had to be told all of it. A half hour later by the dashboard clock and still on the phone with her, he looped onto I-95. He wrapped the call up.

"Lock the doors and the windows, Rhea. Take your weapon to bed. I'll be back by breakfast."

# 24

## DISLOYAL

Monday, December 28
Philadelphia International Airport
Number of days to the New Year's Day Parade: 4

American Airlines flight number 2570, leaving 9:42 a.m. for Miami. The first leg of Frank and Teresa Tisha's holiday vacation, his Christmas gift to her. A flight, then a Carnival Cruise to St. Lucia for New Year's Eve, then back to sea again on New Year's Day, headed to Belize.

They arrived at Terminal B at Philly International seven a.m.-ish via a car service.

The driver hustled to get the door for Frank's bride Teresa, she looking tropical and light and cheerful, so ready for what Frank had described would be the most memorable vacation of her life. Frank managed a small smile when tipping the driver, Teresa fashionably disinterested, facing the glass doors to the terminal, beaming, eager. Their luggage in tow, Frank moved off to the side before entering the terminal, gesturing for Teresa to join him.

This was it. This was where their new adventure would begin, either together or separately. It would be her call. He didn't doubt that what he was about to tell her might not only rock her world, it would open a chasm that separated life as she knew it here, in dreary, cold, urban Philadelphia, from a heavenly existence filled with gentle ocean breezes, azure skies, warm temperatures, and tender lovemaking as regular as the tides.

"You what?" she said, her eyes squinting. "Tell me I didn't just hear what I thought I heard. You fucking *what*?"

He'd short-shrift the parts she already knew: the dead bodies dropping out of the armored car, the number of witnesses to that event in the storm (zero), and the face-to-face follow-ups with Dizzy Punzitore and Big Sal Massimo about it. The issue was—

"I lied to the don."

"Big Sal Massimo? You told Big Sal there was no money when there was?"

"I screwed up, Teresa. If I told them about it, we'd have seen none of it. I'd be out there again today picking up numbers to supplement our cash-flow. Now we've got a chance to live life the way it was meant to be lived. I... er, we deserve this, honey. We'll get our own beachside bungalow. I can sell the house long distance, move everything into storage, have the kids sell things off as they see fit, the car, the furniture..."

"You're talking about our kids, Frankie," she said, frowning. "Our children! Not see them? What about the grandkids? Not see my fucking grandkids?"

Her head shook, her soft gray curls framing her red-lipped frown. She backed away from him, not able to look at him, was crying, then was texting.

"Who are you texting?"

"Our daughter! Stay away!"

"Teresa, baby. Honey. I'm so sorry. We'd still see everyone, we'll just have to get creative about it, will need to make it happen on our end, and see them down there, not up here."

"No. No, goddamn it. This is nuts. I am *not* going with you. Not now, not ever."

"Teresa. Darling." He reached for her, tried pulling her close. She pushed away like he was a leper.

"You—you *bastard*, you! How could you have ever thought I'd leave South Philly, and cold turkey? It's the only existence I've ever known. My family, my relatives... my *grandkids*, Frankie..."

"Please, honey..."

"Get away from me. I'm getting an Uber. You do what you want, but I'm staying. Leave my grandkids? You're a fucking idiot. And why the hell didn't you ever get that eye fixed? I'm tired of looking at it."

He knew it could have gone this way—maybe not this way, with her cruelty—but he wasn't any less crushed knowing to anticipate it.

"It's not what I want either, Teresa. It's... it's what I need to do. They have pictures. Me and the bag of money in the street. I don't know how they know, no one was there, but they do."

But he did know how they knew. Someone in the armored truck had second thoughts and sent photos to his boss that he wasn't aware had been taken. He just didn't know why they hadn't come after him directly instead of sending them to Dizzy. And who were these people that they even knew who he and Dizzy were? Either way, it meant Big Sal probably knew by now, and that meant—

"Frankie—" Teresa moved in and cupped his cheek in her hand in a forgiving gesture. Her touch was melting him.

This was goodbye. Something she would say to him now while she could, while he was alive, rather than have to say it to his lifeless body later if he stayed.

"I'm sorry. I shouldn't have said that," she said, "I feel terrible. I know you need to go. You... I... You take care of yourself. Maybe somewhere down the road, after this blows over, if they forgive you..."

It wouldn't blow over. Massimo could not abide any disloyalty. It was fealty to the family forever. Death was the only way out.

She paced, waiting for her ride, while he continued talking. "You didn't ask me how much, Teresa. The amount that was in the bag. It was a lot."

A blue sedan with a dashboard card that read *Uber* slid into a space at the terminal's curb and put on its flashers the same time a text arrived on Teresa's phone announcing it.

"If I don't know how much, Frankie, then maybe they won't kill me." She was crying in earnest now, her sobs releasing the hurt, the fear, the exasperation, then her anger resurfaced. "And knowing that amount would tell me the price tag you put on us. Our life here. It's like, 'Here, Teresa, this is what it took for me to abandon everyone, everything we ever knew.' Damn it, Frankie, I am—so—fucking—*angry!*"

Her two-handed push to his chest left him lost and speechless. She spun away with her luggage and headed for her Uber, her final good-bye trailing her as she stormed off.

Another car slid in curbside behind the Uber. It was a car he recognized.

~

Philo texted Rhea, *Home in ten.*

Seven-thirty a.m. Five hours, twenty-two minutes on the road. No speeding, and with minimal overnight traffic and only two stops, he'd made great time. He locked the Hummer, hefted his travel gear over both shoulders, grunted a hello at a neighbor, and inserted his key in the back door. Before the push, he checked the pet door insert at the bottom with his foot. The hinged door swung open and closed freely. Business as usual.

More business as usual, his entry through the back door easy and without fanfare, Six not there to greet him, her attack-cat persona a front door routine only. He tended to the security system keypad, then gave a cursory check of the basement on his way up the steps. The dining room then living room were both blurs, stopping for a pull at the front door to check the locks and the alarm system again, then it was up the second set of stairs two at a time. Hallway, bathroom, bedroom. Rhea was awake and rising from his bed. She greeted him with a leap into his arms, a straddle around his waist, a tight hug, and a passionate kiss. Six the Cat vaulted onto his shoulder and purred into his ear.

The bed... Rhea, the image of her safe with him in it, had helped him navigate the last hundred miles. He walked her to it and finished their kiss. No lovemaking, but after they fell onto the ruffled sheets it was the best spooning he'd ever experienced.

"I'm off today," she said. She kissed each of his bloodshot eyes. "You need to be, too. You're exhausted."

"You'll stay with me?"

"Yes."

"Sold."

The time to debrief each other would be later. For now, rest, spoon, purr, sleep.

Teresa's Uber left, Frank staring at it as it pulled away. The four doors of the silver Lincoln limo that had pulled in behind it opened. The only person he needed to see exit was Enzo to know that this was where his new life was going to end before it had a chance to start. Enzo plodded forward, his single focus Frank, his three associates checking their surroundings as they lumbered along the sidewalk with him. Frank remained flatfooted, not attempting to run. They arrived.

"Otherway, we need to talk," Enzo said. "Mister Massimo is disappointed."

"I know. He in the car?"

"Yes. We'll get your baggage. Come with me."

To beg, or not to beg?

Maybe there was some middle-ground wiggle room. "Only a little of the money is with me, Enzo, on me and in the bags. But I can get all of it back."

"Doesn't matter. Let's go." His hand dropped onto Frank's shoulder.

"How did you find me here?"

"Your wife texted us."

Teresa hadn't texted their daughter, she'd texted Dizzy.

With Frank having let his wife know there was an amount of money large enough to take her comfortable life away from her, she had now let him know the price she was willing to pay to keep things the way they were: his life.

Frank was numb, maybe walking, maybe not, moving one foot in front of the other but not feeling them, Enzo and an associate guiding him forward. They reached the car and Enzo opened a door, ducking Frank's head down to help him enter.

Inside the limo, Big Sal worked a plastic spoon at the icy red contents of a waxed cup. Frank sat across from him, Enzo squeezing in next to Frank.

Big Sal spoke without looking up. "Water ice and a soft pretzel, Frank?"

"Salvatore." Frank leaned forward, spoke to the don. "Look, I can fix this. I can get the money."

Big Sal handed him a cup of water ice with a spoon in it. Frank hesitated, then accepted it. He waved away a soft pretzel.

Frank tried again. "Salvatore —"

Big Sal smacked his lips together, favoring a sweet tooth that might eventually kill him, and waved Frank off. He pointed at the cup. Frank understood: no talking until he partook. Frank complied, shoved a spoonful in his mouth.

"There, Frank. Good. Enjoy. No worries about the money, we'll still find it. With Teresa's help. Sorry this isn't much of a last meal, but it will have to do."

Enzo zipped a knife across Frank's throat that turned his neck into a gusher, Frank gripping it with both hands, his eyes wide and terrified until they weren't.

Big Sal swiped at his cherry-lipped mouth with a napkin, replacing Frank's blood spray with another spoon of wild black cherry water ice.

## 25

## WHAT LIGHT THROUGH YONDER MUMMER BREAKS?

Monday, December 28
Northeast Philadelphia
Number of days to the New Year's Day Parade: 4

Five plus hours of much-needed sleep, Philo had been in full crash mode. Rhea snuggled with him off and on in between checking her cop email on a laptop plus making calls to other cops. Philo woke up with her sitting on the end of the bed, on the phone.

"You say it was in a sewer?" she said into the phone. She received a yes answer. "Damn, Carl, that's good police work, bud."

Philo absently scratched his crotch, not realizing he had an audience. She raised her hand in a *"Seriously?"* gesture, directing a squint at him. He shrugged an apology before sitting up. She signed off with Carl.

"I had something delicious in mind for when you woke up," she said, "but that disgusting lapse of yours took me out of the mood."

"Just an itch, nothing contagious. Forgive me? Please?"

"Here's my offer..."

Rhea led him by the hand to the bathroom where she turned on the shower. "It happens in here, lover, after the water gets warm and comfortable, and after I give you a good scrub." She climbed out of her gym pants and sleep top, her eyes on his, her one hand testing the water in the shower, the other finding a bottle of body wash next to it. She flicked open the top to the bottle and squeezed an ample glob of lotion up and out. It oozed sensuously down the side.

"You with me, loverboy?" she said, kissing him lightly.

"Scrub away, baby."

One of the most enjoyable, hottest, and cleanliest showers Philo had ever had. Resting on the ledge inside the shower they settled into shop talk, leaning into each other, the warm water on their naked laps.

"About the cat's collar that was in that one picture, but not found on the cat."

"Jonesy," Philo said. "In that gated community."

"Yes. The trumpeter's cat. Carl pushed Reese into getting some uniforms to do a search of the storm sewers. Sonovabitch if they didn't find a pet collar. Not near the unit, but in a sewer near the community's exit gate. It had a clean cut through the leather, like someone took a knife or a pair of snips to it."

Additional photo analysis would confirm if it was Jonesy's collar, but Rhea already had a good feeling that's what it was. The shower water was beginning to lose its warmth. They toweled off and found gym clothes for themselves. It was nearing three p.m.

"I'm ordering in. Chinese," Philo said. "Join me tonight?"

"Not from Happy House, correct?"

Happy House was where Ed Bounce's severed head was found inside a takeout window, around the corner from Philo's rowhome.

"Okay, be that way, I'll order from somewhere else. This time."

"You're disgusting."

He had twenty minutes to lay out the details of Angus Zorn's New England execution before delivery of their General Tso's chicken and lo mein would banish the gore talk. In hoodies and slippers and other comfort clothing from Philo's drawers, they were at the kitchen table drinking bottled beer, waiting on the food. Rhea had her laptop open and was keying away, Philo sitting next to her, riffing about Zorn and his houseboat, going light on the gore, heavy on the maudlin.

"Zorn, he and I... The two of us... He had leads because he ferreted out where his team members were, steamrolling his way through witness protection programs and their elaborate attempts to disappear. Knowing the potential strike points would have been helpful. We could lie in wait with other SEALs on the list, reduce the threat, or maybe eliminate it... What they did to that man, Rhea, the waterboarding, his body—he was a pain in the ass as a captain, but a good person—if I find any of them, it'll be none of that torture bullshit where they get longer to live. I'm taking them out."

Rhea keyed, listened, sipped, stopped keying, grabbed his hands, and searched his eyes. "First, I didn't hear you say that last part, okay? Second, I'm sorry about the loss of your friend, Philo. Why don't you get the hell out of here for a while. Maybe take another trip to Hawaii?"

"Nah."

"That's it? *Nah*?"

"I'm not running. I can't and I won't. Me and my little arsenal are staying put. I like it around here"—he tugged at the sleeve of her hoodie—"present company included."

"Present company is flattered," she said, "but present company would like another beer, because present company says let's move on to another topic. I have some news. Here, check this out."

He handed her a new beer and looked over her shoulder at a video of a large group of people marching in loose formation on a main street he didn't immediately recognize. The camera was elevated, many stories up, giving little definition to the marchers. He looked more closely. To the right of the street was a narrow boardwalk and sand dunes, and to the right of the dunes, waves from an angry ocean crashed ashore.

"Beach Avenue in Cape May, New Jersey," he said, proud he recognized it. "This is video from a camera atop a hotel..."

"Correct. From one of the old hotels down there," she said. "Closed circuit television. In operation twenty-four-seven."

"Wait. Are those marchers Mummers?"

"Yes indeedy."

"Not a live shot, then. When was this?"

"A *lonnng* time ago. It's the defunct Nor'easter String Band. This is from..." She pulled up an email. "April 1986. More than thirty-five years ago. The string band shuttered in 2001."

"Why are we looking at this footage, and how the hell did someone find it?"

"Answer to the second question first," she said. "Good police work."

"Hahaha. Really? You're going with that? This is needle-in-a-haystack-level police work."

"Fine. We got lucky. My mother cleaned rooms for the hotel when she first arrived in the States from Puerto Rico. She used to take me with her when I was a kid. She remembered watching bands do their routines down in Cape May after the holidays, on themed weekends. There's one incident she wanted me to remember after hearing me bitch about the Mummer murders..."

"Interesting. But why you?"

"Just wait."

Rhea stopped and started the video at different points to get her bearings, then she circled back toward the beginning. "I had the techs enhance the hell out of this thing, but I want you to see it in real time first. Let me move it forward to about eight minutes, twenty seconds. Here."

Philo took a seat and leaned in. He watched the footage full screen on her laptop. Little better than marching ants on the move from this height many stories above the street, but he saw the mishap she wanted him to see because it slowed the parade. A child left the crowd and ran into the marchers. One of the Mummers redeposited her awkwardly on the side, then walked backward until he returned to his place in line and rejoined the march.

"Now, enhanced footage and in slow motion..."

Slightly blurred from the enhancement, the video showed the Mummers all dressed like the Joker from Batman, the band's routine a sendup of the sixties Batman TV series. The little girl, maybe four years old, slipped a woman's grasp and ran to one of the Jokers playing a glockenspiel and hugged his leg. He ripped her away from him by her throat, cuffed her hard to the face, and yelled at the crowd. He flung her to the street before rejoining his band.

Philo was speechless, then, "What the hell happened to that guy? Someone should have arrested—"

"Someone did. A Cape May cop arrested him at the end of the route for assault and battery. We found the arrest record."

"That little girl... was she all right?"

"Turned out pretty okay," she said, batting her eyes at him and smiling, "don't you think?"

"That was you?"

"I was four years old. I got overly excited, picked out a random Mummer, and went for broke. I have no recollection of this, but my mother sure has one. The guy saw me as a little brown spic daughter of a Puerto Rican whore. That's what he called us. Know who he is?"

"No clue."

"Irish Jack Maguire. Age twenty-two. Head honcho for The Real Proper Punks. A white supremacist. His early years."

Philo sat back, processing this. The first realization to hit him: "Maguire was a Mummer? Wow."

"Yes. Back when the Mummers were, shall we say, not on their best behavior regarding minorities."

Philo received a text. Their food was here, the delivery person at the front door. He brought the food into the kitchen, grabbed some plates.

"Forget the food, Philo. Oh my. It gets even better. Look."

The slo-mo footage continued running, but Rhea paused it then ran it back a few frames to the point where Maguire was being an asshole again. The next set of frames advanced. Philo's eyes narrowed. "Why'd your techs zoom in on *that* guy?"

"It says here," she read the email, "the guy next to Maguire with the saxophone... is Lieutenant Lawrence Yonder."

"Assistant to the Philly police commissioner? That Lawrence Yonder?"

"The one and only. A Philly beat cop back then, early in his career. A known quantity as a racist, according to the notes. Cleaned up his act, buried his bigotry, and isn't bashful about how poor his behavior was back then. He's now a poster boy for the department's community activism in the city. Let's put the food out. I'm hungry."

They noshed over egg rolls and wonton soup, then started in on their white meat chicken and noodles, still nursing their beers.

"So, here's where this sits with me, Philo. I don't like Lieutenant Yonder with Maguire here, even though it's thirty-five years ago. I also don't like the coincidence that the lieutenant lives in that community where the trumpeter was murdered. Yonder chairs the homeowners' association security committee there."

"Wouldn't that be what an HOA would prefer, having a cop as the community's top security guy?"

"Sure. Except I already know what's going on with a certain part of that investigation, the safe room alert: nada. Still waiting on answers. The lieutenant sent me to Reese. Reese says he's still working it. We're nowhere with it."

Philo slurped the last of his wonton, then the last of his beer. "You'd think the HOA security guy—a cop, no less—would know all there was to know about safe rooms in his community. How they worked, how a bad guy might beat one, or how someone could get around the distress alert sent to the security company..."

"Right. Except before the home invasion, Lieutenant Yonder didn't know that any of the units in the community had a safe room."

"You know that how?"

"Because he told me, that's how," Rhea said, then slowed her chewing, "and I had no reason to not believe him."

She pondered her own words. "Damn it, even I don't like that answer now. Shit. *Shit.*"

## 26

# I GIVE YOU MY WORD

Thursday, December 31, New Year's Eve
Broadway Louie's Italian Restaurant, South Philadelphia
Number of days to the New Year's Day Parade: 1

Noon, New Year's Eve Day. The curbside space fronting one side of Broadway Louie's corner restaurant had two traffic cones awaiting their arrival. Three men bundled in full-length dress coats and scarves with no hats stood sentry on the sidewalk, ready to check identities.

Magpie Papahani double-parked the Escalade next to one of the cones and put the flashers on. Wally Lanakai folded his hands in the back seat, trying not to look nervous while he eyed the restaurant marquee, aware of its mafia history. The restaurant was small. Quality, not quantity, dictated the attendance at this meeting, the invitation for two Ka Hui players only. Not a neutral location, but Wally accepted, agreeing to meet here out of respect. After all, Massimo's family business in Philly preceded Wally's by sixty, maybe seventy years.

Magpie powered the window down to let the guy look inside.

A simple exchange. "You guys Ka Hui?" he said, surveilling the interior space surrounding the front seat.

"Yes," Magpie said.

"Welcome. Roll down the back window please."

Magpie did as asked. The guy leaned down, face level with Wally. "Good morning, Mister Lanakai." Same scrutiny for the back seat. "Happy New Year. Park your car here, I'll move the cone."

The small blackboard in the restaurant window, next to the front door, read *CLOSED FOR A PARTY* in bold strokes of white chalk, and *HAPPY NEW YEAR* beneath it. Their escort opened the door and gestured for them to enter, no pat-downs involved. *"Bring whatever you want to make yourself feel safe,"* a Massimo mouthpiece had told Wally, so they were both carrying.

Inside looked larger than the exterior suggested, because in the front of the restaurant all but two of the dinner tables had been removed. Two chairs behind one table took up wall space on one side across from a similar arrangement on the other. The seats and place settings at the tables were for four guests only.

So easy to recognize Salvatore Massimo, seated by himself. Pajamas, robe, slippers, his face and hair as whitish-gray as cigarette smoke in a casino. He stood when Wally and Magpie entered, but he stayed behind his table. Two waitstaff had taken positions in front of a bar in the rear of the restaurant, an older man in a suit and a young woman in a white smock.

"Mister Lanakai." Same raspy voice. It hurt to listen to it.

"Aloha, Mister Massimo," Wally said. "And a mahalo for getting my name right."

"Old age often replaces civility with impatience. If I offended you before, I am sorry. Have a seat. I'm letting you know in advance that the restaurant owner, Irv Silberbauer, graciously offered to be one of our waiters today."

"A pleasure," Irv said, bowing to his guests.

Fifteen feet separated the family bosses. Wally unbuttoned his jacket to take his seat, his suit a far cry from Massimo's complete wardrobe surrender.

"The chef here is an old friend, Mister Lanakai."

"Call me Wally."

"As you prefer, Wally. You may call me Salvatore."

Salvatore went off on a tangent about good food from good chefs and good restaurants, but only for a moment, to let Wally know there would be a multitude of pastas, meats, and seafood arriving at their separate tables. He suggested that Magpie sit and partake as well. Wally didn't object. Across the room, Enzo joined Salvatore behind his table.

"This feast will placate these two large men rather nicely," Salvatore observed. "Nowadays my lack of appetite has made me a food teetotaler. Except for dessert. Now, about our grievances with each other. We need to come to some arrangements. Let's do this. I ask you questions, you answer them, you ask me questions, I do the same. This will work only if we're truthful with our responses." Salvatore grabbed a dinner roll, split it in half, buttered it. "I do still like the bread. Let's begin."

First topic, the armored car heist and murders.

"Let's go over this again. Two guards executed, their bodies left in the snow, with one civilian, a Mummer, headless, with a banjo. A bag of money. Not my money, but when I heard about it from one of my associates, I was upset that I hadn't been consulted. Again, I ask, was that you, Mister Lanakai—Wally? I'm looking for your final answer. Did you hit that truck?"

"Same answer as before, Salvatore. No. Ka Hui knew nothing about it. We learned about it in the news."

"Thank you. Any idea who might have done it?"

"I'm hearing nothing on the street," Wally said. He stabbed at some salad, crunched the fresh lettuce. Salty kalamata olives, croutons, and dressing. All good. "I was saddened by it. That one execution... Someone with major issues did that."

"Are you aware that someone on the truck, perhaps that same someone, took a photo at the scene," Salvatore said, "and sent it to us? We didn't receive it that night, it came later. It showed one of my men in proximity to the bodies. The armored car money bag was in the snow with him."

"All news to me, Salvatore. It sounds like someone set your guy up, leaving the money behind. They knew he couldn't resist taking it."

"My numbers runner, Frank Tisha. You ever met Frank Tisha, Wally?"

Wally put his fork down, was finished with his salad, used his napkin to wipe his mouth. "I've heard of him. 'Otherway' Tisha, right, Magpie?"

Magpie nodded.

"Answer this question carefully then, Wally." Salvatore folded his hands together on the table. "Does he do work for you?"

Before Wally could respond, Enzo raised his hand and leaned over to whisper something to his boss.

"I misspoke," Salvatore said. "*Did* he do work for you, in some capacity?"

Wally understood the past-tense distinction had most to do with a past-tense life. Poor Otherway.

"Never met him, Salvatore. We saw him at Resorts the night your grandson was killed. Had you not insulted me on the phone, I would have told you your guy was there and saw your grandson's bad behavior. Now, if you don't mind, I'd like the next coupla questions to be mine."

The two waiters arrived, and so did multiple pasta dishes. When the dining room cleared of the servers, Wally began.

"First, any of your guys lose any fingers lately?" He dipped a breaded chicken parm piece into a side of red sauce, or in neighborhood parlance, gravy.

"I don't follow," Salvatore said.

"I'm tempted to have you line all your guys up so I can check their hands, but I'll ask this next question instead." He chewed. "Was it you who parked someone outside my favorite coffee shop waiting for me with a, what is it called again, Magpie?"

"A lupara."

"Right. With a lupara, a nifty little shotgun supposed to blow my head off, near my house? Because he really screwed up the attempt, Salvatore. That ancient piece-of-shit gun misfired." Wally dipped another piece of chicken in the gravy and consumed it. "My knife lightened his left hand by a coupla fingers."

Salvatore leaned into Enzo, who waved to someone at the rear of the restaurant. "Sorry, Wally, I'm just hastening someone up. No, I didn't send that person after you. I do confess that I had someone lined up for the same purpose, but I called it off."

"I see. And that was because...?"

"Because an associate of mine had lied to me about your involvement in the armored car executions. Which led me to also blame you for the police raid on my bookie operation."

"And to me blaming you for blowing up my club in Chinatown."

The sublime had turned ridiculous, each man giving in to slight chuckles that ended with sips of wine. Salvatore's straitlaced face returned.

"But about my grandson Little Sal." Salvatore blessed himself while keeping his focus on Wally, his aged hands exaggerating their trip around the Sign of the Cross. "I swear to God, Wally, if I find out you had anything to do with it—"

"Again, Salvatore"—Wally raised his hand Scout's honor style—"I did *not* have your family member executed. I give you my word. We were there, and we saw it happen. The guy on a Suzuki or some other flashy road burner took him and the security guards out. But there is something else about it. Magpie, fill him in."

"The shooter raised his hand in a trigger motion at us. It was before he pulled his semi-auto from inside his jacket." Magpie opened his folded hands to accompany the explanation in supplication. "He was there to intimidate Mister Lanakai. Then the shooter saw an opportunity he couldn't resist."

"My grandson," Salvatore said, and squeezed his eyes shut for a second.

Wally nodded. "I think, had I not been there, the assassin wouldn't have been there either. I am sorry, Salvatore."

Salvatore's mob veneer lost out to a grandfather's grief, his pale face coloring, his eyes tearing. "Thank you for your apology." His stoicism returned after one blow of his nose into a napkin. "Tell me this. Why do you think the shooter didn't take you out, too, when he had the chance?"

"You and I are feuding factions," Wally said. "If he kills people from both families at the same time..."

"It would point to a third party doing the killing," Salvatore said, "not two warring families. Goddamn it, some bastard's pitting us against each other."

"Exactly. The cops are working these incidents, Salvatore, busy as hell, thinking there's a mob war in progress. It's keeping law enforcement off balance, too. It's a diversion—"

The armored car, the grandson's death, the police raid, the Chinatown bombing. The over-the-top assassination attempt with a lupara, a traditional mafioso weapon.

"... while someone is out there killing string band people."

The waiter in the suit—Irv, the restaurant owner—arrived with a napkin across his arm and a white plastic container with a dessert scooper on a silver tray. Salvatore straightened up to let him serve him his dessert.

"I'm a slave to water ice," he said to Wally, "but you already know that. I expect you'll want to choose from the dessert cart. Irv, leave the tray here, please, I'll want more."

Salvatore was right. Tiramisu for Wally and Magpie, and Salvatore did want more. He spooned water ice into his mouth while he studied Wally and Magpie.

"You're one big enigma to me, Wally. Why would you even care about the Mummers?" Salvatore shared his gaze between Wally and Magpie.

Wally put his spoon down, finished with his dessert. He composed himself.

"Let me put into words what you're really thinking and try to do it without calling you a racist bastard, Salvatore. How about, 'why do you care, you're not even from around here,' or, 'why do you care, you don't look like the rest of us.' Did I get that right?"

"An unfair characterization."

"If you go far enough back, you're not a Philadelphian either." Wally searched the faces of the other people in the room. "Your real question should be, 'who is killing the Mummers, and why.' So, here's the why, Salvatore.

"They were all people of color. That's what the media is reporting. These executions, they're targeting Black people. Black Mummers. Which means if I were feeling overly racist today, I'd have been the one to ask why *you* would care about these executions."

Salvatore slapped his open hand on the table, annoyed, the water and wine glasses spilling but staying upright. "My roots in this country, in Philly, go back generations! My family helped build this city. They were here when these traditions took root! Let me do you a favor, Wally, goddamn it."

His parted lips were red from his dessert, offsetting the pink of his clenched dentures. He calmed himself. "I'll skip past your insinuations. I'll go ahead and agree with you. It probably *is* because they were Black. Next question is, where does that leave us?"

"With people motivated by a pro-white agenda," Wally said. "White supremacists."

"I'll narrow it down. White supremacist Mummers, not happy about letting minorities march with them."

"Agreed."

Salvatore whispered to Enzo. Enzo left the room.

"Here's what I'm going to do, Wally. We have friends in the Philly Police Department. Enzo will call someone to wish him a Happy New Year. Someone high enough who will share with me where the cops are on these murders." He raised his wine glass. "Truce?"

Wally raised his glass in salute. "Il armistizio."

The old man nodded, impressed. "Eccellente. One last question. Should you be worried, Wally?"

"About?"

"This trend. These supremacists... I mean, for yourself personally."

"Your entitled European-American heritage is showing again, Salvatore. If I played the banjo or a ukulele and planned on marching in tomorrow's New Year's Day Parade, and I wasn't armed, maybe. Otherwise, no."

Nine p.m. Rhea buzzed him up to her apartment.

*Hot.* That was all Philo's brain could register when Rhea answered her door, waved him in, turned, and walked off toward her kitchen. A knockout, Rhea was dressed and ready for drinks and dinner at a New Year's Eve cop party at a restaurant in the city. An off-the-shoulder top in red, and shiny skinny pants in black made of something smooth and silky and flattering to her muscular lower body. Spindle-heeled shoes in red, but not stilettos. It all worked. On the smaller side as far as cops went, women cops included,

Rhea was rocking this New Year's Eve outfit like a runway model. An out-and-out *whoa.* Then he heard her shouting into her phone, cursing at Detective Reese.

"I'm sorry you caught this shift at your precinct but listen to me, you dense fuck. It's not like we're asking the security company to hand over any of their corporate secrets. Did they get that gated community's safe room alert or not?"

She pushed up the volume on her cell to the max after a glance Philo's way, so he could hear. Her raised eyebrows and head bob at his dark suit and tie and black hat said not bad, not bad at all, honey, you clean up pretty good.

"Yes, Ibáñez," Reese snapped, "they got it. And cut the shit, I am in no mood."

"Okay. Then what?"

"It moved over to dispatch. They sent a police unit. It got there in four minutes."

"And?"

"The report says here that... Let me see. It says 'No suspicious activity found.'"

"What? The place was shot up, Reese! What do you mean, no suspicious activity was found?"

"Shot up on the *inside*, Ibáñez. I processed the scene, remember? When we got there, the front door was intact. From the outside, the door would have looked fine."

"'*Fine*?' What the hell does that mean? Locked fine, or unlocked fine, which was it? Did the uniforms check it?"

"Changing pages. Here. The officer's report says..."

Philo watched Rhea pace, waiting. She flashed him a smile and placed her hand over the phone. "You channeling the Blues Brothers tonight, babe? It's New Year's Eve, not Halloween."

He pulled out a pair of sunglasses and put them on. "Glad you like it."

"It doesn't say, Ibáñez," Reese said. "No mention of a check on the entries to the townhouse, either the front door or the back sliders. They should have checked them before they cleared the call. It might have still been good police work, just not good police report writing. We done here? I got my own party to attend tonight."

"Hold it. What car caught the welfare check? Give me that and I'll be outta your hair."

"The report was filed by... Police Officer Yonder. Yonder, Junior. Lieutenant Yonder's kid did the check."

Philo exchanged quick, concerned looks with Rhea.

"And with that, Ibáñez, I am signing off so I can go get drunk and get laid. I suggest you do the same. Happy Fucking New Year."

Rhea crammed the phone into her small clutch. "The commissioner's going to hear about this tomorrow, Philo. I don't like it either. Here." She slapped her small clutch into Philo's chest. "Hold this. I have to pee."

# DRUMROLL

Friday, January 1
City Hall, Center City Philadelphia
New Year's Day

An overcast morning with snow flurries expected to turn into snow showers. The country's northeast just couldn't catch a break, a new cold front gripping the eastern seaboard. Decades of yearend holidays in Philadelphia without snow and then *bam*, the past year ended with a ton of it including a freak blizzard, and the new year was starting out with more. Little to no expected accumulation, but it added flavor and fun and snowflakey Kodak moments to the Mummers parade.

Blankets, gloves, wool hats, tushy cushions, and hot beverage thermoses, and flasks for the age appropriate: seating in the parade's judging stands at 15th Street and JFK Boulevard, near Philly's City Hall, was by ticket only. Twenty bucks each, Philo's treat, but it was Old Time Philly String Band Mummer Teddy Cangelosi who came through by getting them VIP reserved seating in the first row of one of the sets of portable bleachers.

Nine-forty-five a.m. The street intersection was clear, ready for the next string band to run through its paces for the judges. Four bands had performed already, Teddy's the next one up. Philo leaned out from his seat, observing his Blessid Trauma employees Hank, Grace, and Miñoso breathing the frosty air and taking in the spectacle. Rhea was squeezed in tightly next to him.

"Thanks for letting me stay last night, Rhea. And for keeping me from doing shots with your detective buddies. And for talking me out of doing karaoke."

She grabbed his gloved hand, squeezed it with hers. "You poor, misguided boy. I did none of these things. You fell asleep in the restaurant, I had to wake you up for our kiss when the ball dropped, and we left when they started doing the shots. You crashed on my sofa. And it wasn't from too much to drink, you're just a party lightweight."

"You know, a simple 'you're welcome' would have sufficed."

Teddy's wakeup text to him in the morning said he'd never forgive him if he slept in and missed the parade. His band had a few surprises today. One Philo knew about, and one he didn't.

The set of bleachers across from them, on the other corner of the street, held Philly city government dignitaries, TV and radio celebrities, local sports teams athletes, and police department brass including Commissioner Valerie Darnell and the officers in her administration. Rhea pointed a gloved hand at the police delegation. "Do you see who's not over there with all the top cops, Philo?"

"Ah, Frank Rizzo?"

"Haha. Too funny. Sure, that would be one. Another would be the commissioner's right-hand man, Lieutenant Yonder. According to Detective Reese"—she checked a text—"he called in sick. Commissioner Val won't like that. She also won't like it when I confront him on his patrolman kid's safe house screw-up, either. Some big questions left open with that one. But that's tomorrow's headache."

Also across the street, seated in the next set of bleachers down from City Hall, were groups of Mummer families and friends, there to cheer on their parade performers.

Philo's turn to point. "Teddy Cangelosi's girlfriend Harriet Broglio,

Rhea, right there, first row, hanging with the Mummer wives and significant others."

"Can't miss her hair, Philo, plus you can't miss what's parked behind their bleachers. That freakin' road demon car of hers. Christ, she's lucky she's got friends in high places, driving a maniac car like that."

"Connected friends from a former life is more like it. And here I was, about to suggest a double date with Harriet and Teddy, in her car, after he's fully recovered."

"Fine. Let's do it. I like Teddy." Rhea gave Philo a peck on the cheek. "But I will not bail us out of any speeding tickets."

"Deal. Here we go. Teddy's band is set up and ready."

A five-minute routine, Philo knew. It started with spaceships and solar systems and circus apparatus and steam and billboard-sized screening hiding the performers, then all moving in synch, wave after wave of the band's saxophone players jamming the street with the first number that somehow also incorporated hula hoops. More exploding jets of steam presented the next wave of performers in *Predator* and *Alien* costumes lit up with Lite-Brite bulbs playing accordions and banjos and xylophones, the music morphing into the first *Star Wars* bar scene earworm. Then came Rainbow Slinky man, all puffed up with coiled colored appendages and a torso with no visible head, a freaky crowd-pleasing piñata of a character whose arms and legs expanded and contracted with the highs and lows of the music, electrifying the audience. Rainbow Slinky Man and his Mummer dancers moved into their final number, hordes of spent performers on the sidelines, awaiting the finale.

"Any idea where Teddy is in this sea of humanity?" Rhea asked.

Philo scanned the final line of banjo Mummers, all costumed as astronauts, strumming away at "When You Wish Upon a Star" before doubletiming into a circle for their march around the Big Blue Marble globe pulled by cart into the middle of the intersection.

"He's in there somewhere," Philo said, checking his watch, "this is the big finish."

Behind the cart, a drumline of five musicians marched into position, plus a kettle drum on wheels. The five drummers, all Black, their astronaut helmets on but raised to expose their faces, laid down a snazzy march as they strutted up to the globe, then held their places behind it. The audience exhaled a collective breath, then cheered and whistled, allowing for, and supporting, the significance of the drumline. Hoots and hollers and tears coalesced into a crescendo that drowned out the drumbeat.

Cops emerged from the crowd from both sides of the street in riot helmets, four uniformed police in total, one at each corner of the performance, there to serve and protect.

"Those drummers," Rhea said, "bravo." She raised her voice to better the crowd noise. "How'd they get five Black drummers on short notice? Wow, do I love this."

After a minute of noisy audience appreciation, the banjo players stopped their crazy spin around the Big Blue Marble and marched in place, still strumming, repeating the music for the last line of the song, "*Your dreams... come... true.*" The kettle drummer pounded the drum skin, heightening the drama, *boom* boom, *boom* boom, *boom* boom, while kicking off the band's playing of the theme from *2001: A Space Odyssey.*

The globe opened. A man exited, helmeted and dressed like his fellow Mummer banjo players while strumming away, but he walked slowly, more labored than his other bandmates, hobbled by a stiff leg.

Philo hadn't been a Mummer lover for most of his life. Teddy wore him down soon after he returned home from his last SEAL tour in Pakistan, promising him a date with an Eagles cheerleader if he went to the New Year's Day Parade. Philo gave in and was so enamored by the sincerity of the performers that he forgot about the bullshit date Teddy had promised with no way of delivering. Here was another one of those moments, the kind that sent shivers down a person's spine while it was in progress.

The shaky Mummer marched past his banjo line, the string band captain joining him. The two men took a direct route to the edge of the performing area and stopped in front of the stands. The captain approached a spectator, goaded her into leaving her chair, and escorted her by her arm into the street.

"That's Harriet," Philo said for Rhea's benefit. "This... damn, is Teddy really going to do this?"

"It damn sure is Harriet," Rhea said, smiling, "and it damn sure looks like he is."

Teddy as the helmeted, astronautic banjo player reached Harriet, his banjo buddies still strumming chords for the song's last line. When he let his banjo hang loose, the music stopped, replaced by a drumroll. Teddy exchanged his costume helmet with the band captain for a bullhorn. When he lowered himself to a wobbly knee, the screams from the audience rose, became deafening, but soon cut out in anticipation. Teddy produced a small box from a pocket and opened it, holding it up for Harriet's inspection. He raised the bullhorn.

"Harriet Broglio. Please make my dreams come true. Please marry me."

The words brought the house down, Harriet's shaking hands now covering her mouth.

She never got to answer.

*Pop, pop, pop-pop-pop.* Automatic gunfire replaced the drumroll. The shots reverberated, zipping and smashing and ringing and pinging their holy hell off the walls of the tall buildings and the sidewalks and the crowd-control metal railings. Four uniformed police, there "to serve and protect," were firing at will at the drumline, semi-auto handguns in each hand, emptying their weapons at the marchers and their equipment, blasting through drumheads and straps and sticks, striking the drummers repeatedly.

Bulletproof helmets and visors covered the drummers' faces and necks, and under their costumes, flak jackets and Kevlar armored suits protected their bodies. The drummers' weapons emerged, each man shedding his instrument and taking a knee. They returned fire, shredding arms and legs and blasting apart the torsos of all four of the assassins, none protected like the drummers were.

The audience scrambled and trampled each other trying to leave the chaotic slaughter, some struck down in the first few seconds, the others screaming in panic as TV cameras broadcast the melee in living, gruesome color to local households throughout the city and beyond. The shooting was over. Downstream from the judging area the parade was still in progress, the four preceding bands marching the route, oblivious to the attack.

Harriet was down.

Philo and Rhea entered the street running toward Teddy and Harriet, their weapons out.

"You know anything about those drummers, Philo? They look military..."

"Five Marines, Rhea, all part of the U.S. Marine Drum and Bugle Corps."

"*What?* You arranged for these guys?"

"Sure did. Surprise."

Rhea pointed back across the street after they arrived at Harriet's side, at another uniform at the edge of the crowd. He had his gun drawn, an older cop looking as bewildered as hell. After looks left then right, he returned his gun to his duty holster. He produced a cop baseball hat that he slipped on his head, twisted on a pair of sunglasses, and walked calmly against the panicked crowd toward a cop SUV, its lighted bar flashing. He got in the car.

"Philo! There! That cop. That was Yonder! Yonder's here, dressed like a uniform. It's fucking Yonder."

Harriet was on the ground, hit multiple times by random collateral-damage shots, Philo unable to tell how many. She was bleeding out but awake, Teddy cradling her. They heard an emergency siren approaching. Philo eyed her car behind the bleachers.

"Your keys, Harriet. Gimme your keys."

She mumbled, "Purse... bleachers..." The emergency vehicle screeched up next to the crowd, the EMTs disembarking, demanding a clear path.

Philo scooped up her purse from the first row of the bleacher seats, obvious as hell as Harriet's, its reddish-orange leather the same shade as her hair. He found the key fob while sprinting to her car and unlocked the door. The seatbelt on, he cranked the Dodge Challenger SRT Demon to life, the engine roaring, the tires smoking and burning then grabbing the blacktop. It fishtailed away from the curb and crashed through the crowd barriers into the street, the confetti and balloons and shredded ticker tape in the street now swirling in the wake of its throbbing, thunderous engine.

Yonder's police vehicle cruised quietly up the street away from the slaughter. Philo rammed him from behind at forty miles per hour, pushing the cop car forward. The driver stood on the cop car brakes, holding fast against Philo in the Demon, then gave in and caught rubber, heading down 15<sup>th</sup> Street.

His phone out, Philo tapped at a number. "Rhea! I've got Yonder in front of me and he's cranking it up, no interest in slowing down... Huh? Because I rammed his ass once already, that's how I know. We're on 15<sup>th</sup>, now we're on Chestnut, coming up to South Broad. He's in cop SUV number five-seven-one-five. Jesus, he went right, onto Broad. He's heading into the parade. He's gonna ram the parade!"

Barely slowing, the cop SUV threaded a busy crosswalk along the parade route, pedestrians leaping out of the way. It hit its siren an instant before leaving the walk and ramming the floats and pyrotechnic displays and Mummer props directly in front of it. Yonder had entered Broad Street in the meat of the parade and the marching Mummers themselves, with bunch after bunch of performers diving out of his path, hurtling the street barriers to gain the safety of the sidewalk, not everyone surviving the first few seconds of the attack. Bundles of arms and legs mangled by the cop SUV lay in its wake. Philo slowed to avoid the carnage, keen on Yonder ahead of him still following the parade route, past the Academy of Music, the Merriam Theater, the Kimmel, the entire theater district, all shuttered for the holiday parade. Broad Street was lined with spectators, a direct route south with no vehicle traffic, but the street itself was packed with performers. The noise of Yonder's collision with the first band preceded itself, the other Mummer contingents a few blocks farther south now scattering to avoid the oncoming marauding SUV and its pursuer, their screaming vehicles and siren providing a warning.

The SUV skidded left, blasting through a traffic barrier and entering residential Pine Street. Philo followed, the cop vehicle and its siren ahead of him, clearing their paths. A hard right onto 12<sup>th</sup> Street and they were heading south again. The leftover snow, the cold, and the calendar reduced the vehicular and pedestrian traffic. They reached Washington Avenue. Yonder ran another red light, fishtailing onto Washington, Philo following.

"Rhea! He's headed east on Washington. There are mangled Mummers in serious trouble back there on Broad Street, Yonder didn't slow down..."

To chase or not to chase a car in the act of a crime, on a crowded street

—a law enforcement legal dilemma. Not a legal issue for a civilian, but morally...

Philo slowed until he reached the commercial part of Washington Avenue, where he cranked things up again, horn blaring, his eyes on the prize ahead, Yonder still advertising as a cop with lights and siren. Police interceptor Ford SUV vs. Dodge Challenger SRT Demon: crazy boyhood fantasies flashed into Philo's head about fast cop cars chasing street bullies in muscle cars, except here the roles were reversed. His white knuckles were wrapped around the steering wheel, his nerves on edge, his eyesight flicking left and right—he prayed no baby carriages or children on bicycles appeared in the middle of a street that was also a public bus route.

"This is crazy, this is crazy..." he said, scolding himself, then he started pounding the steering wheel in anger. "Where—the fuck—are you going, you prick bastard!"

The police siren ran interference for them east along Washington, past blocks and blocks of short commercial buildings closed for New Year's Day and one-off brick rowhomes and low-rise apartment buildings, running through yellow traffic lights changing to red, sliding into and out of all the lanes like delivery couriers on rocket roller blades. They rubber-banded with each other for fifteen blocks, passing under I-95 until Washington Avenue dead-ended at Columbus Boulevard. Yonder swerved left onto Columbus, paralleling the Delaware River, then...

"Rhea. We're getting onto 95 north. Am I gonna get any help?"

Sounding like she was jumping into a police sedan, Rhea gave him what she had. "Word's out, honey, but without knowing where he's going, it's a bit of a problem, and he's in a cop vehicle."

"Harriet? Is Harriet..." Philo said, afraid to continue.

"I'm following the EMS vehicle with her and Teddy in it to the hospital right now. She was alive when she got in. Listen to me closely. They unmasked the four shooters. They're all dead. Only one was a real cop, Yonder's patrolman kid. Nothing yet on a second one, Caucasian, maybe a cop, maybe not. But the last two, Philo—they're not from around here."

"Meaning?"

"I think we'll find they're Middle Eastern. Stay with me on the line,

Philo, baby, don't you dare hang up, this might be way too big for you, you might need to back off..."

He didn't answer, because he hung up. She called him back, he let it ring through, again and again. He had room to maneuver on Interstate 95's many lanes—he had the horsepower, he had the adrenaline—and right now he was up close and personal behind his target, staying tight to his bumper. He fucking had this.

How did he want to play it—follow him north out of Philly into Jersey, or maybe New York? Try to squeeze him beforehand, push him left into the concrete dividers? Nudge his ass into an accident? The Demon was good for all of it, could outrun the Ford Interceptor engine on the straightaways, but what about the other traffic? What about what Rhea just told him?

Yonder cruised the left-most lane at a hundred and twenty. The Demon had that in the tank and much more. He stood on the accelerator, moved one lane over, was going to get alongside, started to pull up, foot by foot, inch by inch... If Philo could get off a few gunshots, at tires or windows or both, he could slow him down, maybe take him out—

Philo's driver's window exploded, the passenger window also, Yonder with the same idea. *Crash-zip-crash*, the bullet passing next to his head and out the other side, glass crumbling around him, his face and hands showered in glass pellets—Philo needed to back off. He braked and slid in behind him.

The Bridge Street exit was coming up, a fork on the right. He brushed the glass off his hands and lap and felt around his face and neck, looking for blood, felt a sting behind his ear, a minor gash from the glass.

Yonder pulled hard right across all the lanes and made the exit, Philo following. Philo's phone rang again and he decided to answer, to let Rhea know where he was.

"Rhea! I'm off 95 now, on Aramingo. Just passed Bridge, now on Harbison, little traffic. Lieutenant Yonder's ahead of me, blasting his lights and siren. Rhea? Hello?"

"Trout?" a male voice said.

He looked at the phone number. Da fuck? "*Lanakai*? Hang the fuck up, Wally, I gotta go..."

"I wanted to drop something off. Money I owe you. It sounds like you're busy."

"Life-and-death busy, Wally! Some other time. Bye."

"Wait! You said 'Lieutenant Yonder.' Philly police brass Yonder?"

"Look, I'm chasing him into the Northeast, the crazy fucker just shot up the Mummers' parade. I'm hanging up now." But he heard Wally's last comment before closing out the call: *"Yonder's on Massimo's payroll..."*

Oh, what a tangled web...

He jammed Yonder up the ass again, pushing the cop car to go faster. A Catholic church appeared on the left, with churchgoers on foot crossing in front of them, a hundred yards away. The siren and lights scattered the walkers, two vehicles racing past the people gathering at the street corners waiting for the traffic light to change. The cars moved onto a straightaway. Yonder's SUV leaned into the five-point fork, turning right onto a smaller two-way residential side street. Philo called Rhea.

"Sorry about that, I lost the signal. I'm seeing this through, honey. We're on Hawthorne Street, but... I have no idea what the hell he's doing here. Shit! Hold on!"

The police SUV braked and took out the side view mirrors on a parked car on another hard right, the Demon screeching into the same turn, Philo's car lifting onto two tires, slipping left, and that's where Philo lost his phone out the glassless window. His car stabilized on all fours again, Yonder still in front of him but now by many car lengths.

"Unruh Avenue! What the fuck? He's two blocks from my house!" The words left his mouth, but without a phone he had no audience.

Being here, on this street, what registered was it was too much of a coincidence.

Two lanes, a one-way street, cars parked on both sides. The cop SUV gunned the engine up to a four-way stop sign and ran it, did the same at the next intersection and the next. Philo cruised through the intersections at half the speed, keeping him in his sights. Yonder hit the brakes for a hard right into the alleyway near the end of the block he was on, scraping the rear wall of the brick bakery Philo bought his donuts and sticky buns from. The SUV stopped. Yonder was out of the car and on foot, running back up Unruh, his gun raised. He came to a full stop and assumed the position, his handgun aimed at Philo in the Demon on its way past. Philo ducked below the broken window, heard and felt the bullets strike the passenger side door, one making it through the steel panels and the interior padding and ricocheting off the steering wheel, the other going elsewhere. No sting anywhere on his body—he wasn't hit. A hundred feet past the shooter, Philo hazarded a look above the dash to make sure the Demon wasn't going to hit anything, then hazarded a second look behind him. No Yonder, at least not upright. At the end of the block Philo veered right and pumped the brakes, stopping short of striking the traffic light. He cut the ignition, leaned back for another look at where Yonder had taken his stand. He was gone.

Philo crept out of the car, his head down, his handgun still in its holster. He hadn't seen where the bastard ran, but he knew where he was going, the only place that made any sense. He just didn't know why.

## 28

## WHERE'S THE DAMN CAT?

Inside Philo's rowhome—that's where Yonder was.

Philo was sucking air, exhausted, the double set of concrete steps leading to each of the rowhomes looking as inviting as an Everest assault and were now probably more dangerous. He vaulted the first flight at the end of the block, in front of a house five doors away from his own. He flattened himself against the brick. A narrow walkway wide enough for lawn chairs stretched across the space beneath each home's picture window. His head below the windows, he hunkered down, continuing along the front of his neighbors' houses, and reached the second set of steps that led to the landing for his front door. His jacket open, his hand rested on his holstered weapon. He leaned out and peeked up the steps.

The aluminum storm door was closed, the morning sun glinting off the handle, but inside it the front door was wide open. One step up, the living room was visible through a side window, but it was in shadows.

How long had he been away from the house? Seventeen, eighteen hours? Crazy, lovable Six, his feline buddy since he'd left the Navy, had the run of it, all three floors. Belying whatever vengeful damage she'd done, she'd go all berserker on him as soon as he entered—if she could. It was too painful for him to consider what might have already happened to her, so he didn't.

Philo reached into the holster on his hip, goosebumps moving up his arms, onto his shoulders, the back of his neck cold with sweat. His left hand was the best place for his handgun, between his body and the front wall of the house, where it could stay hidden from a trespassing psycho cop and neighbors all. His firearm in hand, his jaw tightening, he hurdled the steps and ripped open the storm door.

The living room was mussed, some pillows on the floor, and the chair facing the picture window was in a reclining position, but that hadn't been his doing, and probably wasn't Yonder's either.

Fuck. Other company.

The security keypad was frozen, dead, and not making any noise, so a police response wasn't coming. No matter, he was here, he could protect his own home.

From one guy, yeah. From multiple trespassers?

Hell, yeah. Hoo-yah, bitches.

The room was empty—no Yonder, but no Six, either.

Maybe Six was outside, on the hunt. Or maybe she was stuck somewhere, in a kitchen cabinet or a closed room, a place where Philo might have opened yesterday then closed before she'd been able to slink out. Or maybe someone hurt her, or worse.

On the hardwood floor, drops of what looked like blood led from the front door. Philo followed them on light feet the length of the living room. He bypassed the stairs to the second floor for now, entered the dining room instead. More blood drops on the rug there. It continued into the kitchen, over to the door to the basement stairs. He opened the door a few inches, then a few inches more, then all the way. Daylight from the kitchen reached halfway down the stairs. The basement lights were off, the bottom half of the steps dark, the stairway empty of Six or anyone or anything else except for more trickles of blood. He flipped the basement light switch. No lights.

He grabbed a Maglite from a drawer. With the flashlight next to his gun barrel, he was going down.

At the bottom of the steps, more blood droplets that led to the middle of the floor. There, blood had pooled surrounding a fur-covered severed leg. At the end of the leg, the paw was missing.

His heart sank. "Six…"

He jerked his flashlight to the wall behind the paw. There, in the shadows, stood a man in full camo, his head exposed, his arms at his side. It was a white guy who wasn't Lieutenant Yonder, smiling.

"We've been waiting for you, Mister Trout," the intruder said. "About your cat. We—"

Philo fired his Sig, intending to empty his magazine into this bastard and anything else that moved. Glass shattered, exploding toward him, the shards crashing back against his chest and face. The lights suddenly snapped on. He was unloading his weapon into a mirror, one of two long mirrors hung inside his large cedar closet, its doors open. He spun left but was dropped to a knee by taser leads to his back and arm and the fifty thousand volts they delivered. His muscles contracted but didn't fully incapacitate him 'cause he'd felt this before, knew what to expect, and willed himself to hold on, to let the cramping pass... *Aghhh...*

He twitched and growled and spun his way to his workbench, lifted a screwdriver, spun again, and plunged it deep into the jugular of someone who'd approached him from behind. Screams in blood-gurgling Arabic ricocheted around the room while hands descended on him from all angles, until one hand dropped him into a heap with a punch from a set of brass knuckles that loosened his jaw. Yonder and his smiling, old-guy, dentured teeth hovered over him after delivering the blow, Philo now most of the way incapacitated because someone had plunged a needle into his thigh. He drifted away...

When he regained consciousness, groggy and thick-tongued, he found himself seated, restrained by bungee cords tightly wrapped around him but not around the folding chair he sat on. He was still in his basement. His head was swimming, and had it been years ago, a different place and time, he might have enjoyed whatever chemical they'd syringed into his thigh. His mouth was duct taped. His arms, from his shoulders to his wrists, were wrapped tightly against his stomach by the bungee cording, but his hands were not, his sweaty palms touching each other in a pious prayer position from inside the duct tape used to keep them together. The left side of his head throbbed, and the bridgework inside his fractured jaw was hanging. *Fuck,* did his jaw hurt, even with the drugs. The one attacker he'd eliminated with the screwdriver was MIA, but his blood was everywhere. Philo's heavy eyes blinked hard to keep them open, he had to get his bearings...

A jarring, anxious memory.

*Six... They tortured poor Six...*

Philo shuddered, tried to stand, was shoved back down. Bookending him were two men in black and gray scarves like he'd seen in crude video executions, also like he'd seen overseas just before their demise by his own capable, lethal hands. A third was Yonder, smoking a cigarette and leaning against the paneling. Philo smelled camphor, and cedar, and musty clothing, plus blood, plus piss that was probably his. The fourth guy in the room stood above him. Philo had trouble looking up but forced himself to, the light in the suspended ceiling blinding.

"Dude. You're awake. Cool. I'm Jack. You might know me from my appearances on stage and screen as Irish Jack Maguire, Grand Poohbah of America's leading nationalist group The Real Proper Punks. And you are the infamous Philo Trout, bareknuckle boxing terror of the local bar scene."

His Irish brogue was less cultured than the lieutenant's, but it was no less odd that the two of them were slinging hash with the bozos standing behind Maguire, speaking to each other in heavy Middle Eastern accents. Jack Maguire crouched in front of Philo. This was the guy he'd shot at in the mirror, his eyes now a sparkly brown and showing their delight at Philo's return to consciousness. Maguire smiled as smug as all fuck.

"So. You're wondering what the hell is going on."

Philo winced and dragged his head in a visual sweep that found his white *LAUNDRY* cabinet with its door ajar. In it, maybe, was his salvation: a loaded 9mm behind his gun cleaning equipment. A lot of good the gun did him now, restrained as he was, but he had to have an out, a goal, some hope, something, anything. A POW always needed a goal.

His captor noticed the object of his attention. "Oh. The metal cabinet labeled 'laundry,'" Maguire said in air quotes. "Yeah. Let's talk about your guns."

A hooded thug dragged over a large gym bag, turned it upside down in front of him, emptying it of multiple handguns, his short-barreled rifle, and his shotgun, spilling them onto the floor near Philo's feet, close to him but not close enough to be of any help.

"Yeah, sorry. Demoralizing to see this, right? Lieutenant Yonder knows his way around the database for the Firearms Division of the Pennsylvania State Police. Your state's gun registry. What a great little citizen you are," he said, his tone mocking. "You own twelve guns legally, and we found ten of them scattered throughout your house. Your ankle gun and the one in your holster made numbers eleven and twelve. Your entire private arsenal, Trout, all present and accounted for, all now unloaded and sitting conveniently just outside your reach. Bet you're getting hard, seeing all these guns, huh? A real gun orgy for a tough guy like you. Ha! So, Trout—let's get this show started.

"*Two of these people are not like the others*," Maguire sing-songed, off key. "That would be Lieutenant Yonder here, and me. These other two guys here, they've got some serious Islamic terrorist agenda we'll talk about in a minute. But Larry and I have known each other since the eighties. Both Mummers back then, but you might already know that. Problem is, the Mummers in this city think they need to change. They want to move away from the good-natured, good-timey, old-fashioned ribbing of, you know, niggers and other minorities. The subhuman mongrels who think they can infiltrate these white Philly institutions, like today's parade..."

Philo keyed on that in his head. The Marine drum corps absolutely annihilated their ambushers. He cracked a smile beneath the duct tape, his eyes giving away the joy this thought gave him.

"Oh. That's right," Jack said. "Feeling good about that performance today, aren't you? Had a good time? To be remedied shortly, asshole. These guys are handling it, and you, Philo, are personally going to get the brunt of it. They're U.S.-based Al Qaeda types. No worries, no ideological surrender here on my part, Trout. My domestic extremism is still intact, although these guys keep pushing me toward a militant Islamic version of it. Nah, not for me, and not for The Real Proper Punks. We simply have some common enemies and targets is all, so we find it convenient to work together.

"Mummer clubs and bands are now on notice that adopting more... *diverse* Mummers' performances will not be tolerated. How are we doing so far, you ask? We started a mob war as a distraction, and it's working just fine. They're all idiots, even the cops.

"The armored car heist? Us—The Real Proper Punks. Videoing it and snitching to Big Sal Massimo, that ancient wop in the bathrobe, about the money? Us. To get some coin, we had to give some up. Killing Massimo's wop grandkid at the casino? Yep, the Punks. The raid on Massimo's bookie operation? We called that one in on the Philly Cop Hotline. Croaking those nigger drummers and that trumpeter? Us. Bombing that clubhouse in Chinatown, the one where that pineapple nigger Wally Lanakai does business? Us again. The attempted hit on that poi-faced fat schmuck? You win some, you lose some, and that one didn't work out. Our guy paid for that screw-up with part of his hand, then his life. We jettisoned him when we got rid of the armored car. He became a liability.

"The stuff that didn't hit the papers, the beheadings that have Homeland Security wrapped up in knots—your SEAL buddy Zorn—that was these guys, my Al Qaeda buddies. I'm not into that shit, but for the right money, let's just say we were okay with it, and we let it happen.

"I'm doing all the talking here, boasting my ass off, aren't I? Too fucking bad, 'cause I ain't done..."

Maguire moved onto a different level of terrorism: cooperating with Al Qaeda to capture and execute SEAL members "because it's in the service of getting back millions from these guys, payable today, Trout, for helping them move more easily undetected in the U.S. Supplying them with American guns and cover, and intel from access to the cop databases... that came courtesy of my good buddy Larry Yonder here, isn't that right, Lieutenant?"

Yonder took a prolonged, tough guy drag from his cigarette, sucking it down to the filter, and bowed. He flicked the butt at Philo's chest. Philo didn't react, couldn't because of the drugs.

"Damn straight, Jack," Yonder said. "I hate niggers. And kikes. And spics. Wops for that matter, too. And the people who hang with them."

In Philo's head, but with no way to vocalize it: *your racist kid is dead, Yonder, you sick fuck, so fuck you.*

"So let's sum this up for you," Maguire said. "I'm not here to do you any harm, but my Al Qaeda friends are. You with me so far, Trout? Oh yeah, the duct tape. Sorry. Just nod for me."

Philo was nodding but not in agreement, was still too drugged. He tried focusing on his abductor. Real Proper Punk head honcho Jack Maguire was even uglier in person. Acne facial scars, pug nose, tiny ears, probably maimed and killed pets and other animals as a kid.

*Pets...*

*Six. Poor Six.*

"I'll take that nod as a yes, even though it's the drugs. Why don't we review where we are? First, we're in your basement. Second, Osama Bin Laden's dead, his body dumped in the ocean, and these gentlemen are really upset about that. That was *your* doing, Trout. You and your twenty-two other hotshot Navy SEAL friends, the rest of them getting tracked down and, like Al Qaeda likes to boast from that Islamic bible of theirs, they're doing some major smiting to their necks.

"Aziz," Maguire called over his shoulder. "Is your livestream app ready?"

"Yes." The sober answer came from the taller of the two Al Qaeda pricks left in the basement with them, the words spoken through a hood. He was keying at a cell phone.

"Good," Maguire said. "Let's get down to business. Look this way, Trout, so you can see yourself in the mirror."

Philo heard "necks" and "smite" and "livestream." They were going to behead him live on the internet. On American soil, in his own house. The message this would send, the damage it would do, this show of Al Qaeda's reach, and of American weakness... the propaganda... It all blasted through the drugs they'd given him, straightening him right the hell up. He turned his head, to see what Jack Maguire wanted him to see.

But what—who—was in the mirror? Something not possible: Pop, his father, right there, in front of him in USN officer whites under the bungee cording, seated in a chair, facing the cedar closet, his Navy officer's cap tilted on his head like a bon-vivant. Alive.

The drugs, they were confusing him.

He peered into the open cedar closet with its mirrors on the inside of each door, one shattered from Philo's bullets, the other intact. In the intact mirror was Philo, not his father, dressed as his dad looked as a younger Navy man in uniform. Camphor, mothballs, musty clothing, the smells all combining to storm Philo's nose like smelling salts. Also in the closet was his father's open USN steamer trunk, standing upright, the trunk's interior decorated with wallpaper and fabric and side drawers. These SOBs had beat his ass, drugged him, and dressed him up for this humiliation. This execution would be so demoralizing on so many levels—and yes, this image, he did look like his father...

*Love you, Pop. Sorry for my behavior, all the trouble, our fights. I was wrong. You, your racism, you were wrong too. But I cleaned up real good, Pop, honest. My last mission got me the Presidential Unit Citation. You'd be proud, Pop, and so would Mom. The obscenity that's gonna happen, the indignity, the shame this will bring to the uniform and the country—I am so, so sorry, Pop.*

Maguire snugged up the officer's cap on Philo's head to make it fit better. "Nice touch, right, Trout? The uniform's an unexpected perk we found in the trunk. You cut a mean military figure under all that wrapping. Quite the American hero. Fellas," he called, "a little help over here, please."

They lifted Philo's chair and dropped it closer to the open cedar closet and the steamer trunk on his right, Philo still wrapped tight as a mummy in the bungee cords, sitting unattached to the chair. "Aziz! Is your page accessible? You live yet?"

"Yes, we are live," Aziz said in a heavy Arabic accent. "We are broadcasting from a TikTok page. Sixteen thousand visits already, my brother. We will need to do this quickly, before the authorities take the feed down."

"Okay then. Mister Trout," Maguire said, "let's get you into a more subservient position in front of the mirror."

The masked ones lifted Philo off the chair and onto the floor, then made him kneel. He teetered forward, was pulled back upright. Maguire produced a camo ski mask, slipped it over his own head.

"I'm masking myself because, you know, foreign terrorism doesn't play well in Peoria. You're Catholic, right? Oops, sorry, hold on, I forgot." Maguire ripped the duct tape off Philo's mouth. "There, that's better. So, raised Catholic, correct?"

"Fuck you, Jack." Philo's dislocated jaw grunted his answer, garbled but still understandable. It felt good to say it, but dissing his captors hurt like a motherfucker.

"Ouch. The nuns wouldn't like that language. Catholic it is, then. Here, let me help you out a little more." He motioned Aziz over.

Aziz leaned in, lifted his machete, and inserted its sharp tip under the duct tape that attached Philo's wrists together. He sliced it off from the wrists to his fingertips, an imprecise cut that drew blood. Philo's hands were now exposed, freeing him to point them heavenward.

"Now you'll be able to pray—to beg—to God, Trout. Good. Wow. You look so choir-boyish, all kneeling and shit. So Catholic, so Christian. And in that uniform, so 'murcan."

Maguire stepped up to Philo's side to admire their reflections in the closet mirror together. "I like it. Good stuff. One little issue we need to clear up, though. Your cat. Where the hell is it?"

This was the best—the happiest—question he'd been asked so far. They didn't have her. The blood in the house... Asking this meant that maybe the blood wasn't Six's, or the leg without the paw. Another gift to her master from Six, probably a squirrel part. A small relief, considering what was still in store for him, but he'd take it. The other question was, was anyone coming for him, because the cavalry didn't know where he was.

Another hooded man came down the steps to the basement. He spoke in Arabic to Aziz, the two scowling and grunting dissatisfaction at each other. Disgusted, Aziz turned to Philo.

"My incompetent soldier here has... investigated your house, Mister Trout, and has not found the cat. Where is the cat?"

They were really, really interested in Six, and Philo had no idea why. Except—

Jonesy, the cat in the safe room, her collar missing.

Random pictures of Six and other SEAL team pets that his Rear Admiral contact showed him, retrieved from Al Qaeda darknet addresses.

And now Maguire's interest in Six. As interested in the cat as he was in Philo.

Maybe more so.

Six was a whiney pet found wandering the Bin Laden compound after SEAL Team Six completed their mission. For Philo, his feline pet warrior was a small comfort, an unexpected spoil from the assassination.

"Gone," Philo managed. "Might not see her for days. Let me outta these bindings, I can help you find her. I know where she likes to hunt..."

"The only way for you to get out of these bindings, infidel, is in two pieces, separated at the neck," Aziz said. One more person joined the party through the back door. He whispered to Aziz, Aziz's expression unchanging. "Other cats and roaming dogs are out there, but none of them is yours. Tell me the places she would go."

"Tell me why you want her," Philo said.

Aziz slapped him in the cheek, then slapped him in the other cheek. He loaded up for a third strike. Maguire grabbed Aziz's arm.

"Calm down, Aziz, Jesus. Let's do this instead. It's your lucky day, Trout. You get to learn about the keys to the kingdom. It's info you'll take to your grave, no harm, no foul to us. I fill you in, then you tell us where to look. Easy-peasy. Aziz, tell him about the cat."

Aziz relented. The facts, per Aziz.

Bin Laden had a cat. The cat wore a collar. The SEAL raid killed Bin Laden and four other people, but Al Qaeda knew it didn't kill the cat. When the raid was over, Bin Laden's dead body left with the heretics. The cat left with them, too, alive, along with her collar.

The facts per Philo: he had that cat, and she and he were buds.

Aziz wrapped things up. "No one remembered the cat well enough to tell us what he looked like—or her. But they all knew about the collar. We do not want the cat. We want the collar."

Al Qaeda's double secret mission, per Aziz, was securing long-term financing. The cat's collar contained a computer chip with the locations of millions in Bin Laden's money. Bank accounts and crypto, back when digital money was in its infancy, in Pakistan, India, Afghanistan, Switzerland, and elsewhere. Beheading the assassins was tied as much to finding which SEAL had the cat, so they could retrieve Bin Laden's money, as it was to avenging his death.

"Good to know," Philo said.

Another slap. "Where is she, Trout? My soldiers and The Real Proper Punks are looking to get that pay! Her collar is the ticket! Tell now, and when we find her, we will not kill her, we will just take the collar. You have my word."

"Yeah, no. Fuck you."

If they found her, she'd go down fighting, just like him. He was feeling more together now, less fuzzy, but the broken jaw was still a problem. So were the tight bungee cord restraints. He now found it hard to breathe.

"Aziz," Maguire said. "Send both men out to find the cat. You can do this next part in here on your own. Move over here."

Maguire took the phone, trained its camera on Aziz and Philo. The image also appeared on Aziz's laptop, open on Philo's workbench. "Perfect. Aziz, take it away."

Aziz lifted the machete waist high. "And now, with Allah directing my hand, I will avenge the murder of Osama Bin Laden by this infidel, and the other American infidels who continue to defile Mohammed and His teachings with their pagan existences. So epic an event, my Jihadists! My brothers! The execution of this executioner, on American soil, *live!* So *righteous!* Join us, America. Watch now as your hero dies in his father's uniform on his knees, near his weapons, the ones he used against our religion, the ones America uses every day to carry out its campaign against Al Qaeda. Against Islam! I feel so joyous, so beautiful, so alive!"

The steamer trunk, open next to them in the closet, contained Pop's complete USN existence. Hanging loose from interior drawers were mussed clothing, a slashed American flag, uniform shoulder boards, ripped newspaper clippings, medals, and a gold watch on a chain.

Aziz squared himself above Philo, who was now on his knees. Philo smelled urine mixed with the camphor. These sonsamotherfuckin' bitches, they'd pissed on his father's belongings, defiled his military service, the urine stream still glistening, running down the inside of the trunk, reaching an edge near the bottom and emptying into a drawer.

A drawer that was still closed.

Twelve guns in that pile, all unloaded, his and only his, no one else's, but what about—

"Pray, Trout! Pray to your god for forgiveness. Point your hands to your heaven. *Pray!*"

Philo lifted his hands heavenward, gazing into Aziz's stern eyes. Philo silently moved his lips in pious mimicry, the drugs taking the edge off, but it was all he could do with his jaw dislocated. He closed his eyes, started slumping, was fainting...

*Jack... Aziz... yes, YES, I am so totally fainting, it is a marvelous faint, I am so totally selling it.*

"Aziz! Straighten him up!" Maguire said.

Philo slumped into the trunk shoulder-first, then slid farther down. When he reached the floor he ripped the closed bottom drawer out of the trunk by its knob, his praying hands coming away with Pop's Navy-issue Colt sidearm, which was loaded because, well, "*Japs, Philo, you can never know what those sneaky little Jap bastards are up to, son.*"

The .45 was now the only gun in anyone's hands in the room. Seven bullets, three targets.

Shots to the chest then the head of one man, Lieutenant Yonder—*thrup, thrup*—dropped him, his protests clipped in mid-sentence. Aziz's machete whipped past the ducking Philo and caught steamer trunk leather behind him, the blade embedded in the trunk, immobile. Philo's shot entered one of Aziz's eye sockets, Aziz dropping dead-weighted to the floor, the machete staying stuck in the trunk.

Maguire now showed a handgun and leveled it at Philo, except head honcho Jack Maguire, of The Real Proper Punks, was already really, properly dead, he just didn't know it, a bullet entering his forehead and leaving behind an ear, blood spraying the wood paneling that his body slammed against before sliding to the floor. But Maguire had gotten a shot off, a ricochet off Philo's knee and into his shoulder, jamming him backward, into the lighted cedar closet. He clutched the gun but was out of breath and bleeding, and still wrapped in these fucking bungee cords.

Three dead, a fourth body around here somewhere, and two other Al Qaeda soldiers unaccounted for, the ones sent outside to look for Six. Whenever they returned, he'd need to be ready. The phone was propped against Maguire's inert foot, still filming. Philo shimmied away from the closet and stuck his brutalized head into the camera. He saw his mess of a face livestreamed onto the Al Qaeda laptop on his workbench.

A noise behind him. He rolled onto his back, screaming in pain, his weapon raised, his finger curling the trigger. The pet door stopped swinging, a furry orange and white blur soft pawing her way toward him.

*Six*, with blood on her fur. Philo lowered the weapon and choked up while he spoke to her. "Six... sweetie..."

When she cuddled with him, he stroked her neck, her collar still around it. She horked up a hunk of something onto his pantleg, him not able to do a thing about it.

*Meow.*

Philo lifted the streaming phone into his hands and spoke directly into the camera, at the internet audience. "They're dead," he grunted, the pain in his jaw excruciating with each syllable, but he had to get this out, garbled or not.

"Fuck you, Al Qaeda, and fuck you too, Punks, you racist degenerates. Hoo-yah, SEALS." His breaths were halting, he was getting lightheaded, his father's Navy whites blooming red florets around his knee and shoulder wounds. He had additional breathless words for his audience. "Someone… needs to get here soon. There's more of 'em, they're coming back, and I'm fading."

He clicked off the livestream so he could fat-finger 911. "Ambulance, now, 3228 Unruh. I'm in the basement. Three dead in here. I'll be the one wrapped in bungee cords who shit his Navy officer whites. Careful when you enter, the place might not be safe."

He lost the 911 connection. Six purred into his other shoulder, warming him on the cold basement floor. The race was on. Who would get there first, the EMTs, the cops, or Al Qaeda?

He drifted off, was jolted awake when the back door to the basement creaked open. Al Qaeda numbers three and four entered. They lost it when they saw the carnage, screaming to each other in Arabic. Philo pushed Six into the closet, but she wanted nothing to do with that and bit him. She came bouncing back out.

Gun—Pop's gun—where was it?

He'd never be able to reason with them. This was it, this was fucking it. It was over. At least he wasn't getting beheaded.

One of them reached for Six. She bit and scratched him but only one time each, the guy's handgun now pressed into her ribs, jamming her calico body hard underneath it, against the floor, Six squealing in protest. Philo found Pop's Colt too late, the second guy stepping onto his hands before he could lift it. He shoved the barrel of a weapon into Philo's mouth. Philo waited on the trigger pull.

"Infidel! Allah condemns you!"

Why did they always need to talk shit before they did the deed…?

More Arabic from the guy, breathing hard into Philo's face, seething at him, Philo not understanding a word, then English again. "You murdered our prophet. I sentence you to—"

A cannon went off behind them, twice, the booms in the basement deafening, and both intruders jerked forward from headshots that exploded out their foreheads, spraying Philo's face with gray matter and blood before their bodies dropped dead-weighted onto his chest. Six jumped like a surprised little kitty almost as high as the suspended ceiling, then sprinted to the steps and up to the first floor.

Magpie Papahani, the massive Hawaiian, stood over them, his gun raised in both hands, a high-caliber magnum, ready to do more damage if the job wasn't already done. Wally Lanakai entered behind him. Sonovabitch.

"Trout—Philo—you're hit. Magpie, call nine-one-one."

"Wunnerful, the calv'ry, the fuckin' Hawaiian calv'ry," Philo managed, smiling, pretty sure he'd just evacuated his bowels. "Glad you didn't knock. I already made that call, Magpie. Wally, how'd you… Why…?"

Wally shoved a shoebox inside the open closet. "Here to pay what I owe you, Trout. It's in the box. For arranging the Massimo meeting. Although it looks like this meeting here"—Wally surveyed the basement—"might have been more productive. My phone call to you today, you not able to talk… It made us get here a little faster than I'd originally planned."

Wally got into a crouch, eyed Philo's mangled body and his wounds up close, the bungee cords still tightly wrapped around Philo's uniformed body. Wally produced his knife and began cutting through the bindings.

"Hell, Trout, there's three other dead guys in here," he said, eyeing how tight the bindings were wrapped. "How'd you manage—"

"Funny story. Short answer, my pop. Check the internet, it was livestreamed, it might still be up. Owww…"

Magpie spoke, finishing his phone search. "Already three million views on TikTok, boss."

Wally placed his hand on Philo's chest. Philo closed his eyes, reopened them, and mustered what little he had left in his tank.

"This does not mean we're new best friends, Wally."

Wally scanned their surroundings, Philo's basement looking like a pit where enemy war dead were thrown.

"Understood. But now you owe *me*. Listen, about this mess in here." Wally managed a smile. "If you need a referral, I know a guy. He runs a crime scene cleaning outfit..."

# 29

The thirty-two-hundred block of Unruh Avenue was blocked off at both ends with emergency vehicles and police cars and "... Homeland Security SUVs," Rhea said to Philo, him strapped in and wired up to a machine, "with your Navy brass buddy here, too. Your 'Rear Admiral.' That's it, simply 'Rear Admiral.' You'd think he'd go with a last name, or a title a little less suggestive?"

Philo was in the back of the ambulance on a collapsed wheeled stretcher getting saline and blood in IV bags, already fortified with a shot of loopy juice for the pain. Two news helicopters hovered, and additional news reporters and cameras gathered at the barricades, wanting past them. No one was allowed anywhere near the front of his house or down the wide back alley behind it without an ID check.

Before Philo answered her, Rhea yelled to the ambulance driver again. "We're all tucked in back here, fellas, so, if you want to crank things up a notch and get him over to the hospital, like, soon, that might be a good idea. This guy's got at least one bullet in him, remember?"

"I don't remember his name," Philo said. "I'm not sure I ever knew it. They should give him clearance to hang out, he means well. He'll want to talk with me."

"Sure, when he gets there. Right now, he's back there hanging out with the forensics team from this police district. With, you know, the bodies."

"He's a Grim Reaper type," Philo said, snickering. "He talks in code. A funny guy talking funny code, now I think about it." He found his comments entertaining, then realized his perception might have been medicinally influenced. "Maybe he wants to put another bullet into those crazy fuckers, just to make sure they're all dead." That one was especially humorous to him for no reason, Philo chuckling until he was out of breath.

"Calm yourself, cowboy, your laughing can't be good for the bandaging."

"Rhea?"

"Yes, doll?"

"Don't do the detective thing with me, just do the girlfriend thing, okay?"

"Fine, no repeat of our last ambulance ride together." As in when he'd first met Detective Rhea Ibáñez, who worked a case that also ended with him in an ambulance.

"Correct," he said.

"Done. Wrong precinct, so you're in the clear, it's not my case. But a warning, bud. She's good, and she'll grill you until she gets everything right."

"Who?"

"The detective in this precinct who caught the case. She's giving you room, *us* room, right now, like the docs told her to, before she pulls out the notepad. She'll want to know how you managed those last two gunshots. The ones in the backs of their heads, before those two Al Qaeda collapsed onto you."

"My Three Stooges rifle. It has a curved barrel."

Hell, he was so killing it.

"Hush. We'll need to decide how to work in whatever help you had without giving up any names, if possible. Which is what I assume you want."

"Best if they're kept out of it. They did a good thing. They shouldn't have to suffer for it."

The ambulance pulled away from the curb. The other victim of the attack in there with him, who'd been quiet to this point, started to fuss.

*Meow. MEOW.*

"She comfortable in the kitty carrier, Rhea?"

"Six is doing fine. I'll get her to your vet right after we get you checked in."

"Her collar." Philo was really fading now, his eyelids like weighted blankets. "I told those guys about it—"

"'Those guys' were Homeland Security. The agent who de-collared her got some nasty cat-fang and scratching action from her. One more thing, before you nod off. Check out this TikTok post."

No, no, please, not the attack...

"I don't wanna see it, Rhea. I'm enjoying the drugs, I don't need any more PTSD right now."

"Oh, honey, no. That thing's already gone from the internet. This is a different video. She said yes, Philo. You never saw Harriet's answer, you were gone. She told Teddy yes, she'll marry him."

One of the Mummer wives had filmed it before they loaded her into the EMS vehicle, Teddy joining her there. His Mummer buddies surrounded them, clapping and crying and smiling and hugging each other, the post still accumulating likes.

"That's nice," Philo said, "wake me in time for the wedding."

*Meow.*

## Binge Killer

**A town with its own dark secret...**

After serial killer Randall Burton is diagnosed with a terminal disease, he decides to jump bail and go out in a blaze of glory.

One woman stands in his way.

Her name is Counsel Fungo, and she's an exceptionally talented bounty hunter, if a little eccentric. Officially, her two canine companions are therapy dogs. But she considers them partners. Counsel will do anything to stop criminals from preying on the vulnerable, and she's intent on stopping Randall Burton.

Randall's trail leads to sleepy Rancor, Pennsylvania. Named one of the "Safest Towns in America," it's a quiet town tucked away in the Poconos. Its citizens are mostly widowers, bowlers, and bingo players.

But there's a reason no one in Rancor has reported a major crime in the past 50 years.

And neither Counsel nor the killer are quite ready for what this town has in store...

**Get your copy today at**
severnriverbooks.com/authors/chris-bauer

# ACKNOWLEDGMENTS

The South Philadelphia String Band, first place performers in the String Band division of the 2022 Philadelphia Mummers Parade. The "Old Time Philly String Band" is a stand-in for this perennial Philadelphia Mummers powerhouse.

Mark "Frog" Carfagno, legendary Phillies stadium greenskeeper, a Mummer with the South Philadelphia String Band, and crooner with the Mickey Finn Band in South Philly. Mark continues to champion voting Dick Allen (a.k.a. Richie Allen, a.k.a. Rich Allen), former Philadelphia Phillies and Chicago White Sox superstar baseball player, into Major League Baseball's Hall of Fame. Many thanks for spending time with the author on this, Mark. Keep up the good fight.

Dick Allen, one of the greatest baseball players to ever play the game. Rest in peace, Dick. Most of the people alive today who saw you play will never forget you.

Jared Brey, for his 10/20/2016 article in *Philadelphia* magazine on Philadelphia's Northern Liberties development.

William J. Donahue, novelist, editor, and friend, for his "dancing nerves" mention.

Vin DiLauro. Vin, when you read the book, you'll eventually understand the reason for this acknowledgment. I never had an uncle with so interesting a nickname.

The Rebel Writers of Bucks County. Russ Allen, Dave Jarret, Martha Holland, Jackie Nash, and posthumously, John Wirebach.

The Bucks County Writers Workshop chaired by Don Swaim. A writers group I have been a proud member of for more than twenty years.

Beta readers Daniel Dorian and Melissa Sullivan.

Randall Klein, of Randall Klein Books. One chapter title came directly from your editorial feedback. And your content edit suggestions were pretty good, too. Thank you, sir.

Stephanie Farr, journalist. One observation of yours on Twitter about the Philly Mummers made the cut.

All my friends and relatives in South Philly from days gone by, some of you—okay, more than some—with direct connections to people known for making offers that you can't refuse.

# ABOUT THE AUTHOR

"The thing I write will be the thing I write."

Chris wouldn't trade his northeast Philly upbringing of street sports played on blacktop and concrete, fistfights, brick and stone row houses, and twelve years of well-intentioned Catholic school discipline for a Philadelphia minute (think New York minute but more fickle and less forgiving). Chris has had some lengthy stops as an adult in Michigan and Connecticut, and he thinks Pittsburgh is a great city even though some of his fictional characters do not. He still does most of his own stunts, and he once passed for Chip Douglas of *My Three Sons* TV fame on a Wildwood, NJ boardwalk. He's a member of International Thriller Writers, and his work has been recognized by the National Writers Association, the Writers Room of Bucks County (PA), and the Maryland Writers Association. He likes the pie more than the turkey.

severnriverbooks.com/authors/chris-bauer

Printed in the United States
by Baker & Taylor Publisher Services